Dedalus Original Fiction in Paperback

Prague 1938

Dara Kavanagh is a writer, academic, translator and
poet. A native of Dublin, he spent more than a decade
working in Africa, Australia and Latin America
before returning to settle in Ireland. He is the author
of several books and poetry collections.

D0271079

Dara Kavanagh

Prague 1938

Dedalus

Supported using public funding by
**ARTS COUNCIL
ENGLAND**

Published in the UK by Dedalus Limited
24-26, St Judith's Lane, Sawtry, Cambs, PE28 5XE
email: info@dedalusbooks.com
www.dedalusbooks.com

ISBN printed book 978 1 912868 51 3
ISBN ebook 978 1 912868 52 0

Dedalus is distributed in the USA & Canada by SCB Distributors
15608 South New Century Drive, Gardena, CA 90248
email: info@scbdistributors.com   www.scbdistributors.com

Dedalus is distributed in Australia by Peribo Pty Ltd
58, Beaumont Road, Mount Kuring-gai, N.S.W. 2080
email: info@peribo.com.au   www.peribo.com.au

First published by Dedalus in 2021
Prague 1938 copyright © Dara Kavanagh 2021

The right of Dara Kavanagh to be identified as the author of this work has
been asserted by him in accordance with the Copyright, Designs and Patents
Act, 1988.

Printed and bound in the UK by Clays Elcograf S.p.A
Typeset by Marie Lane

A C.I.P. listing for this book is available on request.

Kolik řečí umíš, tolikrát jsi člověkem
– Czech Proverb

Contents

I   The House on Nerudova Street   9
II   *U Černého Slunce*   17
III   Old Meisel   25
IV   The Thief   33
V   Meisel's Granddaughter   41
VI   Katya   47
VII   'Pequod Mutiny'   54
VIII   *Národní Obec Fašistická*   60
IX   Heinrich Heine   65
X   Pickaxe Handles   75
XI   *Orlando Furioso*   84
XII   Three Card Trick   92
XIII   Chess Pieces   99
XIV   Apprenticeship   105
XV   Exodus   113
XVI   Scenarios   118
XVII   Reckonings   123
XVIII   The Letter   133
XIX   On the Bridge   138
XX   September 1938   144
XXI   Witness   153
XXII   The Carve-up   160

XXIII   Bloodlines   167
XXIV   Susannah and the Elders   176
XXV   Suspicions   182
XXVI   Endgame   189
XXVII   Through the Looking Glass   196
XXVIII   Complicity   204
XXIX   Showdown   211
XXX   Christmas Eve   221
XXXI   Christmas Truce   228
XXXII   New Year's Eve   238
XXXIII   Flight   247
XXXIV   Degenerate   258
XXXV   *Cigno Nero*   268
XXXVI   New World   277

I

The House on Nerudova Street

Maman came from Turin, necropolis of statues and long colonnades where Nietzsche finally went mad. Perhaps, as a girl, the chill of Alpine melt-water entered her veins. She had little of the hot-headedness one associates with her compatriots. Her anger, such as it was, took the form of headaches and withdrawals.

In fact she was Papa's second wife. His first, the soprano Elsa Mörschel, had run off with her voice coach and, as was said in those days, had come to a bad end somewhere in Moravia. A laudanum overdose. Along with a stack of recordings on the *Ultraphon* label and a baby-grand that dominated the music-room, she left two young children in my father's charge: my half-brother Klaus, twelve years my senior, and Katya, closer in age if not in appearance. It may have been that responsibility that led him to act so precipitously. Within months, rather than installing a regular governess in the house on Nerudova Street, he'd brought Maria Teresa Tedesco from Turin to Prague, where she knew not a soul and spoke not a word of Czech. I can only assume she'd been his mistress, one of several perhaps.

Papa travelled a lot in those days. He was an art dealer, and it was not unusual for him to be gone for weeks at a time, to Nuremberg or Dresden, to Vienna or Venice, to Basel or Turin. As the years went by he visited Italy less and less. He declared he could no longer abide the preposterous posturing of the 'Hairless Ape', as he called him. What Maman thought of *Il Duce* I've never fathomed. Papa's antipathy meant that I'd only been to Turin once, on the occasion of my grandfather's funeral. I was five. I recall a gloomy interior inhabited by whispers and ladies' fans and great quantities of lacework, and the powder on my grandmother's cheek that came away when you brushed it, like dust from a moth's wing. I've no doubt that dusky interior has coloured my memory of the city.

Because of the places business took him, Papa was something of a polyglot. We all were. It wasn't unusual, in Prague, in those days, to speak several languages. Maman always addressed me, and I her, in Italian, though why I'd always called her Maman and Papa, Papa, I've never understood, unless it derived from her penchant for reading French novels in yellow covers. Even after sixteen years, her Czech was error prone and heavily accented. Father Kaufmann, a Sudeten Jesuit who was my Latin, German, History and Mathematics tutor and also Maman's confessor, was a frequent visitor, and in his presence *hochdeutsche* became the lingua-franca in the living room. At other times we'd entertain one or another of Papa's business associates, a far-flung bunch, so that occasional smatterings of Polish, Ruthenian, even Yiddish would pepper the talk. It was like an illustration of the old Czech proverb he'd had Maman embroider for over the lintel: *Kolik řečí umíš, tolikrát jsi člověkem* – 'Your humanity is as plural as the number of tongues you speak'. At one such evening, Father Kaufmann shook a celery stick and baptised our house in Mala Strana the 'Little League of Nations.' The maid and cook, though, spoke only Czech, as, by choice, did Klaus.

Klaus, you see, was a nationalist. He was just old enough to remember the Old Habsburg Empire, whose collapse gave birth to a clutch of new nations, each eyeing their neighbour with deadly jealousy. So it was a surprise to hear the ardour that animated his voice when he spoke of the Berlin Olympics – he'd been the star member of the Czechoslovakian sculling team. At the closing ceremony – this he told us on his return – once the flame was extinguished and the stadium plunged into darkness, there was a moment's awed silence and then one hundred thousand voices called out in unison, *Sieg Heil, Sieg Heil*. 'It was no use to resist, you were swept along by the power of it.' Eyes ablaze he stood and mimicked the Roman salute, but that was for the benefit of Katya, who stared daggers. Had Father Kaufmann been there, I imagine his performance would have been more muted.

As for Katya, she was far happier working on her charcoals, montages and engravings in her attic studio. Whatever her opinions, and whatever language she thought them up in, she kept them largely to herself. Or she let her art speak for her. The prints and collages she produced, several of which had featured in avant-garde journals like *Exploze*, *Pásmo* and even once in *Revue Devětsilu,* were dark, angular, monochrome, jagged – curious distortions of the human form that Klaus castigated as perverse. 'Why give your time to producing such ugly images?' he'd ask, genuinely baffled.

'You used to draw so beautifully.' She might have pointed to the war-cripples who, all through our childhood, begged on every bridge and under every archway. Or to the wine-stain birthmark that discoloured one side of her brow. But she chose not to.

Papa indulged her, to an extent championed her work, which is all the more surprising given the persistent rumour that she was not, in fact, his child. Maman could never understand her husband's somewhat decadent taste in art – for her, art started and ended with the Renaissance masters. And so she rarely visited the *U Černého Slunce* Gallery on Karluva Street which, to me, was an Aladdin's cave. 'Contemporary Czech and International Art', read the business card with the black sun logo. By 'International', Papa meant German, Swiss, Italian and, occasionally, Hungarian art. I don't recall ever having seen anything from further afield.

At the time of the events I'm to relate, I'd just turned fifteen. Father Kaufmann SJ had been my mother's confessor, and now that I was entering adolescence, he was to be my spiritual advisor. I didn't mind. I quite liked him. He had a long, desiccated face with large eyes that made me think of Don Quixote. Besides, he'd taught me the rudiments of chess when we should have been studying algebra. The one black mark against him was nineteenth-century history. Where I wanted to learn about the Risorgimento and the Franco-Prussian War, all he seemed to be interested in was surplus value and the emancipation of the serfs. I also had him to thank for the family name. I was Guido Salvatore Hayek. It was his steadfast banter that finally led Papa to raise his hands in mock surrender and agree to 'allow Maria Teresa make an honest man of me'.

You might have thought Prague would have been scandalised by so prominent a figure as Emil Hayek living openly with his mistress and having a child by her. But Papa was genial, forceful, well-liked, and moved largely in artistic circles where such arrangements were common enough. Besides, it had been his young wife who had abandoned him. True, as Catholics, he and Maman had had to await news of the demise of Elsa Mörschel before remarrying. But that news had come two years earlier. The wedding, a private affair, took place the very year of Maman's return to Turin to bury her father. That trip would be all the honeymoon she ever got.

In any case, Father Kaufmann had always intrigued because he was such a mix of contradictions. A chain smoker in a soutane, one with a taste for the finer things, though he never hid his communist leanings, an outspokenness which raised eyebrows and occasional rebukes within the military hierarchy of the Society of Jesus. A bon viveur, though he'd taken a vow of poverty and ran a soup kitchen out of the great Church of St Niklaus. A Sudeten German who had no time for the Sudeten Germans then agitating to be incorporated into *Grossdeutschland*. A Jesuit who could fire off a ribald joke or colourful anecdote any time Maman was out of earshot. He must have been in his late sixties, though he behaved like a man of forty. Papa called him Hans or Hansi, to the rest of us he was Father Kaufmann. Only to Maman was he Johannes.

I wasn't devout in the way Maman was. I was a believer, though. Moreover, I had that hunger for devotion to a cause peculiar to adolescence. But there was one other reason I was looking forward to having Father Kaufmann as my spiritual advisor. In all things, Klaus excelled. He was the complete athlete, and the trophy cabinet teemed with cups and medals for soccer, shooting and chess as well as rowing. His results at the Gymnasium had been first class, whereas I'd been tutored at home, since I'd inherited from my mother's side a congenital irregularity of the heart, an arrhythmia that had cost her only brother his life while he was still a seminarian. It was Uncle Guido I'd been named for.

In all things, Klaus not only excelled. He'd also preceded me. It had been Father Kaufmann who'd taught him, too, the rudiments of chess until the day his student out-played him. When Alekhine beat the great Capablanca for the world crown, they'd play through the moves together, inventing endings for the games that had been drawn, which Klaus would invariably win regardless of which side he took. It had been Father Kaufmann who'd introduced Klaus to canoeing – the Jesuits ran a youth club on the Moldau, or the Vltava as Klaus insisted. But Klaus didn't have a religious bone in his body. Nor the sort of philosophical curiosity that I'd always had. The spiritual would be an area of Father Kaufmann's attention that would belong to me, and to me alone.

Don't imagine it was sibling rivalry that was driving me. I'd never seen Klaus as a sibling. He was fully twelve years older, so to me he'd always been an adult. As for what he made of me, I've never really known. Did the teenager resent the arrival of this intruder, the illegitimate child of his father's mistress? If he did, it wasn't apparent. True, he rarely called me by my Christian name, always Kašpárek, after the diminutive puppet. But I think that was because I was so much younger than he, and wasn't much given to sports. He didn't appear to begrudge the presence of his father's mistress in the house, either, but that may be because all his scorn was directed toward the mother who'd abandoned him.

On one occasion, while Papa was away on a trip to Basel, Klaus brought me up to Krčský woods together with Papa's hunting rifle. There, we shot at a line of bottles. It was exhilarating. All the same, I came away with a feeling of total inadequacy, of how cosseted my upbringing was. Papa had regularly taken Klaus on hunting trips when he'd been that age. Incidentally, Papa once asked Klaus to teach me how to make a rudimentary crystal radio set out of copper wire, aluminium foil, a safety pin, and lead taken out of a pencil. I marvelled to hear the thin strains of the Prague Philharmonic condense out of the ether. But Klaus' heart hadn't been in it. At twelve you pick up such things.

For a while we did share one passion. That was for stamp-collecting. It was through these miniature stained-glass windows that I first got a sense of the wider world around us: *Sverige, Helvetia, CCCP, Polska, Magyar Posta*. It was no harm at all that Papa had so many foreign correspondents. My favourites were those that had been overprinted – the British Monarch overwritten by *Saorstát Éireann 1922*, and *Deutsches Reich* stamps overwritten with Danzig or bearing fantastic sums, 75 Tausend, 2 Millionen. When I turned eleven he gifted me the entire collection. Klaus had moved on.

The mystery was that my father always spoke with a kind of amused irony about Elsa Mörschel. 'I came home one day,' he'd say, 'to find the pair of them practising the duet out of Don Giovanni.' He'd even play, on occasion, one of the several recordings she'd left behind of Heyduk's *Songs My*

Mother Taught Me, which invariably prompted Klaus to leave the room. Through the static of the old gramophone I found her voice thin, almost ghostly. Most visitors, though, agreed with Papa that she could have been a very fine soprano indeed, had she but kept it up.

II

U Černého Slunce

I may have given the idea that I was something of an invalid.
Not so. The arrhythmia meant that I had to take a few basic
precautions, that was all. Not to get overtired, not to get
dehydrated. No sudden or prolonged exertions. When an
attack came on, and the frantic double-pulse fisted at my
throat, I had to lie down and raise up my legs until it passed,
even if it meant lying in a doorway on the street. That had
only happened twice, though. Another time I'd fainted. But
that was as likely down to anaemia, brought on by my recent
growth. Maman was overprotective, but given the untimely
death of her beloved Guido, it was difficult for Papa to gainsay
her. He did his best, and I loved him for it.

He didn't have it all his own way, either. Sometimes I
heard raised voices. As I had grown gangly over the last few
months and my voice had broken to something of a croak, as my
skin was bad and my imagination worse, I sensed instinctively
I was the root cause. Sometimes I heard Papa shout words
like 'mollycoddle' and 'mama's boy'. For her part, Maman's
headaches and silences became daily features of Nerudova

Street. But Papa persevered, and anytime he persevered, Papa prevailed.

So it came about that every Tuesday and Thursday he'd take me to the *U Černého Slunce* Gallery, 'The Black Sun', on Karluva Street. 'It'll be a good apprenticeship for the boy,' he announced at the dinner table. And so it was. There was so much to learn. Not merely developing an eye for art trends and an idea of the prices a particular artist might fetch, but framing, restoring, touching up. Talking to customers and gauging what it was that they most wanted to hear was a skill in itself, one at which Papa excelled. Only rarely did a customer meet the asking price. The asking price was no more than an opening gambit in a game of bargaining and haggling that might take an hour or more, during which biscuits and a samovar of tea or even a bottle of absinthe were produced. 'Guido, go and see if the little green fairy is home,' he'd say at such times. And then there were the ledgers, with their double-entry accounts and balance-sheets that had to come out identically when you totted up income against expenditure. Mostly, I was an errand boy. This delighted me. I loved Prague, that fairy tale city. Papa placed an injunction on informing Maman of this aspect of my apprenticeship. Maman would not have approved.

He gave me an allowance to cover these days, not quite a wage, but given how little I spent beyond old stamps or an odd second-hand book, it was sufficient for me to begin to amass a nest-egg in an old biscuit-tin I kept hidden at the back of my wardrobe. 'You should never be without a little something put aside,' he'd say, unpeeling a few twenty koruna notes. 'Fate has this nasty habit of springing surprises on us out of the bluest of skies.'

Because he had the only set of keys and had to let in the cleaning woman, Darja, who came three mornings a week, and Jan, who'd lost part of his arm in the war and worked half-days, we'd rise before dawn. We'd set off having had nothing but a glass of water and maybe an old crust – later, I'd be sent out to the corner café for hot bread-rolls and coffee, which I'd carry back in a pewter flask, but never before ten o'clock, when the gallery opened its doors to the public. I loved the walk down Mostecka and over the Karluv Bridge before the city had woken up, with the mist low over the river and the roofs and cobbles glinting as though they were newly washed. The gallery was always cold to begin with, though by the time we opened up to the public at ten, it had warmed through our activity. I loved the very smells of the place, which the cold air and our hunger pangs made more distinct – the heady volatility of turpentine and white spirits; the rich savour of linseed oil; the burnt tang of sandalwood and beech shavings from Jan's lathe.

It was as well we set off so early. Papa could never pass an acquaintance without exchanging pleasantries, gossip, or the latest off-colour anecdote. *Always remember, Guy, our business is people.* I think his philosophy went beyond the gallery. Papa was a social animal to the roots of his being. He had a sonorous voice that came from the diaphragm, and he loved nothing better than to exercise it. He was the king of banter, of flirtation. At any other time but seven in the morning it might have taken him thirty minutes to cross that bridge. As it was, we were often fifteen, even thirty minutes late to open the shop for Jan, who scowled and muttered, and Darja, who couldn't have cared less.

In the workshop I'd watch Jan out of the corner of my eye. He was missing his left hand, and in place of a hook or a regular prosthesis, a sort of metal loop protruded from the sleeve. This he managed with considerable dexterity, as well as the crook of his left arm, so that he was able to manoeuvre and hold an awl, say, or a chisel just ahead of the mallet. It was Jan who had crafted the black sun pendant, finely gilt, that hung out over our doorway. He invariably wore a forage cap from his army days, which he'd whip off with his good hand to dry the sweat with his sleeve in the same movement as though every second counted. He worked fast, as if to demonstrate that the amputation had done nothing to diminish his usefulness. In all the time I'd known him, I'd never seen him smile.

By the back wall was a work-bench with a vice and wooden-jawed clamp. Above it, their outlines traced in inks, hung an entire taxonomy of tools – chisels and mallets and saws of every variety. These were Jan's tools. Beneath the work desk was a bucket which contained such tools as Papa had accumulated before he'd taken him on. On the facing wall hung a great selection of frame corners, in every design, wood and tint. Several of these, Papa would place in turn for a customer on the corner of a canvas. His skill was to find the precise form and thickness and shade that would bring to life the painting, picking out a highlight hitherto subdued.

Jan must have been a master-joiner before the war, but he was so parsimonious of speech, begrudging words as a miser would coins, that I never verified this idea. Where one of Papa's maxims ran 'Measure twice, cut once', Jan had an eye that gauged, by a single glance, lengths and cuts and fits to an uncanny snugness, so that glue was scarcely required. It was fascinating to watch, fascinating to see the finely bevelled lengths of frame emerge on a bench so rough-hewn. At the pedal-driven lathe he was also a master wood-turner. Besides framing, the gallery ran a sideline in plinths and custom-made display tables which helped when business was slack. Papa's philosophy was that every mouse should have two boltholes. That philosophy had seen the gallery through the lean years at the start of the decade.

Within the workshop, the contrast between Jan's rapid handiwork and Papa's painstaking, meticulous methodology was something to behold. Though the *U Černého Slunce* Gallery was known for its line in contemporary Czech art, Papa took in old paintings that required cleaning or restoration. He'd set them, unframed and naked, on an easel, then examine the brighter border that had been concealed for maybe centuries beneath the frame. As he worked, I marvelled to watch the tiny coins of pure colour emerge from under the yellowed varnish, coaxed out by a cotton ball dampened in a Petri dish. 'When the solution might be too strong, you know what you must use?' he asked me, a jeweller's eye-piece squeezed like a monocle in his left eye. I shrugged, and was startled to hear him gargle up a froth of saliva and tap his lips. 'Go on, try it!' With a glance toward Jan, to make sure I wasn't being made a fool of, I spat, tentatively. 'Don't pussyfoot, boy!' He spat. I spat. It became a race. Within minutes the entire canvas was marbled in our saliva. I glanced again to Jan. He'd remained impervious to the whole game.

On a couple of occasions my father had taken me on overnight trips – to Hradec Kralove or Český Krumlov. It was far more difficult to bring Maman round on such occasions, and taking 'the child' beyond Czechoslovakia's frontiers was absolutely out of the question. Out of the question, Emil, I won't have it! And yet, secretly, Papa had secured a passport for me, a treasure I kept hidden in the biscuit-tin to the back of the wardrobe. *One of these days, Guy! And the first Maman will know of it is when she receives a picture postcard from lake Geneva. How would that appeal to you?*

It was on our trip to Český Krumlov, or more correctly on our return journey from Český Krumlov, that my father confided that he was training me to one day take over the business. 'Keep it under your hat for the time being, Guy,' he said. 'You see it's no use leaving it to Klaus. I hate to say it about my own son, but he's a Philistine. Klaus' idea of beauty might do for the National Socialists, but it will never do for Bohemia.'

I was confused. I blushed, with embarrassment, but also with pleasure. After all, Klaus was making decent money as a sports instructor and had done a course in radio engineering. He'd never shown any real interest in the gallery. 'Don't say anything to your mother,' he tapped his nose, 'not a word.' Then he added, 'Not as yet.'

'Why not?'

'Because my dear boy, Maman may have other plans for her little Guido.' Though nothing had been said in the house, I had an inkling of what he meant. Papa had nothing against the church, not as such. But neither had he any great devotion to it. Once, I'd overheard him say to her 'you won't be happy until you have your Guido Salvatore dressed in a priest's frock.' All the same, when she'd insisted on my having a spiritual adviser, it was he who'd insisted it be Father Kaufmann. 'Tell me,' he squinted one eye, always a sign that a *bon mot* was on its way, 'How are you getting along with our irreverent Reverend? By the by, did you ever wonder why his hair isn't white, or silver?'

I pictured momentarily the priest's mane of hair and pencil moustache, which were the tawny colour of old ivory. I shook my head.

'Too much of this!' He made a gesture of smoking. 'So how are you two coming along?'

I smiled, weakly. Because what he was probing was none of his business. I suddenly became interested in the evening countryside sweeping past our carriage window.

'Do you know, I think that old rogue is an atheist!' Papa began to drum his fingers and hum a merry tune, *barump-be-dum, barump-be-dum,* and I could see his reflection still eyeing up mine.

'But what about Katya?' I asked, in part to move the subject away from something so private as my confessor, something which should be untouched by the mild raillery I could expect from Papa. But partly, too, because when we are met with sudden good fortune, we try to forestall any possible obstacle by naming it at once. 'Surely Katya is the artist of the family.'

'Poor Katyenka,' he sighed, which surprised me. 'Her art is all very well, but she has no head for business. No feel for it. And where talking to people is concerned, well! She's a disaster, isn't she?' He leaned forwards and fixed me with his gaze in a manner I'd only rarely seen. 'Promise me, Guido, that you'll always look out for her.'

I promised. Of course I did. It made me feel like a man to

make such a promise. But at fourteen going on fifteen, I had no idea what it was I was promising.

III

Old Meisel

1938 is a catastrophic date in the history of the Czech people, a people who have never lacked for catastrophic dates. It was a pivotal moment for all of Europe, a year during which the course of history might have gone any number of directions. For the house on Nerudova Street, too, it was a time of unlooked-for change. As the bells of Our Lady of Týn rang in the New Year, and the crowds in the Old Town Square embraced one another with apprehensive smiles, we had little real idea of just how bad things would get before the year was out.

All through spring, the Marconi wireless was turned far less to music, as it always had been. In previous years, the main battleground had been whether to tune into Munich or Prague or Vienna, to classical or jazz, to Italian opera or Django Reinhart or Smetana's *Ma Vlast*. Now, bulletins and political broadcasts were the order of the day. 'That machine,' declared Father Kaufmann, rather more sententiously than was his wont, 'is the tabernacle in everyone's home. And we must be careful, or demagogues of the stamp of Dr Goebbels are like to become the new household gods.' If Maman had

had her way, the wireless would have remained unplugged, displaced by the old phonograph it had usurped. 'At least such a rasping voice would never make it onto a record label.'

Political discussion, which often grew heated, was unavoidable, particularly when we had guests. Maman would have been far happier if these soirees had, as in former times, remained musical affairs, with card games and talk of artistic fashions and the latest town gossip. Katya had learned the clarinet to grade six, and though I loved the Hebraic airs she'd coax from it, it was a shame she could never be induced to sing outside her attic studio – she had inherited a sweet voice from her soprano mother. There was usually some guest who could bring to life the baby-grand to accompany Maman or Klaus, who had a fine baritone voice. But that year, there was an element of the ostrich burying its head in the sand about such frivolous entertainment.

One evening in late spring, around the time of the partial mobilisation in the wake of the Austrian Anschluss, the talk turned again to the problem of minorities. The question hinged on this. With the map of Middle Europe such a hotchpotch of ethnic groups sitting inside the towns and borders of larger polities, should the borders be moved to accommodate the minorities, or the minorities moved to consolidate the borders. Klaus took the latter view. Curiously, given Konrad Henlein's increasingly vocal demands for full autonomy for the Sudeten Germans, his antipathy was aimed chiefly at the Poles. After all, the Germans you could understand. They'd been badly done by with the Treaty of Versailles. Some of their territorial claims were justifiable, particularly around Danzig. Henlein and his SdP would have to be accommodated in some way, but they'd have to be reasonable in their demands. No castle under siege could reasonably be asked to surrender its castle walls. But as for the Poles, they were damned opportunists who'd carve up Bohemia at the drop of a hat. When Marshal Piłsudski had died, he for one had shed not a tear. Not one.

'And what,' asked Father Kaufmann, 'if *mein lieber* Konrad won't come round to your way of seeing things?'

Klaus was leaning against the piano, punctuating his thought by depressing a B# key again and again. It was an annoying tick. *Plink!* 'He'll have to.'

'But if he won't?' Father Kaufmann, lighting one cigarette from the butt of the previous, was squinting against the smoke. It was a sacred mystery where he got his cigarettes, since Jesuits are not permitted to have their own money. 'What if Herr Konrad and his SdP cronies simply refuse to be *accommodated*, as you put it?'

'Then they'll have to leave.' *Plink!* 'If they want so much to be a part of a *Grossdeutschland*,' *Plink!* 'then let them go and live there. And I say to them, *auf Wiedersehen und viel Glück.' Plink!*

'Leave at gunpoint?'

'If necessary.' *Plink!* A vision came to me of Klaus as he had appeared at the time of his national service. He'd remained in uniform all the while he was on home leave, even when attending mass. It had seemed to my seven-year-old mind admirable, romantic. This time round, though he'd long been a reservist and had recently enlisted in the Signal Corps, Maman had prevailed on him to dress in evening clothes.

Father Kaufmann nodded slowly. 'All three million of them.' This was more dismayed statement than question.

'If it comes to that, all three million.' *Plink! Plink! Plink!* QED. One, two, three.

'Stop drumming on that one key, Klaus, it's infantile.' The interjection was from Maman, who was at the card-table. Her back was to the piano, so that she didn't see the glower that darkened his features at being admonished in front of his fiancée. Through the partition, she and Katya made up with Maman the party of skat players. Maman's upbringing in funereal Turin must have been a nineteenth-century one, and she still subscribed to the tradition that women should withdraw after dinner to allow the men to discuss politics over port or whisky. It was a concession to modernity that the partition to the drawing-room remained open.

Rather than answer Maman, Klaus turned his chagrin on me. 'Guido wants to abolish borders. Make Europe into one big Switzerland, as advocated by his beloved guru Stefan Zweig. Isn't that right, Kašpárek?'

I flushed. 'If it means an end to minorities…'

'A brotherhood of nations!'

'Why not a brotherhood?'

'All marching happily to the Radetzky March, I suppose. And ruled over by a family of inbred degenerates. We tried that before, Kašpárek. And look where it brought us.' Klaus had meandered through the partition and over to the card-table, and now placed his hand on the shoulder of his fiancée, who was looking up at him admiringly. 'I tell you, if I had been there in Sarajevo that day, I'd have put a bullet in Franz Ferdinand myself.'

'There's something in it all the same,' said Father Kaufmann. 'Love thine enemy. And couldn't they just as well march to the *Internationale.*'

'Congratulations, Guido Salvatore mundi, you have the support of our Marxist priest! You know what they call him down in the rowing club? Red Johann.'

'*Il prete rosso,*' put in Papa, winking at me.

'Klaus!' said Maman, smiling. 'Johannes is no Marxist.'

'Marxist, no,' declared the Jesuit, raising an exclamatory finger. 'Communist.'

'There's a difference?'

'Certainly, there's a difference. From each according to their abilities, to each according to their needs. Doesn't it have the very cadence of the apostle? The early Christian communities were communist, thousands of years before Comrade Marx ever dreamed up his manifesto.'

'I daresay the first Christian communities had no need of Comrade Beria and the NKVD. But just try telling the farmer and factory worker to share what they have with the poor and the idle, see how far you get.'

'You prefer the world to dress up as boy scouts? *Die Fahne hoch, die Reihen fest geschlossen...*'

It seemed that Maman was to get her musical evening after all.

'I prefer Czech lands for the Czech people,' declared Klaus. 'If you can't sign up to that, you have no place in our country.'

His eyebrows raised conspiratorially, Papa, who had remained aloof from the exchange, pushed the brandy decanter across the table to our guest, a diminutive art dealer from Bratislava whose name escapes me, though I can still see the hooded eyes, the sensual lips and the thick beaver collar on the overcoat that enfolded the back of his chair as though some species of bear were about to overwhelm him. Nodding slyly, the man took Papa's gesture as an invitation. 'And what would you say about the Jewish question?'

It's difficult to quantify the effect the interjection had about the room. There was an all but imperceptible gasp at the card-table, and Father Kaufmann and Papa exchanged hurried glances. Even Klaus winced. An unspoken taboo, one of the very few to be observed at the house on Nerudova Street, had just been breached. If, as was widely assumed, Katya was not Papa's child, and after all she alone of all the household had eyes so brown they were almost black, then she was the daughter of Mordecai Gans, the voice coach with whom Papa's first wife had absconded a few short weeks after giving birth. From what Papa had said to Katya, I understood that he'd died a few years after Maman. I'd never seen him, but I'd seen his photo in the atrium of the Rudolfinum Concert Hall. The eyes were carved of the same mahogany.

'What do you say, Hans?' said my father, to break the silence.

'I didn't know there *was* a Jewish question, Emil,' sighed Father Kaufmann. 'I live such a cloistered life, you see. Would our friend mind spelling it out for an ignorant Jesuit?'

The art dealer, oblivious to the sardonic, heard nothing disingenuous in this. 'By all means. The Jew has no country. The Jew has no nation, not for two thousand years. It follows that the Jew has no loyalty. None beyond his own people...'

'The chosen people.'

'As you wish. I'm not a believer.' He raised his brandy glass with his stubby fingers, smelt, sipped, savoured. Papa's brandy was always of the finest. All this time I was aware that Father Kaufmann was watching me out of the corner of his eye, and I blushed. 'You see, Father, it's this way. You may have Polish Jews, and Russian Jews, and Hungarian Jews, who knows, you may even have Bohemian Jews. But these are labels, nothing more. First and foremost they are always Jews. That is what sets them apart.'

'Where would you have them go?' The question came from Katya. We all turned to look at her. For Katerina was morbidly shy.

'Let them have their New Jerusalem! Isn't their promised land supposed to be somewhere in British Palestine? Let them go there.'

Now the silence was more pronounced, so much so that even our obtuse Bratislavan merchant must have noticed it. This time it was Klaus who broke it. 'That reminds me. I ran into my friend Novák, who works down in the Town Hall. You'll never guess who's putting in for the necessary documentation for travel. I suppose he must be getting ready to up sticks.'

'Who's that, Klaus?' asked Maman, since Papa seemed lost in reflection.

'Old Meisel.'

Once again Father Kaufmann's eyes were on me. Once again I blushed, more deeply yet. I had no real fear that he might break confidence, joker that he was. But I was mortified that Papa might notice. He was always alert. Or Klaus, because he had such a mocking tongue, and would enjoy nothing more than having a dig at 'little Kašpárek'. The irony was, with last year's spurt of growth, I was now taller than Klaus. Not so robust, but taller. He had no right to call me little Kašpárek any more.

'Meisel, the merchant?' enquired our guest.

'You know him?'

'Everyone knows old Meisel. Has that shop on Bilkova Street, isn't that it?'

'That's him.'

'And so he's selling up shop!'

'I imagine he realises what way the wind is blowing.'

'Where will he go, did your friend say?'

'He didn't say. Perhaps... Odessa? That's right Papa, isn't it? Didn't he originally arrive here from Odessa, all those years ago?'

At last Papa was motivated to speak. It was as though he'd been pulled from a trance. 'You say the Jew has no loyalty. Well, there's one Jew who gave up his only son in the last war.' That was the second taboo broken. The Great War was never mentioned in our house. Papa had lost both of his brothers to the catastrophe. He'd quite literally lost them. They were part of the Czech Legion that had wandered for so long in the wilderness of Siberia, caught up in another conflict. For years, Papa would ask the stragglers and survivors if there was any news of his two brothers. But there never was.

'Izsak,' he went on. 'Ezra Meisel's only child. A fine lad, too. When news came of his death, the old man almost went out of his mind with grief.'

'The more fool him,' said our guest. 'To lose a son. And for what, eh?'

IV

The Thief

Old Meisel wasn't an art dealer. His business was antiques and fine arts. Furniture, silverware, old books and maps, even clothes. During the long endgame of the Habsburg Empire in the run up to the disastrous conflagration that swept it away, he'd made his fortune visiting the estates of the distressed nobility and buying up family heirlooms for perhaps a third of the price they'd later fetch. Any time a work of art came into his possession, he'd send his card around to my father – to father and a half-dozen others in the business, who would be invited to the backroom of the shop on Bilkova Street to view the exhibits and make their offers.

I'd accompany Papa on these visits. Bilkova Street is in Josefov, the Jewish Quarter that sits under the elbow of the Moldau. But the ghetto had been pulled down and the area greatly improved since the time that Ezra Meisel first stepped off the train and settled there, in a tenement basement near where the Old Shul used to stand.

The bidding process was never straightforward, and since the backroom was always crowded and stifling, I took to wandering about Josefov while I waited for my father to conclude his affairs there. Although the streets were nowadays as wide as anywhere in Prague, it felt like a different world. The shops, whose air held the tang of different foodstuffs, and which had a tiny box screwed into the doorjamb that customers touched as they entered, had signs and posters in a language I took to be Yiddish. But more exotic yet was the script that adorned the synagogues, like an unknown musical notation. The quarter teemed with people, some in tight black suits or in skullcaps and woollen shawls, the men bearded and with long locks of hair, and on every stoop sat urchins who stared up from undernourished faces. That was my impression, at least.

Returning to Meisel's premises from one such excursion the previous October, I'd been surprised by a girl sitting behind the counter, eating soup. She was perhaps a year or two older than I. Her mass of dark hair was long and unkempt, her pale face streaked with dirt. She watched me from sullen, sloe-black eyes, as though she resented my daring to look at her. At that time I was acutely self-conscious. I was gawky, having shot up the year before, my voice had broken, I had large hands and it seemed to me that my Adam's apple was colossal, as though a billiard ball had lodged in my throat.

'I'm here for my father?' I tried. 'Emil Hayek?'

She shrugged. Then abruptly she dropped the spoon into the soup bowl, rose, and disappeared through a doorway immediately behind the counter.

After we left, I asked Papa who she was. He at once gripped me in a headlock and rough-polished my scalp with the knuckles of his free hand. 'So, you scamp! You've met the old Jew's granddaughter, have you? And I suppose she already

34

has you under her spell.' Annoyed, I pushed and pulled till my head was at last free and made a show of straightening my hair. 'You'd want to be careful, Guy. She's an alley-cat. You don't want to let her get her claws anywhere near a mouse like you.' Normally I enjoyed his horseplay, but hearing my loud breathing and seeing my face flushed with anger, he decided to hold fire on whatever quip he'd readied. Instead, he suppressed the mirth that characteristically lit his features. 'You did notice she's lame?'

'Lame?' I replayed in my memory her rising from the soup-bowl and exiting so abruptly that half the soup was left in the bowl. 'Don't play games, Papa.'

'I'm not. Some childhood illness. Polio. Or rickets. Really, did you not notice the little contraption she has on her leg?'

I hadn't. But that didn't mean anything. She'd been behind the counter, and the doorway through which she'd exited was immediately to her back. We returned to the gallery in silence, a strange turmoil in my gut that returned on and off all that day and the day after, and the day after that.

I took to keeping an eye out for her, any time that I was in Josefov. My wanderings took place not only on such occasions as Papa had an engagement with Old Meisel. Any excuse I could find, I took. If I was to meet Katya outside the Rudolfinum, or at the typing-pool of Meier & Nedvěd, where she worked, I'd set off early enough to take a detour up past the Old Cemetery or the Klausen Synagogue. But she was hard to encounter. Once, I saw her sitting on a wooden box by the corner of Milosrdnych Street, the centre of a group of youths her own age. I was too distant to make out if there was anything strapped to either leg, and shrank back into the crowd for fear she'd see me. On another occasion I saw her pale face in the window of a passing tram. It was the strangest of encounters. She appeared to be staring straight out at me, as though singling me out from all the other pedestrians.

The fact that the girl might be lame did not bother me. Quite the opposite. Her lameness was a godsend. It was the first thing that Papa had said about her. Was that how the world saw her, then? First and foremost, her lameness, and only then, her incidental beauty? Well I did not. In my case it was the opposite. And she might come to see that. To appreciate that. Here was someone who saw her beauty. That fact must make her feel… what? Gratitude? It was the wrong word. It was I who was grateful. Without her lameness, her defect, she might have no cause to notice a clumsy adolescent.

Such were the thoughts of a fifteen-year-old.

I thought of her constantly, so constantly that I knew I should inform Father Kaufmann about it. Ever since he'd become my spiritual advisor, I'd determined not to hold anything back from him. Not the essentials, in any case. From the first, I'd told him that I was a prey to 'impure thoughts'. I wasn't so much surprised to learn that that was perfectly healthy for boys of my age as to hear him ask whether I engaged in 'self-abuse'. It was such a bizarre term. I of course said that I didn't, but his brow was so lit up with irony on hearing my denial that it dawned on me what he intended by the term.

Now, as it happens, the fantasies I had about Old Meisel's granddaughter were among my more innocent. Something held my imagination in check, a restraint that derived from a form of reverence. I imagined mildly erotic scenarios in which

I might in some way come to her rescue, earn her admiration. One secret, which caused me feelings of exquisite shame, I held back from imparting to my confessor. It was this. To the back of the *U Černého Slunce* Gallery were some cases with many drawers in which were held prints and charcoals. Often I'd idle through them, if my father was dealing with a customer. Now, among these I was astonished to come across a handful of nudes that were so like the Jewish girl of my memory that I blushed to look at them. It wasn't the curve of the body, which of course I'd never seen outside my adolescent imagination, nor the hair, long and bedraggled. It was a sort of wanton defiance that stared out from the charcoal eyes, as if inviting and at the same time defying the viewer to keep looking.

For his part, Father Kaufmann took a philosophical view. It was a natural instinct, to raise a girl on a pedestal. 'Think,' he said, 'of Dulcinea del Toboso,' and at that moment it was impossible not to think of him as Don Quixote. To wander streets in the hopes of catching a glimpse of her? Well, he'd done as much himself when he was my age. He'd never seen Old Meisel's granddaughter. But he'd heard of her. When she was younger she'd knocked about with a gang of street-kids that were up to no good. 'The point is, Guido, I'm not telling you what to admire and who to pant after. But remember this. Whatever it is we *choose* to desire, it's our free choice. Some men like gems. They invest stones with value, and the stones become sacred to them. It's the same with Klaus and sports. Or for the chess player. Nothing is so important to the chess player as the next tournament. I had a brother who collected coins. A rare coin had more importance for him than music or fine wine. And for your sister, it's making art. Remember your Matthew?'

'Matthew?' I shrugged.

'The tax-collector. *The kingdom of heaven is like unto a man who finds treasure hidden in a field. He hides it again, and in his joy sells all he has to buy that field.* We're not told what the treasure was, just that he hid it, then sold all he had to buy the field. Incidentally, I always thought that he wasn't being entirely honest. Wouldn't it have been more correct to inform the owner of the treasure rather than perpetrate a deception?'

'I don't think I'm with you.'

'Always be on your guard. Desire can be a form of madness. In Holland many years ago, there were some who sold up their entire estates to buy a single tulip bulb!'

'What has this to do with Meisel's granddaughter?'

'I realise I'm asking you to take the word of an old celibate. But it's no different when it comes to girls. Matthew doesn't tell us what the treasure was, just that it was precious to the man. We invest in a girl the desire that makes us desire them. We choose one out of the mighty throng and set them apart, raise them on a plinth, unique. Then come to believe in their uniqueness. But always, though we might not realise it, this is an act of will. Of wilfulness. Always remember that, Guy.'

'And girls? Is it the same for girls?'

'How could it not be?'

That conversation and others like it were the background to my exquisite discomfort at that soiree in late spring when I heard Klaus mention old Meisel's preparations for departure, and knew the Jesuit's ironic grey eyes were on me.

There was also this. It had come to me one day, as I was peering secretly at the nudes in the gallery, that Meisel couldn't have a granddaughter. Or if he had, it couldn't be the girl that I'd seen. When I'd quizzed him about the family, Father Kaufmann had told me the merchant had only one child, a son Izsak who'd been killed in the war. So that if this girl were Izsak's daughter, she must needs be in her twenties. Yet this girl I'd glimpsed can't have been more than seventeen.

Could it be that my father had been mistaken, and that the girl in the shop wasn't Meisel's granddaughter? If that was the case, then perhaps she wasn't lame. Perhaps she wasn't the notorious alley-cat of whose delinquencies even Father Kaufmann had heard, and who might sink her claws into my adolescence.

I decided to broach the Jesuit the next time we were to meet.

It so happened that on the very morning of that meeting, a breezy Saturday, I was walking by the Vojan Park on the Mala Strana side when I caught sight of her mass of dark hair. She was seated just inside an entrance. I ducked back at once, took up a position behind a tree. She appeared to be reading, though it was too far to see what alphabet the book was written in. There was a basket beside her, open, with what looked like dirty linen inside it.

Now, though I hadn't paid it any notice, that entrance was directly across from Laszlo's Jewellers. I'd been there for no more than a couple of minutes when, from the door of the jewellers, there erupted a commotion of street kids scattering in different directions. One sped past me and on through Vojan Park. They were followed almost at once by Laszlo himself, in apron and green visor, who chased another in the direction of Karluv Bridge yelling, 'Stop, thief!' Several seconds later, another figure emerged from the shop, a man in fedora and overcoat. He made at once for the park, hurried past where the girl was seated, and as he passed I saw him drop something small into her basket of linen. He then set off abruptly in pursuit of the street kid who'd sped past me, he too calling 'Stop, thief!' It was all done in the blink of an eye.

Slowly, almost leisurely, the girl rose. I must have stepped out from the tree in all the excitement, because she was looking straight at me. She lifted her basket and looked about, as though considering which way to go. Then she began to make straight for me. I saw that she moved her right leg with a restricted motion, as though there were a stone in the shoe. My instinct was to bolt. But something held me. Apprehension? Fear. The closer she came, the more paralysed I was. At last she stood before me, so close that there was nothing else in my field of vision. 'You were watching me. Why?'

My limbs were as though paralysed. My thoughts, too. I opened and closed my mouth, swallowed dryness. How she must despise the obscenity of my huge Adam's apple, bobbing up and down like a float on a fishing-line. Involuntarily, my eyes drifted down toward the basket of linen.

'I've seen you before,' she said. When I didn't reply, her hand swooped out of nowhere and smashed across my face. The smart was appalling, shortening my breath and blinding my eyes with hot water. I turned my face from her. To anyone in the vicinity it must have appeared a domestic squabble.

'I don't like to be watched,' she hissed. Then, unhurrying, though Lazlo was by this time pacing back and forth in front of his shop like an agitated hen, she raised her basket and proceeded through the park in the direction of the river.

V

Meisel's Granddaughter

This is what Father Kaufmann told me that same evening.

'I've only heard the story second-hand, you understand. You should really ask Emil. He's had dealings all his life with Ezra Meisel. But what you heard is true. Meisel only had one son, Izsak. There was a daughter, but she died a young child. The mother, too, not long after Izsak was born. Puerperal fever, I don't doubt. So that Meisel raised Izsak single-handed, which was quite a feat, particularly in the days before they cleared out the old ghetto.

'The ghetto I've seen with my own eyes. A rabbi from the Spanish Synagogue organised a tour for some of us seminarians just before the tenements were to be pulled down. A more overcrowded and degraded den of humanity it would be difficult to imagine. Disease was rampant, cholera, tuberculosis, typhoid fever. There was no sewerage to speak of. Poverty has a smell, you know. A mixture of old laundry and cabbage-water and stale piss. But this was far worse than anything I'd encountered. Ragged children stood in doorless houses that gaped like ruined mouths, windows of broken glass

41

or boarded up, entire families living in a single room, owning no more than a pram to hawk their goods in. One water-pump might serve an entire slum of maybe forty families. And yet it wasn't all misery. There was life, there, too. All this I'm telling you so you can imagine how it must have been for Ezra Meisel to be left with a young family. The daughter died. Izsak he took away when he was scarcely more than an infant. I've little doubt that's what saved him.

'We move on twenty years. Old Meisel's business has prospered. Izsak, his only son, is to be married, to the daughter of Rabbi Jakobs. A fine woman, renowned for her beauty. Izsak and she have played together since they were children. He loves her, and she him. Dinah is her name. It was a splendid wedding, by all accounts. But they were not blessed with children.

'The war came. Like so many others, like Emil's two brothers, the uncles you've never met, Izsak became a soldier. I heard it said that when she saw him in uniform, Dinah threw herself onto her knees to beseech him not to go, and hugged his knees so that he had to drag her out of the door. It was the last time she ever saw him. When news came that he had been killed, Ezra Meisel was not the only one to go out of his mind with grief. Dinah, too. She refused to believe a mere telegram could decide that her beautiful husband had been killed. She took to questioning everyone who had been at the Italian front, even the blind and the crippled who begged at every street corner. This was a time of great turmoil, even after the war ended. All through Europe, the old empires had collapsed. The new republics were in the process of being born. In such confusion, was it not possible that God had spared her Izsak?

'Gradually, she relinquished hope. I say relinquished. Because it was as if she were relinquishing her hold on the world. She took to wandering the streets, a lost soul. She took up with men. Don't misunderstand me. She never became what they call a streetwalker. She never looked for money, so far as I have heard. Perhaps it was that she could lose herself only in the embrace of a stranger. She still had vestiges of her beauty, a strange, tortured beauty that hunger had sharpened. She became a great favourite with artists, a model who would pose and not ask anything but the sour wine and black bread they allowed her to share. You of course don't remember. The last years of the war were years of starvation.

'I saw her, once. But by then the consumption was already well advanced. The cheeks were hollow, the skin lifeless. She coughed blood constantly into a filthy rag, it was painful to see. But her eyes were lit by that wild intensity, demonic or angelic, that the disease sometimes brings in the final throes.

'Of course, leading that life, she was often pregnant. Who knows how many miscarriages she'd had, a woman in her pitiful condition. But one survived. She took the child to her father, the rabbi. Rabbi Jakobs drove her away. He had no such daughter! And where the rabbi forsook the infant, Old Meisel, the merchant, took it in. It was, after all, the child of the woman his beloved son had taken to wife. A baby girl.

'Leah, he named her.' He paused, dampened a finger, and traced the strange writing on the kitchen window, which had fogged. האל 'Jacob's wife, one of the four Matriarchs of Israel. The name signifies unwell or sickly, as I imagine the infant must have appeared.' He stopped, as if he had just become aware of how much he'd been speaking, and he slowly wiped away the letters with the sleeve of his soutane.

'And so, the girl I saw in the shop...?'

'...was Leah. Leah Meisel. Ezra arranged for her to take his surname. Dinah Jacobs had no blood of his. And who knows who the father was, or even if he was a Jew.'

I considered. All this was new to me, yet oddly, it was as if a story was being told whose outlines I already knew. 'There's a picture,' I said. 'A charcoal. More than one. In father's gallery. Do you think they can have been of her, the girl's mother?'

He considered. 'I don't see why not.' He squinted an eye, assessing me. 'Nudes?'

I blushed, and deflected my eyes.

'Nudes,' he concluded, roughly tousling my hair. 'Have you heard the story of Lilith?'

I replied I hadn't.

'It's an old tradition from the Talmud. The legend says that Adam, before Eve was created from his own rib, was smitten by a female creature named Lilith, who was born at the same time as Adam and of the same clay. She was as much demon as woman. A wanton, so the legend goes. She left the Garden of Eden herself, having coupled with an Archangel. Again, you need to be on your guard. Beauty is not always the same as attractiveness. There can be no doubt Eve was the more beautiful of the two women. But I've always had the feeling that, to poor Adam, Lilith was the more attractive.' He winked a grey eye. 'Be careful you've not encountered your Lilith.'

'I saw her, today.'

'Today? The girl?'

44

'She was sitting in Vojan Park.' The way, all at once, you decide to take a dive so that the limbs are what decide, not reason, that was how I decided to recount the scene that I'd witnessed that morning, everything, with the exception of the slap whose smart I could still feel. *I don't like to be watched.*

'So it's true, the stories they tell about her.' He tut-tutted, mildly. 'For shame. And on their Sabbath, too.'

After the escapade in the park, my fantasies became more sexualised. This, too, I kept secret from my confessor. There was something of the masochist in my adolescent imaginings, but also its opposite. In the games of humiliation I'd dream up, roles were swapped, first I'd be the victim, then the perpetrator. There was little sadism in the scenarios, little pain that was physical. They were fantasies of domination and shaming, of mortification and exposure. Mild enough fare. I might well have spoken of them to Father Kaufmann but that the old priest was becoming increasingly hard of hearing. The house was never empty. The merest chance that my masochistic fantasies might be overheard by the cook or maid, by Maman in her bedroom or Katya in her attic, put a padlock on my tongue.

I also took to sneaking longer looks at the nude portraits of Dinah Meisel, the half-dozen charcoals and aquatints that my father held in the display cases to the rear of the gallery. Visually I caressed them, pored over them, examined them so intimately that I knew every square inch of that body, and could play with its orientation at will, substituting the face of Leah Meisel for that of her mother, the model. It was a public space, where I might be discovered at any moment, but that threat merely added to the guilty frisson of the activity.

With trepidation, with anticipation, I awaited the arrival of the card, the note to advise Papa that some pieces of art had fallen into Old Meisel's possession. What if she were there, in the shop? Would I be able to meet her gaze? Would she read the dark and twisted desire in my fifteen year old face, and know what shameful scenarios I nightly dreamed up for the two of us? But weeks passed, and the card never arrived.

Then came the soiree when the bombshell was dropped. Old Meisel was making preparations to leave. Klaus' friend Novák, who worked in the Town Hall, had witnessed it with his own eyes. I could no longer sit around, waiting for a note to my father that might never come. I'd have to seek her out on my own initiative.

What I was to say to her, once I tracked her down, I hadn't the slightest idea.

VI

Katya

That summer, it happened that Katya and some of her colleagues were mounting an exhibition in a disused cafeteria on Hybernska Street. Up to that year, I'd been largely ignored by Katya. Now that my voice had broken, she finally appeared to notice me. I'm not being entirely fair. Unlike Klaus, Katya had gone to a boarding school, so that throughout my childhood we really only saw her one weekend out of every month, and during holidays. It was her own choice, apparently. More recently she worked in a typing-pool for Meier & Nedvěd. I can still hear the din of the great room where the typewriters were set out in rows and columns like so many lathes or sewing-machines, except that here what they manufactured was text. It all made a terrific racket, like a torrential downpour on a zinc roof. Given her speed and accuracy, Maman couldn't understand why she wouldn't look for a position as a stenographer, but Katya was happier with the anonymity of the typing-pool.

Even when she was home, she spent long hours up in the attic, which Papa had altered into a studio for her. Sometimes you'd only realise she was there from the lovely woodwind of a clarinet moving through the scales. Growing up, she felt more like an occasional lodger than a regular member of the household.

She wasn't formally trained as an artist. She'd dropped out of college after a single term. But somehow she'd fallen in with an artist's collective that squatted in a derelict tenement in the Vyšehrad area that had thus far been overlooked for demolition. They were an odd bunch. Misfits, political radicals. How Katya had been inducted I have no idea, because she was desperately shy. It wasn't only on account of the birthmark, though she was morbidly conscious of that. One self-portrait she'd actually overwritten with the words: *A blackbird, startled out of a raspberry bush, spatters shit on the artist's head*. She wore her hair low over the brow like a crow's wing to hide it. But her reticence was more deeply engrained, and she never looked anyone in the eye, not even Papa. I've no doubt Dr Freud would have a term for what afflicted her, and a pathology to match.

With me she was easier, especially now I was a gangling youth with a cracked voice. Perhaps she sensed a kindred spirit. Having been home tutored, I knew just about no one my own age. I wasn't shy, not the way she was. Awkward, yes. Self-conscious. But from as far back as I can remember I'd babbled constantly to Maman in Italian, I'd pestered Marta, the cook and Jula, the maid in Czech, and now I was older, I engaged Father Kaufmann in long German conversations on everything under the sun. Papa too.

In the run up to the exhibition on Hybernska Street, Katya had handed in her notice at Meier & Nedvěd. For the present she'd live on her savings, give the artistic life a real go. The

exhibition was being organised by a character named Václav
– they didn't seem to go in for surnames in the commune. He
had a thick mane of hair, a goatee, and round wire glasses
that I assume was intended to suggest a soviet revolutionary.
He wore, moreover, even in the heat of summer, an army
greatcoat with epaulettes dating from the war, though he was
far too young to have taken any part in it. In fact he can't
have been more than twenty-one or two, Katya's age. I daresay
nowadays I'd have thought him a preposterous figure. On the
morning that Katya brought me into the Vyšehrad tenement, I
was enthralled by him.

I assumed they'd slept together. I assumed this not merely
because there was an ethic of free love in the commune – all
doors had been removed from their hinges, there were old
and stained mattresses on every floor and graffiti in several
languages declaring all property was theft – but because as we
walked there that Sunday morning, she asked me whether I
was still a virgin. And then there was Lizaveta, a large-boned
blonde who hovered protectively in the vicinity of Václav and
gave Katya the evils every time Václav joked with her. So
much for free love.

Father Kaufmann had said that poverty has a smell – an
admixture of old laundry and cabbage-water and stale piss.
If so, this place was poor indeed. Add into the mix the waft
of smoke from an open wood fire above which some gloopy
porridge-like substance was bubbling, the dampness of
diseased masonry, bird droppings, dry rot, and the acrid tang of
printer's inks. Such art as they engaged in appeared to consist
chiefly of screen-prints and fliers, dozens of which were
drying on strings suspended across doorways and windows

like bunting on a river-boat.

Katya had brought me along ostensibly to help move load after load of their wares from Vyšehrad up to Hybernska Street. I say ostensibly, because there seemed to be no shortage of bodies milling about. On the other hand they only had one handcart, so that the process was laborious and inefficient in the extreme, though for all that filled with high-spirits. Václav gave orders which were ignored or superseded, so many and various were the languages of the party. There was a giant, a dray-horse of a man, to pull the handcart each time it was loaded up, so high and heavily that the axle groaned plaintively while the high mounds of papers, boards, ready-madges, plaster-casts and assorted paraphernalia shed fliers, papers and million Reichmark notes like so many leaves in late October. Ivan, they called him. He was a Serb, a long-haired, bearded, greasy figure with wild eyes who grunted or boomed out single words, monosyllables for the most part – adjectives or nouns unencumbered by syntax. It may be that these were all the Czech he knew, though he gave the impression he'd be contentedly tongue-tied in any language.

Seven trips all told it took us, each round trip perhaps three miles. To add to the general merriment, an accordion and tambour danced along in front of the charivari, played by a brother and sister who hailed from Dresden. Roma gypsies, so they were scarcely Aryan types. It was a Sunday, and we received many a look of reproach from the good citizens of Prague as we traipsed up and down, a ragtag assortment of street-kids trailing like kite-tails behind, gathering the worthless banknotes. The cafeteria on Hybernska Street must have belonged to a relative, presumably of Václav. It's difficult to see how else he would have got permission to use it. It might also explain the paper which Václav flashed to the gendarme who arrested our merry procession and held up its progress for twenty minutes.

It was after ten by the time we got back to Nerudova Street. Little had been achieved beyond moving what was required to be moved from the Vyšehrad squat. Everything had been dumped on the floor of the cafeteria. It would take most of the week to sort through it, house it properly, arrange the space, hang the exhibition. I looked forward to the week, for Papa was all for my being involved. No harm for the lad to get out there into the real world, he said. And to be fair, Maman was no longer for wrapping her Guido up in cotton-wool.

There was another reason I was pleased to have a week away from the *U Černého Slunce* Gallery. About a month before, Papa had taken it into his head that Jan should teach me the basics of woodturning. The ex-soldier was at once suspicious. At such times, his scowl was something to behold. 'You think I'll teach the boy all I can do?'

'Ha! A few pointers, Jan. The basics.'

'For what would I do this?'

Papa put his arm around the veteran's shoulders. 'Tell me, how many years have you worked for me now, Jan?'

'I've worked here for eight years.'

'Eight years. And in all that time, have you ever heard me complain about your work?'

Jan's scowl, if anything, tightened. But as it did, he stood more erect.

'Not once. Because your work is first class. Now tell me. Do you really suppose I'd have you train up a clodhopper like

Guido to take your place?'

He squinted, assessing and dismissing me.

'I'm thinking of the boy, not you. Suppose another war were to come, eh? What then? It will be good for him to have a skill.'

'But Papa, if a war were to come along, I'd be a soldier.'

'You, with your heart wired up wrong like a panicky clock? No, no. I've made up my mind.' His arm released his worker. 'Yes, Jan?'

Jan doffed his forage-cap and clicked his heels together. It may have been some relic from his military days, or more likely a parody of that time.

'It's settled. Jan will teach you the basics of woodturning for one hour every morning.' And so it was, for the next three weeks, which is to say six hours. And such hours of torture they were, Jan squinting at me as though I were a cuckoo raring to push him out of the nest, barely throwing me a word, pushing me aside with his strange prosthesis shaped like a magnifying-glass without a lens, and wielding deftly the tools whose names I scarcely knew.

I was mightily relieved to have a break from that lathe. And of course, it wasn't lost on me that Hybernska Street wasn't a hundred miles from Bilkova Street, where old Meisel had his shop. I'd have many an opportunity during the course of that week to slip out and wander in search of the alley-cat who'd slapped my face. Katya had said that one of our main tasks, while the others mounted the exhibition proper, would be to distribute fliers and paste up posters announcing, rather grandly, *The First International Exhibition of 'Pequod Mutiny'*. She herself had designed the poster, a bizarre photomontage of disarticulated dolls and mannequins overwritten by texts in various fonts and at various angles. They were merely awaiting the arrival of a mimeograph to crank out copies by the hundred. As the city was to be divvied up for distribution, I'd be making the case for being assigned the Josefov quarter. The only question was whether to let Katya in on my dark secret. After all, she'd begun to treat me as an adult.

I decided to hold off, for the moment. I didn't want her to veto my working the streets of the Jewish quarter if she decided the infatuation was bad news. After all, everyone else did. Time enough to broach the subject after the exhibition.

VII

'Pequod Mutiny'

The next day was given over to hard graft. There were fewer of us about, and putting the disused cafeteria into some sort of order took up the bulk of the day. The hundred chairs had to be stacked somewhere out the back, though the tables, ornate marble-top affairs on wrought iron legs, were fixed to the floor and immoveable. Václav, whose uncle it turned out owned the place, gave orders liberally, just as he had done the day before, and just as liberally the orders were circumvented. And at every circumvention, imposing as any Wagner heroine, her blonde tresses braided into bread-like spirals, Lizaveta frowned her deep displeasure. Brunhilda, Katya called her behind her back. In fact she had secret names for all of the company. Václav she dubbed Trotsky, and once I heard that it was patent which revolutionary he was emulating; the brother and sister from Dresden were Hansel and Gretel; a stubbly character who always wore a peaked cap was the Good Soldier Švejk; and the giant Serb was Rasputin, and now that she said it, the pale eyes in his weather-cudgelled face were lit by the same crazed magnetism as the mad Russian monk.

To give him his due, Trotsky seemed too caught up in the bustle to be greatly bothered by the indiscipline. The one black mark I scored against him was when, laden down with the machine, myself and Hansel, the Dresden accordion-player, asked where he wanted the mimeograph to go. 'That's not a mimeograph,' he corrected. 'That's a spirit-duplicator.' As if our muscles gave a damn what the contraption was called. At length, after much toing and froing, it was deposited in the old kitchen which was to serve as office and command centre.

Periodically, Ivan would arrive outside with another cartload of junk. 'Good!' he'd grunt. Or 'Nice!' The most curious load arrived toward evening, just as Katya and I were setting off homeward – a party of eleven naked shop mannequins, their limbs in a variety of agonised contortions. Trotsky was particularly animated to see these arrive, though what precisely he had in mind for them he hadn't imparted to a single soul, with the possible exception of the formidable Lizaveta.

They must have worked on them all through that night. When we arrived the following morning, they were variously dispersed about the cafeteria, standing in twos or threes at the tables or propped against the counter. It was how they were dressed that startled. In the first place they had been bewigged and garishly painted. Acquisitive, piggy eyes and huge, leering grins. Some had furs or stoles, some jackets, and there was an impressive variety of feathers and hats on display. Several wore gas-masks and one, moustached and with wire glasses, wore a chamber-pot which somehow called to mind a German *Stahlhelm*. Each had a miniature Czechoslovakian flag taped to its right hand. None, though, wore anything below the waist apart from shoes and stockings, their genitalia suggested by pubic scribbles.

One figure caused me discomfort. Over by the toilets stood a mannequin the head of which had been replaced with an actual pig's head. It was dressed in the garb of a priest, a crucifix rather than a flag tied to its right hand by a rosary. To complete the tableau, by the door, just as one entered, a figure on wheels held aloft a begging cup, legless and with dark glasses, a war-cripple in the uniform of the Austro-Hungarian army. A placard strung around its neck read 'Pequod Mutiny', in faultless Sütterlin script. It was as if a Georg Grosz painting had come to hideous life.

I was impressed. Katya too. Immediately, she had the idea that we must add music to the atmosphere, so she dispatched me back to Nerudova Street to fetch the old phonograph from her attic studio. I was only vaguely aware that she had one, so rarely had I been allowed into that sanctum. 'See what you can find that's modern,' she said. 'None of Maman's Italian operas, Guido, you understand? And no Schubert. And *definitely* no Smetana. Bring the Kurt Weil opera that Father Kaufmann gave me for my twenty-first. You know the one. The Seven Deadly Sins? And bring that blues record you like so much.'

'And Papa's collection of Carlos Gardel tangos?' I was only half-joking.

'Yes!' she clapped. 'Bring those!'

'Ok,' I said, doubtfully. 'I'll see what I can do.'

That afternoon and all day Wednesday, the other artists of the commune added their various wares, turning the cafeteria by degrees into a menacing Spiegeltent. Ivan, it turned out, had spent his time collecting a range of plaster-cast faces, including his own and Katya's, which now adorned the walls like so many death masks, presiding from closed eyes. Katya's contribution consisted of a range of jagged collages and photo-montages, over-stamped with lettering in various alphabets that spelt out nonsense words. There were also a couple of her oils, distorted self-portraits that would have been grotesque but for the bizarre humour of the titles she'd dreamed up for them.

The two Dresdeners had compiled an endless series of streetscapes, all painted thinly on sheets of newsprint so that the text showed through. These, together with thousands of the old Reichmark notes they'd brought with them in suitcases, they pasted up about the walls like cheap wallpaper. A plan to have the streetscapes overlaid with a screening of F.W. Murnau's *Faust* had to be shelved at the last minute when the Hvězdné Kino failed to furnish the projector they'd promised. Given what was to transpire, it was probably just as well.

Among the other exhibits, a Chinese lantern that cast shadows of grotesques, and a giant, rusted mantrap from the war stood out. And all the while, *Mi Buenos Aires querido* slowed entropically, with no free hand to wind the phonograph, valiantly and vainly contesting the indefatigable clatter-clank of the mimeograph, or spirit-duplicator, as Václav insisted. Back in the kitchen-cum-office, Brunhilda was cranking off hundreds of copies of the *First Manifesto of Pequod Mutiny Collective* in time for the grand opening.

Klaus had been home when I'd arrived for the phonograph, and though I tried my utmost to dissuade him, he'd insisted on carrying the thing as far as Hybernska Street. His reaction to the Wunderkammer was entirely predictable, though he waited until we were briefly back outside to give voice to it. 'Why must you always celebrate what's ugly? It's perverse! It's childish. Besides, it's old hat. Isn't this precisely the sort of rubbish they mounted in the Cabaret Voltaire twenty years ago?'

Katya looked to the pavement. 'I suppose you'll tell Papa.'

'Why would I want to hurt Papa? You live in the most beautiful of cities, and all you see is ugliness. You disappoint him, Katya. But I expect you know that, right?'

'I disappoint you, Klaus. It's not the same thing.'

Good for you, I thought. Klaus simply shrugged and walked away.

The grand opening was to be on Friday evening. That left all day Thursday and Friday to distribute the fliers and posters. Though it raised a few eyebrows, no one objected to my taking on the Josefov quarter, together with a spry little chap from Brno I'd seen back in the Vyšehrad squat – the one whom Katya dubbed the Good Soldier Švejk. We set off with a brush and bucket of paste each, and one knapsack apiece – one for fliers, which were monochrome, the other for posters, which were larger and overlaid in three colours. It was a windy day, thin high clouds skitting across an otherwise clear sky.

Most of the morning was spent pasting posters to lamp-posts and pillar-boxes, pressing fliers on unwilling passers-by, and cadging water so as to keep the thick gloop from setting, so that it was well after lunch before we got to Bilkova Street. Meisel's green van was parked at the laneway to the side of the shop. But even had it not been, that wouldn't have been a cause for concern. He was often gone for days at a time, scouting the

country for auctions and bargains. At such times he'd leave
the shop in the charge of his nephew, whom everyone called
'Hookworm'. It was widely known he had connections in the
underworld. Another nephew drove the van and did the heavy
lifting. As for Leah Meisel, that demon-child whom Father
Kaufmann had dubbed my Lilith, there wasn't the merest sign
of her that day, neither at the shop nor anywhere else in the
Jewish quarter. It was a pity. I would have liked her to have
seen me at our activity, glamourised by association with a
bunch of misfit artists who, as Václav put it, were throwing a
custard pie into the faces of the bourgeoisie.

VIII

Národní Obec Fašistická

On the Friday morning, the very morning of the grand opening, Katya and I arrived to a chaotic scene. A crowd of onlookers had gathered outside the cafeteria. We elbowed through to find that every one of the windows had been put in. In the gloomy interior, Trotsky was pacing about, the army greatcoat billowing behind him, the grind and tinkle of broken glass under his boots as he inspected the damage. Even from the street I could see there was paint daubed on the walls, and that the mannequins had been kicked asunder.

He glanced toward us as we stood in the open doorway, a wry smile playing on his lips. 'Seems like we've had a visit from Gajda's thugs.' He pointed to a red scrawl daubing the door. *NOF*, the National Fascist League, and beside it, a stencilled image of the axe in its bundle of rods. Behind his back, on the wall the two Dresdener Romas had pasted over with their newspapers overlain with watercolour streetscapes, enormous capitals of dripping red paint spelled out the word: DEGENEROVANÉ – which is to say, degenerate.

Once inside, the extent of the devastation became apparent.

The mirror had been daubed with a Star of David and the word *ŽIDÉ*, though so far as I knew, Katya was the only one of the commune who carried a taint of Jewish blood. Strips had been torn out of the Reichmark wallpaper, Katya's two canvases had been slashed with a knife, the Chinese lantern kicked in, the jaws of the mantrap daubed with red paint. There was even a childish swastika burned into the marble countertop. Only Ivan's death masks had been spared, these and the phonograph and records, which serendipity had placed for the night in the kitchen-office to the rear of the premises.

Katya stood by her two slashed canvases, touching the wounded fabric. 'We'll have to cancel the opening.'

'Not a bit of it! This is perfect!'

'Perfect?' For once, she eyeballed her interlocutor.

'It could not be better!' His face lit with madness, Václav laughed toward one of us, then the other. 'Don't you see?' He shook his mane, the glasses flashing in the sullen light. 'Now we've had our pogrom! Our very own bonfire of the vanities!' And somehow, amidst all the debris and ruin, his laughter was contagious.

A reporter came, and Trotsky was in his element. Then a photographer, whose flashbulbs froze the scene with sudden lightning. Sometime later Ivan arrived. 'Goths,' he opined. Then 'Visigoths,' nodding as though it were an improvement on 'Goths'. Lizaveta came in next, Brunhilda with broom and dustpan. Václav, taking his leave of the reporter, watched her setting about clearing the floor. 'You know, I'd love to leave all that glass lying exactly where it is. Just listen to the crunch of it!'

'No good,' growled Rasputin.

While the rest of the collective put the exhibition back together, I set off to finish canvassing the Josefov area. That morning, the Good Soldier Švejk was a no-show, so Katya came with me. She'd given up on any possibility of properly repairing the two canvases in time for the opening, and took the sanguine view that it was better to stitch across the gashes with black thread in such a way as to highlight the sutures over the scarring. She'd even argued, with eventual success, that they shouldn't clean off the mirror. All the same, I could sense that the violence of the defacements had disturbed her. So, to keep her mind from dwelling too much on the NOF hoodlums, I decided the time had come to let her in on my secret passion. We were nowhere near Meisel's shop, so I had little fear of encountering its object. I even went so far as to include the resounding slap which had crowned the incident in the park. Everything, even the fact she was slightly lame.

'She sounds like quite a girl.'

'You might say that!'

'Does Papa know?'

'Not really. He may suspect.'

'Klaus?'

'Of course not.'

'She's only vicious because you saw her weakness. That she's lame. That's what made her strike out.'

'You think so?'

'I feel like I know this girl. And you haven't spoken to her?'

'When I tried, all that came out of my mouth was ah, uhm, uh…'

'I see.' We were standing at the corner of Kaprova and Maiselova, trying to unload the last of our fliers. Those who took them, and they were few and far between, tended to ball them up and drop them while still within sight. 'Suppose you were to write to her?'

'Write!' The thought had never occurred to me. Even now it seems fantastic. 'What on earth would I write?'

'I don't know. What would you *like* to say to her?'

I shrugged, weakly.

'At least if you wrote, it wouldn't be ah and uhm and uh.'

She had a point. Still, I wasn't sure. 'Father Kaufmann says there's nothing inherently special about anyone. That it's we who decide to set them up on a pedestal because we're desperate to be enthralled by something. You believe that?'

'I don't know, Guy. It sounds to me like you're pretty smitten.'

'And you really think a letter might work? What I mean, would a letter work in your case? Suppose someone you thought was a bit of a fool wrote you a letter…'

'That would depend.' There was a clock-face visible in the office across the street, and as it was already after five, she suggested going home to get ready for the launch.

'But really,' I tried once more, as we stepped onto a tram, 'you think a letter might do the trick?'

'I don't see what you have to lose. That's all I'm saying, Guy.' Then she added, 'At least your cheek will be well out of range.'

The launch was a fiasco. On either side of the doorway stood the two Dresdeners, she dressed as a *Mädchen*, he in lederhosen and Alpine hat, but each so rouged and mascaraed that they resembled two puppets. Now they really looked like they could be Hansel and Gretel. He wheezed a salutatory riff on the accordion and bowed to every attendee, she carried her upturned tambour as a tray on which were lined in neat rows miniature salted breads interspersed with shot-glasses of cheap vodka. Entry was free, though attention was directed to the begging mannequin cripple in military dress holding aloft a tin can.

In fact, Václav and Lizaveta had done a commendable job in restoring all eleven mannequins. The problem was there were very few attendees, so few that for much of the evening the mannequins outnumbered them. Those that were there consisted largely of derelicts who were attracted by the bustle and the possibility of free shots of vodka. As the night progressed, Ivan had to remove more than one of them as their petulance took a rowdy turn.

It was a fiasco. And yet, when I look back at that summer of 1938, that is the image that stays with me. For Václav was right. In its own way it was perfect – a *tableau vivant* of tramps and beggars shifting about the gaudily costumed mannequins, bickering, cadging such vodka as they could; Hansel and Gretel standing sentinel at the entrance, two figures from a mechanical clock; and all the while, drifting through the hubbub out through shattered windows into the city night, the discordant music of Kurt Weil from Katya's phonograph where she kept it wound up in the corner.

IX

Heinrich Heine

Katya, Katya. What exquisite agony your suggestion cost me.

All the long night I tossed and turned, wondering what on earth I could possibly write the girl. A simple note? A declaration? But I'd scarcely turned fifteen, and she was seventeen at the least. Two years in the difference, but such years. Besides, I was an absurd figure. A gangling youth who'd been tied to his mother's apron-strings and scarcely knew the first thing about real life. No. It was hopeless. Hopeless.

By the following morning, Saturday morning, reports of the sabotage had made the papers. Papa met us at breakfast with an interrogative stare. Before him lay *Národni Politika*, *Vlajka* and even *Rudé Právo,* which surprised. Each was opened to the account of the vandalism, varying considerably in length. *Vlajka* carried the headline 'DEGENEROVANÉ' over a centre-spread of photos that made the place look like a crime-scene. Seeing them, I experienced a tiny thrill.

'I see Radola Gajda paid you a little visit. Isn't that his calling card?' Papa's finger was on the bundle of fasces that had been stencilled on the door. Other photos in the spread included the mirror with its Star of David, the crudely burnt swastika, and the pig-headed priest. 'I don't imagine Hans will be too enamoured of this character.' And then there was a photo of Katya, who stood with Václav by her two slashed canvases. *'Katya Hayek, the artist, considers her damaged paintings.'* He read. 'It's fame of a sort, I suppose.'

We exchanged shrugs. *'Degenerované,'* said Papa, at length, when neither of us deigned to comment. 'The German term for degenerate is *'Entartete'*. Last year, in Munich, the National Socialists mounted an exhibition. *Entartete Kunst.* I know. I visited it. Not my cup of tea, but still, some interesting stuff. But I can tell you one thing, the Third Reich is not a good place to be seen to be a degenerate.' He looked from one of us to the other, waiting for a reply. When none was forthcoming, he went on, 'It seems our *Národní Obec Fašistická* is keen to afford you the same recognition.'

We were still tongue-tied. I wanted to meet Katya's eye, but she was staring mutely at the table. Papa folded away the newspapers. 'I think it might be better if you don't go back there.'

'Don't go back!'

'You know what the poet Heine says? *Dort wo man Bücher verbrennt, verbrennt man auch am Ende Menschen.* You see the way it's going in Germany. Where they burn books, they will end by burning people.'

'So you think we should just... agree to be silenced?' I'd never seen Katya talk like this, not to Papa at any rate.

'When I see a wasps' nest, I don't go poking it with a stick. What do you think you're achieving? Tell me, Katya. I want to know.'

But now she clammed up. Under her crow's wing of dark hair, I could make out a frown corrugating her brow. 'Can I be excused,' she murmured, not having touched her breakfast.

'By all means.'

She sprang from the table and left the room, not replacing the chair under the table. But it wasn't petulance. She was furious with herself for her own inarticulacy.

Papa's talk had one unforeseen consequence. I decided to take down our *Ausgewählte Gedichte von Heinrich Heine*, to see if I could track down the quote about burning books. Unwilling to cross Papa, and in any case quite exhausted after the last couple of days and last night's insomnia, I decided to spend an afternoon of lassitude in the study, surrounded as ever by bookshelves of volumes in four languages: Czech; German; Italian; and French. It was no harm. Reaching up for the volume, I must have moved too suddenly, for all at once I took a turn. Blood drained from my face and my throat hurt. Heart tripping crazily, I lay on the floor. Deep breath. Deep breath. I rose slowly, poured and drank a glass of water, lay back down, raised my legs onto the chaise-longue. At length the heartbeat flicked back to a regular pace.

I decided not to mention the turn to Maman, but spent the balance of the day leafing through Heine's Romantic verse. *Ich weiss nicht, was soll es bedeuten, Dass ich so traurig bin…*

In a flash it came to me. I could write Leah Meisel a poem!

The next couple of days I spent agonising over the poem, scratching out lines furiously that were appalling and maudlin, or so clichéd as to be laughable. On Tuesday I was back in the *U Černého Slunce* Gallery, so that it was Wednesday before I had come up with a sonnet I was moderately pleased with. I decided to run it past Katya. After all, it had been her idea to commit my thoughts to writing. But when I tapped on the attic door, there was no answer.

Now I thought about it, I hadn't seen Katya since she'd abandoned the breakfast table that Saturday morning. But then, there was nothing unusual in that. She was always secretive. But it made me doubt the efficacy of the poem, and even whether the idea of a poem was itself disastrously flawed. Ok, I said to myself, in an effort to steel my resolve. Ok. What did I have to lose? She'd said it herself. And at least my cheek would be at a safe distance.

I re-examined the sonnet. It was a poor imitation of Heine. The only part of it I remember, at this distance in time and space, is the opening quatrain. I'd laboured so long and laboriously over that part that it has remained with me down the years. *Her eyes were moons, rising from the ocean / That in the half-light shone like gypsy rings / And were as foreign. In the dark / They became caverns I would not enter.* In my defence, it must be remembered that I'd quite recently turned fifteen – on Valentine's Day, of all days.

Damn it, I thought, I'll do it! So as to give myself no time for the sort of cavernous self-doubt that characteristically stymied my every action, I took out a sheet of foolscap and copied it out in faultless copperplate, folding it into an envelope upon which I wrote the beloved name. I decided to leave the verse unsigned – perhaps it would be the first in a long series of anonymous tributes, as if I were a Provençal troubadour and she my secret lady.

I had just crossed to the Staré Město side of the Karluv

Bridge when I was once more afflicted by doubts. This would be a disaster. I would be a laughing-stock. No, no! A thousand times no! Far better to tear it into a hundred pieces. I took out the envelope and made to a parapet overlooking the river. Then, I thought, if Katya wasn't in the attic, probably she was ignoring Papa's injunction. Like as not, I'd find her in the cafeteria on Hybernska Street. And if she wasn't there, time enough to tear the offending sonnet.

My hunch was correct. I found her sitting at the counter, listening to the Good Soldier Švejk recount some anecdote or other that had his stubble cracking open into high wheezy laughter, hee-hee-hee. I could see Lizaveta in the back-office, cutting up newspapers with a scissors. Now, the presence of the Good Soldier Švejk was not something I'd foreseen. He was a genial chap, but irreverent. Pretty much the last person you'd want to learn that you'd written a love sonnet. So from the doorway I gestured to Katya to come outside for a quick word.

She looked at me with suspicion. 'Papa hasn't sent you?'

'No. Not a bit of it.'

'You're sure?'

'Swear to God!' My hands opened as though to show I concealed no weapon. Still looking as though she did not quite trust me, and to the merriment of the Good Soldier Švejk, who was wiping a tear from his eye, she slipped off the stool and came out onto the street.

'Guido,' she said, 'promise me. Papa hasn't sent you.'

'It's nothing to do with what happened here. On Friday. In point of fact, he doesn't even know I'm here.' Stop beating about the bush, Guido! 'I decided to take your advice. I…'

Unsure of how to complete the sentence, I produced the envelope.

'You've written to her!'

'A poem.' My cheeks flushed painfully. 'A sonnet.'

'May I?' Awkward as hell, I nodded. The envelope was unsealed. Fighting a smirk, she took it from me, opened it, read.

'That's sweet.'

'Sweet.' Sweet was about the last word in the world that I wanted to hear.

'What's wrong with sweet? It's nice.'

Nice! I took it back from her. 'Not bold? Not brilliant?'

'I think she'll like it.'

'Really?'

'Sure. But you need to sign it.'

I flushed crimson. 'No way!'

'Hold on,' she said, touching my forearm. She ducked into the cafeteria, returned almost at once with a fountain-pen. 'Sign it "Orlando".'

I stared, puzzled, but accepted the pen.

'Orlando? Come on, Guy! From *Shakespeare*? He woos the lovely Rosalind with poems.'

I grimaced at her, doubtful. 'Does he win her?'

'Course he does! It's Shakespeare.'

I scrawled the word hurriedly, replaced the envelope in my inside pocket, handed her the pen, and began to walk away. 'Guido,' she called. 'Remember! Faint heart…'

I thought sincerely of dumping the envelope into the nearest bin. But she was right. *Faint heart never won fair lady.* Annoyed at myself, annoyed at having shown it to her, annoyed at my ridiculous youth, I determined at once to go through with my plan. It was twenty past eleven. I remember that clearly.

The time I'd encountered Leah Meisel in the shop eating soup had been around midday. On one other occasion I'd seen her making for the shop just shy of twelve. Was it not likely then that she always took her lunch there at around noon?

There was a café several doors down from the shop on the opposite side of Bilkova street, so I determined I'd take a coffee there by the window and await her arrival. That much was clear in my mind. But what to do next? Was it really possible that I was going to march into Meisel's shop and hand her the envelope. And then wait around like a shy schoolboy while she read it and probably laughed in my face. Or worse, dismissed it as 'nice'? It didn't bear thinking about. And yet I was damned if I was going to skulk off home and leave the poem undelivered.

It happened as I walked along in exquisite anguish that I caught sight of the Serb giant, towering above everyone else, pacing along in the contrary direction, no doubt making for the exhibition. 'Ivan,' I waved to him, a plan born instantaneously in my breast. He marched across the street as though the traffic weren't there and beamed down at me. 'Ivan, you have a few minutes?' I showed him my wristwatch, tapped its face. 'Minutes.'

He considered, and nodded his long, greasy locks. 'We go for coffee?' I asked. In the pantomime that followed, my Czech came out in loud, slow fragments, as though I were the one who was a foreigner here. I pointed toward the café from which Meisel's window display was visible. 'Coffee?' I made a drinking motion.

'Beer.'

The place was quite empty, so it was easy to get a table by the window. Now, how to explain to this monosyllabic ogre what precisely I had in mind? 'There's a girl,' I began. 'A girl?'

'Girl.' A grin bloomed.

'In that shop. There.' But of course, it was unlikely she was there so early. I tapped my wristwatch. 'Not yet.'

'Jew girl?'

'Yeah. A Jewish girl. We wait here. Wait to see her enter the shop. Yes? Understand?'

Still grinning he nodded, his pale eyes intense. He lifted the beer bottle and all but drained it in one draft. Now for the tricky part. 'When she goes in, the girl,' I reached into my inside pocket and produced the envelope, 'then you give her this.'

He lifted the envelope, peered at it, weighed it, held it up to the light.

'Give it to the girl. Yes?'

He shrugged. It was affirmation enough. And for a while my spirits soared. The thought of this outsized Rasputin marching into the shop and thrusting the letter into the hand of the astonished orphan took all the adolescent sentimentality out of the gesture. So it seemed to me as I sat across from him.

The beer bottle was drained, my coffee cold, and the hands of the clock had crawled toward noon, but there was still no sign of her. For ten minutes we'd been sitting in uncomfortable silence, exchanging occasional nods or smiles. I scoured my barren brain for something to say, but nothing lived in my imagination's desert that morning. Once, he put his huge fingers under my chin, raising it. 'Mask,' he said.

'I'm sorry?'

'Mask,' he nodded. 'I do.'

A vision of the eerie array of death masks on the wall of Pequod Mutiny came to me. 'Yes,' I grinned enthusiastically, touched my face. 'Mask. Ha ha! Why not?'

He nodded, twice. Then silence perched again at our table, clacking its beak. At five past twelve I suggested a second beer. He shook his locks. 'I go,' he said, making to rise.

'No. Please!' I gestured to the waiter. Another beer. The thought he might abandon me and force me to give the missal directly into her keeping filled me with dread. He shrugged, pointed to the clock, his features darkening.

At twenty past, I caught sight of her. She was in the company of a redhead in a thick boa and huge hat. I grabbed Ivan's forearm. 'There!' I whispered. 'That's the girl. Not the redhead. The other one.' He at once rose from the table, swept up the envelope, and made to intercept her. 'No! Wait until she's alone! Wait until she's gone into the shop. Then give her five more minutes.' I flashed five outstretched fingers. 'Five minutes, ok?'

He nodded. But he wasn't happy.

At length the two girls parted, and I watched my beloved limp into the antique shop. After precisely two minutes, the Serb marched out of the café, strode across the street, and disappeared in after her. Scarcely a count of ten after that he re-emerged, waved generally at the café without looking, already striding purposefully in the direction of Hybernska Street. I sat, alone, my heart pounding, tiny fireflies dancing about my peripheral vision.

What happened next was uncanny. So it has always seemed to me. I saw her head and torso appear in the shop-window. It was a blurred vision, washed of colour and with ghostly reflections of passing traffic sustained across the glass, as though somehow the gloomy interior were underwater. I thought of the legend of the Lorelai, who lure sailors to their death on the Rhine. She didn't once look about, that was what was so strange, but from the very first gazed directly at me. It was as if she knew I'd be precisely there.

Slowly, like something from a Fritz Lang film, I saw the white sheet of paper swim up over her pale face. The eyes were sockets, emptied by shadow. When the paper was aloft over her head, she began to shred it, then let the scraps fall all about her black mass of hair like so much confetti. The vision then sank back from the window into the dark interior.

Five minutes, perhaps, I sat. I wasn't dismayed. I felt calm, so calm that it seemed to me the whole world had slowed down. The opening shots of the campaign had been exchanged.

I rose and paid the bill, then all but laughing I made for the exhibition. I was keen to apprise Katya of all that had happened.

X

Pickaxe Handles

Some sort of foreboding must have overtaken me as I turned onto Hybernska Street, because I was already jogging as I saw the thin crowd gathered outside the cafeteria. There was a police car drawn up, and several uniformed officers were milling about. Ivan's head towered above them. He was striding about, his hands tearing at his hair, giving out, in a voice that cracked soprano with emotion, a stream of garbled recriminations aimed toward himself.

If the scene I hit upon wasn't quite as chaotic as the morning after our Kristallnacht, it was far more disturbing. The Good Soldier Švejk was seated on the pavement, bloodied, a bandage being wrapped around his head by Lizaveta. I called to her, and when she turned toward me I was shocked to see her left eye swollen shut like an obscene fruit. 'Where's Katya?' I cried. But she shrugged, and returned to the bandaging.

Inside the shop, Václav was talking to one of the police, his face more bloodless than I'd ever seen it. It was clear that whoever had entered the place had really gone to town this time. The mannequins were a tangled mass of limbs and collapsed torsos, the phonograph, records and duplicating machine were in fragments, and the floor strewn with torn papers and bits of plaster. Even some of the marble table-tops had been chipped.

I found out later that, not very long after I'd left, two open trucks had pulled up outside the place. Some eight or nine thugs in paramilitary uniform, bandanas pulled up over their faces, had jumped off and rushed the exhibition, wielding billy-clubs and pick-axe handles. Švejk had been the first to go down. Then, while the others set about smashing up the mannequins, three of them cornered Katya and set on her with clubs and boots without mercy.

'For Christ's sake where is she?' I cried. The policeman scowled, unused to any interruption from a mere adolescent.

'They took her away,' said Václav. 'Lizaveta did everything she could. But she wasn't able to stop them.'

Christ! I thought. Christ! What to do?

Instinctively, I ran. The gallery on Karluva Street was a good half-mile away, but I ran at such a sprint that by the time I arrived my heart was pounding dangerously at my throat. 'Papa!' I cried, but it was all I could get out, doubled over as I was and gulping great drafts of air into my lungs.

'What? What is it, boy? Take your time.'

'Papa! They've got Katya!'

'Where?'

'The exhibition.'

He marched so fast toward the cafeteria on Hybernska Street that it was all I could do to keep up with him. As he proceeded he fired questions toward where I was trotting behind him.

'So what happened?'

'They came back.'

'The same thugs?'

'I don't know. I think so.'

'What was Katya doing there?'

'I don't know.'

'What were you doing there?'

'I went to find Katya.'

'But she was gone?'

'No. Earlier. This morning I went.'

'You *left* her there?' Momentarily, he stopped. I gasped for breath, but also for mortification. 'Guido, you left her there?'

Mortified, gasping for breath, I nodded.

'Klaus wouldn't have left her there.'

It was a blow to the solar plexus. If he had tried, he could not have found a more hurtful thing to say. Papa, whom I'd always loved. Papa, whom I'd always striven to emulate. Hot tears blinded me. After that, I fell fifteen or twenty paces behind my father where he marched ever onward, every so often breaking into short trots.

When we got there I crouched, my fingers at my jugular to feel the mad pulse. All blood had drained from my face. Papa made straight for Václav, who was now alone, his head in his hands. 'Where's my daughter?'

'Sir?'

'Katya Hayek. Where have they taken her?'

Václav looked up, confused. He looked around for Lizaveta, who had been there during the attack, motioned rapidly for her to come over. Apart from the clammed-up eye, it looked like she'd taken a crack to the mouth, which had begun to discolour and swell to one side.

'Where have they taken Katerina Hayek?'

She shrugged. 'Hospital.' It clearly hurt to speak.

'The hospital.' He held her shoulders. She winced. 'Which hospital?'

'I don't know. The hospital.'

'You get home,' he barked at me. 'Get home, and stay home.'

I wasn't allowed to visit the hospital for two days, but after that I visited every day. When at last I saw her, I was shocked by Katya's appearance. She'd taken more than one blow to the head. Her skull had been fractured and in order to stitch up the wounds they'd had to shave her scalp. When her head wasn't bandaged, it was covered with a convict-like stubble through which the sutures showed like lines of ants. One blow in particular had left a hand-sized half-moon mark, as though she'd received a back-kick from a horse. Her right arm stuck out from her in plaster. It had received multiple fractures where she'd tried to ward off the blows. Her collarbone, too, had been broken. Her bruised ribs were tightly wound in bandages, and one lung had been punctured. Her jaw had been dislocated, and the white of one eye was so bloodied that it was difficult to look at her.

To give him his due, Papa had told me before we arrived that he'd been too harsh with me. What could I have done, faced with a half-dozen men with pick-axe handles? He had one child laid up in hospital, what great benefit would it be to have two? But the damage had been done. *Klaus would not have left her alone there*. Besides, there was something else gnawing my breast. It was something I was ashamed to tell him. Had I not engaged Ivan on my childish quest, he'd have been at the café. That's where he'd been heading when I'd intercepted him, and forced him to wait with me in the café far longer than he was comfortable with. I was scrawny, but I had big fists. Who knows but that the sight of the giant Serb beside me might have made them think twice about setting on three defenceless artists.

My spirits were listless all that week and I moped about the house, skin lifeless, hair limp and dark thumbprints of insomnia pushed under each eye. It was as if the gears in my head had disengaged. Everything, even the most minor task, took on monstrous proportions. Maman must have had a word with Papa, because as we made our way to the gallery that Thursday morning, he brought up the subject again. 'Don't beat yourself up over it, Guy. There was nothing you could have done.'

I said nothing. There was nothing to say.

'Sit down,' he said. I didn't understand. We were crossing the Karluv Bridge. He gestured toward a bench in one of the alcoves. This was a first. Never before had we interrupted our descent to open up the gallery for a parley.

'This is something I've never told you,' he began, standing before me and looking up at the statues towering over us as though they were some sort of graven jury. 'In fact, it's something I've never told anyone. Not Klaus. Not even your mother. Did you never wonder how it came about that both of my brothers were lost in the war, but that I remained unscathed?'

I fidgeted uncomfortably, the taboo of the subject was so deeply entrenched.

'Well I'll tell you. It's time you learned about your old man.' He paused, his eyes on the statuary, the anguish palpable.

'You don't have to tell me anything, Papa.'

'I know. I know I don't.' For the first time, he glanced at me. 'I want to.'

'Ok.'

'We were three brothers. I was the middle brother, did you know that? Rudi was the eldest. So by rights, Rudi would have inherited the business. And Franz, Franz was only sixteen when news came that the heir to the throne had been shot in Sarajevo. Franz actually lied about his age to enlist. And I was the middle boy, neither clever as Rudolph nor as full of fire as Franz. I wasn't a coward. Or at least, I had no reason to believe I was. I had no great love for the Kaiser, but then, what Czech ever had any great love for the Habsburgs? But I'd nothing against him either. Franz was the nationalist of the family. But, I was engaged to marry Elsa Mörschel…' He stopped. He shook his head, and I thought for a while he wasn't going to resume. Then he sat, his cheeks in his hands, staring directly across the bridge at the far alcove. Perhaps he was seeing the figures there, the ghosts of his past, all of them dead. 'Elsa Mörschel. The singer. My father, Rudolph Snr, didn't think much of the idea of my marrying her. But there you have it. I was infatuated. I was in love, why not say it? And that, I can say, changed my perspective on everything.

'Franz jumped to the colours, without ever informing our parents. And Rudolph too was called up. But as for me, Emil Hayek? I was in love. My young wife-to-be loved me, or so I believed. I had too much to lose. It wasn't so much the idea of death that I was fearful of. It was the idea that I might come back crippled, or disfigured. Then Elsa might not love me any more. And so I let old man Mörschel find his future son-in-law a good position in one of the ministries. We even brought forward the wedding. Mörschel was from an old aristocratic family which still had a lot of pull. I had no skills essential to the war effort. I wasn't a train-driver. I couldn't mine coal, or repair aircraft engines. And so I was assigned to munitions, rubber-stamping train timetables to keep the troops supplied up at the front. You see? I kept myself as far as I could from danger while Rudi and Franz set off for the Galician front. And they never came back. Then my parents died in the flu epidemic, but I know they really died of a broken heart. And so I came to inherit the business which should by rights have been Rudi's. Do you think I could ever again look Rudi's widow in the face? Or little Rudi, who grew up without a father?

'But you know what it is that haunts me most? It was a simple look. A look of hurt disappointment. Not from Rudi, which might have been expected. But Rudi had a way of taking things in his stride. If a dodge like munitions had come his way, he'd probably have jumped at it. No. It was Franz's look. When he was home on leave, in uniform while I was dressed in civvies, he gave me a look that I will never forget. Growing up, he'd always idolised me, you see.'

He turned to face me, almost surprised to find he wasn't alone. 'So you see. You mustn't be too hard on yourself.' He leapt to his feet. 'Come on – you know Jan. He'll be furious if we kept him waiting.'

The entire household had been there that first evening I was allowed to visit Katya – Maman, Papa, Klaus and his fiancée,

Eva. Even Father Kaufmann, though he and Papa were taking their leave as I arrived. Katya regarded each of us from uncanny eyes – the one red with blood, the other with the preternatural luminescence brought on by morphine. It was so odd. The morphine had loosened her tongue, though the weak wheeze of her voice and dislocated jaw made it difficult for her to speak, or for us to interpret what she said. When at length I swam into her vision, there was no mistaking the salutation. 'Orlando!' I looked around guiltily to see if my secret had somehow been outed, but no one seemed to think it any more than the raving of the drug. Only Klaus raised an eyebrow.

She was lucid enough, Katya, despite the beating and whatever cocktail of painkillers they had her on. Her main preoccupation that evening was in regard to the impending wedding of Klaus and Eva Špotáková. Eva had asked Klaus to ask her to be one of three bridesmaids. Would her hair have grown back sufficiently for her not to look like some sort of lunatic, or escaped convict? 'That's not for months yet,' said Maman. 'Eleven weeks,' smiled Eva, putting a hand gently on Katya's cast. 'By that time your hair will be as thick as it ever was and down to about here.' 'Here' was a line just above the nape of the neck. I didn't want to say it, but what most bothered Katya was that she'd be on display in front of the entire congregation without the crow's wing to veil her birthmark.

Papa had done the decent thing, trying to raise my spirits. But it was actually the conversations I had with Katya over the subsequent weeks that finally lifted my depression. On the occasions I visited alone, she was always eager to hear how matters progressed with Leah Meisel. I told her in minute detail all that had happened on the fateful day of her beating, of the agony of sitting across from the shop trying to entertain Ivan, of the sight of her arrival with the redhead, of the weird apparition in the shop window when she held my literary efforts aloft and turned them to confetti. 'So you see, she's no Rosamunde.'

'Rosalind,' she corrected. 'So maybe Heinrich Heine isn't her kind of poetry.'

'Maybe Guido Hayek isn't her kind of Orlando.'

'Don't tell my you're giving up after the very first round. Do you think Joe Louis would be world champion now if he'd simply given up after losing to Max Schmeling?'

Momentarily I had a vision of two years previously, the whole household clustered around the wireless, listening to the electric commentary from Yankee Stadium. 'You're sounding like Klaus now.'

'And you're sounding like a defeatist.'

'So what do you suggest?'

'Try a different poet. Model your next attempt on Rilke.'

'Rilke?'

'There's a volume up by my bed. *Das Buch der Bilder.* Father Kaufmann gave it to me to help my German. Take it. Look especially at 'Song of a Drunkard' and 'Song of the Dwarf'.'

'Ok,' I said, doubtfully, wondering whether it was as a dwarf or a drunkard I was most likely to come across.

XI

Orlando Furioso

The verse modelled on Rilke fared no better than the imitation
Heine. But at least it presented me with a poet to admire. As
I entered Katya's attic studio to locate it, I experienced a tiny
bat-squeak of jealousy that Father Kaufmann should have
given it to her rather than me. I'd felt something similar the
previous year about the Brecht-Weil records he'd given her on
the occasion of her twenty-first. He was my spiritual adviser,
not hers. I was prey to that curious ownership that adolescents
feel for their confidantes.

I felt I was entering a curious shrine, climbing up into that
attic. It was a misshapen space lit by two skylights, the ceiling
cutting across at an intrusive angle. In an alcove to one end
was her bed, a wrought-iron cot not unlike the hospital bed she
was in at present. There was a dresser with an enamel basin, a
wireless set that Klaus had given her for her twenty-first, and a
stool from which I had removed her old phonograph. All about
the walls were plates cut out of books and journals – bizarre
photomontages by Hannah Hoch, monochrome prints and
lithographs amongst which I recognised Munch, and Goya,

and Käthe Kollwitz, long her favourite. When you are up here alone, are these your dark companions, Katya Hayek?

To one side of the space, Papa had installed a large ceramic sink with a mirror behind it. It was colour-stained. Jars with paintbrushes erect like porcupines stood variously around it, and a palette with little turds of colour dried hard. To this end of the loft Katya had strung up a few of her own works. I recognised immediately the poster she'd designed for 'Pequod Mutiny', though here, the prints were monochrome, and printed onto paper that was red, yellow or blue. To my eye, these were far more arresting than the prints in three colours that Václav had had us run off his spirit-copier.

About the floor, in stacks, were a good number of her charcoals. These were dark visions, human forms in angular contortions with outsized mouths and crazed eyes – grotesque figures in a nightmarish city. To an extent Klaus was right. Katya had developed a taste for the ugly. When she was home one weekend from boarding school, she'd executed a couple of portraits of Papa and Maman. She'd caught perfectly Papa's patrician profile, the tightly curled hair, the slightly snub nose, the jovial crow's feet. Maman, in lace décolletage, wore her hair stacked high with a single ringlet escaped across her brow like something out of Versailles. To this day, in oval frames, they were on the wall above the baby-grand, two profiles such as might dignify coins or medallions. She'd long since turned her back on that kind of elegant portraiture.

Towards the other end, through the scaffolding of various easels, was a bookshelf, and beside it a chair and music stand. There stood Katya's clarinet, its silver skeleton glinting in a shaft of dusty sunlight. While I struggled through exercises on the baby-grand, butchering them with clumsy fingers, she gave life up here to the haunting strains of Bruch's *Kol Nidre*. Katya, Katya. If only your tongue were half so eloquent.

The Rilke influenced verse – in fact there were two – I sent by post to the shop on Bilkova Street. I didn't dare venture into the shrine myself. These, at least, were purged of the sentimentality of my first effort. I took pleasure in the jarring images I cobbled together. As to their efficacy, I was left in little doubt. I saw her, standing by the corner of the old Jewish cemetery in the company of 'Hookworm'. I'd seen Meisel's nephew on several occasions. He had a perfectly round, hairless head marked by a deep chevron for a brow, and wore a long leather coat even in summer. Instantly, as always seemed to occur, she was aware I was on the far footpath. She squeezed Hookworm's forearm, directed him to look at me, then put her hand to his ear and whispered something that caused his head to burst into a gormless watermelon grin in which a trio of gold teeth spangled. I walked on. ...*aber mein Herz, mein verbogenes Blut*...

'You really think that a girl like Leah Meisel will be impressed by poetry?' I asked Katya, the next time I was in.

'I think a girl like Leah Meisel will be impressed by persistence.'

'Hunh! Doubt that. But talking of persistence, you know who I see most days I'm here, standing across from the hospital?'

Concerned, she shook her head.

'Rasputin.'

'No!'

'I think he's standing sentry, or something. Maybe he's

afraid those thugs will come back to finish the job.'

'But for God's sake! Tell him to come up!'

'I always do. He just shakes his shaggy locks. He takes it very much to heart that he wasn't there to protect you that day. Which is crazy. It was my fault. I had no right to take him with me on that mad mission.'

'And who was it that sent you on that mission, Guy?'

'So you really think, perseverance?'

'Faint heart…'

And so, the third poem was posted. *Manchmal glaub ich, ich kann nicht mehr –*

I was walking home from a hospital visit one afternoon when I was arrested by the acute sense of Leah Meisel's eyes upon me. Sure enough, she was sitting in the very alcove where Papa had told me his secret shame. There was a man in a pin-striped suit seated beside her fanning his face with a light grey fedora, the very figure, I felt sure, whom I'd seen emerge from Laszlo's jewellers and drop the tiny package into her bag. 'Hey!' he called.

I ignored them, made to go on across the bridge.

'Hey Orlando! Hold up!'

I felt my heart pound. So he too was in on the joke. I marched on, but at length felt his hand upon my shoulder. 'Hold up, would you?'

I turned, squinted at him. He had a single, joined, jet-coloured eyebrow. That was the first thing I noticed. Swarthy, like an Italian, and irises that were almost as black as the eyebrow. But a smile was playing about his lips. 'Leah wants to have a little word with you.' His eyes were animated by something approximating mirth. But there appeared to be no malice in the mirth. Candour, rather. 'Wouldn't you like to have a little word with Leah?'

I felt my gut turn a somersault. Oh God, what humiliation had she planned for me this time, and in full view of every passer-by? I could see, over his shoulder, her dark form in the middle of the bridge, still as a stone in the centre of a moving stream.

'What's your name, boy?' she asked, when finally I retraced my steps to where she stood.

'Guido.'

'Guido what?'

'Guido Hayek.'

She nodded. I chanced only furtive glances at her. 'So who's Orlando, uh?'

I burnt crimson.

'Orlando furioso,' said her companion, who was standing just behind my shoulder.

'What's he?'

I smouldered.

'A knight in shining armour,' came the man's voice.

'Is that it, Guido Hayek?' Her fingers reached out toward my chin. I winced, as though she were about to scratch my cheek. She smiled, tried again, raised my face. 'Look at me, Guido Hayek.' I did so. She was more real, more beautiful, than in my imagination. This day, there were none of the dirt-streaks or tangled locks that I'd witnessed in old Meisel's shop. 'Is that what you want? You want to be my knight in shining armour?'

I looked to the cobbles for help. I was acutely aware of

my burning skin, my clumsy fists, my ridiculous Adam's apple bobbing up and down.

'What would you do for me, Guido Hayek? Would you go on a quest?'

I swallowed. My eyes were hot. I nodded twice.

'You see, Zak. He's not such a schoolkid as you thought. So you'd really go on a quest for me, hey?'

Again I nodded.

'Ok,' she said. The sun cast a lovely light on her as she shaded her brow and peered along the riverbank in the direction of Nové Město. 'There's a little jewellers on Masarykovo nábřeží. Lowenthal's. Maybe you've seen it? In on the left, about half way along. Go in there and steal a ring for me. We'll wait for you here.' Her hand reached out to push through my hair, and again I winced away. 'Will you do that for me?'

'*Steal* a ring?'

'Or is it just poems that you're good for, Guido Hayek?'

The walk to the jewellers was trancelike. I remember nothing of it save the unreality, and the breathing that seemed so loud that I was amazed no one heard it and guessed my guilty intention. I hadn't the slightest idea what I was to do once I got inside Lowenthal's, a pokey corner shop not much bigger than a bathroom. All I knew was that I was determined to see it through, and drove all thoughts and doubts out of my head as I bore down on the jewellers.

Behind the counter was a middle-aged woman with a tight mouth and half-moon glasses who was examining an engraved pendant of some kind for a customer, a huge grandmother in furs. Hearing the bell clatter, the shop assistant glanced up, sized me up, and with a dismissive tightening of her lips, returned to the engraving. They were conversing in German. A minute crawled by. Two. I coughed. She interrogated me with her pencilled eyebrows. 'Rings?' I croaked. The be-furred customer turned a filthy glare in my direction.

Another minute crawled by. I leaned over a glass display as far away from her bulk as I could manage in the tiny shop. There were trays of rings, each with a miniature tag tied on with thread. I tried to make out the prices. It occurred to me that if only I had my biscuit-tin with all its savings, I could purchase a ring and bear it back as though I'd stolen it. But the wardrobe with its biscuit tin was far away, on the castle side of the river.

For a while the shop assistant watched my breath fog up the glass as I peered into the case. 'What is it you want?' she snapped, in Czech.

'Ein Ring, bitte,' I managed. *'Der Ring ist für meine Schwester.'*

'I'm sorry about this,' she said deferentially to the enormous Frau. 'Two seconds.' She came out from behind the counter and jimmied a little key into the lock. 'How much were you thinking of spending, son?'

I mentioned a figure I'd seen on one of the tags that seemed to me to be fantastic. She hesitated, looked at me with something more like solicitude. 'Is it an important occasion?'

'She's to be married.'

'Ah, married!' The corners of her mouth twitched into an approximation of a smile. 'A wedding present. Perhaps one of these?' She pulled out a drawer, it contained some of the cheaper rings, and set it on the glass top of another display cabinet. 'Take your time. Now, madam...' and she shuffled back behind the great mother bear at the counter.

'You see!' cried the latter, triumphant. 'You've spelled it wrong!'

'I never heard it spelt that way.'

'It's *ie*, it's not *ei*.'

'Well I never heard it spelt with *ie*.'

'But it's *ie*. I wrote it down for you...'

My heart pounding at my throat, my sight blurred, I fumbled one of the rings into my hand, thrust my hand into my pocket, and bundled out the door. It was pure instinct, all done before I had a chance to make a conscious resolution. The door slammed, the bell jangled horribly, calling out to all the street that here was a thief. By chance there was a bread-van passing at that instant. I leapt onto the running-board at the rear, as I'd seen countless street-urchins do, then clung on for dear life. At the junction of Legil Bridge the van slowed to a halt and I jumped down, sprinted to a tram-stop and leapt aboard a tram just as it was setting off.

I collapsed into a wooden seat, my heart pounding dangerously and all blood drained from my face. I had to fight, long and hard, to bring the wild palpitations back to anything like normal. When at last I succeeded, I was miles away from the river. The tram was empty.

Klaus would not have left her alone there. Maybe so. Well, now I'd proved, if nothing else, at least I was no coward. Stupid, maybe. But no coward. Slowly, I pulled my hand from my pocket, slowly unfurled the fingers. There, sitting on my palm, was a gold ring with a tiny jewel winking like a red eye. I shut my own eyes, and laughed aloud.

XII

Three Card Trick

By the time I got back to the Karluv Bridge it was early evening. They were long since gone. But I didn't mind. I was still basking in the glow of having carried out the risky task she'd set me. The only question to consider was how to get the ring to her.

Later that evening I decided on two things. To post it to her at old Meisel's shop, wrapped up in paper to disguise the contents, and to leave the price-tag attached. 'Is it just poems that you're good for, Guido Hayek?' she'd asked. She'd have her answer, and what a fine way to convey it!

Should I write a new poem, another tortured quatrain in imitation of Rilke? No. This time I'd go one better. I was sending her a stolen ring. I might just as well wrap it in stolen verse. So I took down a copy of Rilke's *Neue Gedichte* and copied out the following lines:

> *Und da trifft du deinen Blick im geelen*
> *Amber ihrer runden Augensteine*

Unerwartet wieder: eingeschlossen
Wie ein ausgestorbenes Insekt.

Should I translate it for her, the prehistoric insect caught in the amber of her cat's eye? Let her find out the meaning herself! Aware of the swagger in the gesture, I sealed the envelope. It was only after it was sealed that I thought of adding the signature, *Orlando Furioso*, and had to find a new envelope to reseal the package.

Very pleased with my day's work, I slept the sleep of the just.

What I hadn't envisaged was that she'd be so hard to convince. I allowed two days for the envelope to arrive, then on the third day stationed myself in the café across from old Meisel's shop. Sometime after twelve, I saw her appear at the corner with the redhead, just as she had the day of the attack. I sprang from the table and made to walk past them, doffing my hat with an elaborate bow as I did so. The redhead gave out an astonished snort.

'He's looking very pleased with himself,' said Leah.

'Perhaps he's drunk?' said the redhead. She had sharp features, something animal-like in her mien, but not unattractive for all that. I put her age at about twenty or twenty-one. Surreptitiously I examined Leah Meisel's slender fingers to see if any tiny red jewel winked from their loveliness. But they were bare. 'Might I enquire if the lady received a package?' I said, in a poor attempt at bravado.

'Phhth!' She turned to her companion. 'Some trinket or other arrived in the post, Ada. I don't doubt this character bought it from a huckster.'

Suddenly I rouged. For once it wasn't embarrassment. I was furious at the thought that she had so easily seen through my valour. My first thought had indeed been to fetch the biscuit-tin so that I could buy the accursed ring. 'I t-took it!' I stammered.

Ada laughed, her mouth like a cat's.

'You told me to take it. I took it!'

'Can he prove it?'

'How can I prove it?'

'Can he describe, in detail, everything that happened. Lowenthal is bald, isn't he?'

'He may be bald for all I know. The assistant in the shop was a woman. She spoke German.'

'So what?' Leah turned to Ada, taking her arm as though they were about to go on their way. 'That still doesn't prove he didn't buy it from her. He's devious, this one.'

'All schoolboys are devious.'

'Look,' I said. 'This is how it was.' And I described in detail everything that happened: the old Frau dressed in furs; the misspelled engraving; the story about a sister's wedding; the mad charge from the shop; the passing bread van; the ride on the tram. 'That's how come I didn't bring it to you in person, on the bridge.'

'Clever little monkey!' said the redhead. 'Do you believe him?'

'Phhh! He's had three days to cook something up!'

At that moment I hated redheaded Ada. I hated both of them. But I'd misjudged her. 'I know,' said Ada. 'Why don't I pay the old widow a little visit? I'll say I was passing by her shop on Tuesday evening when I saw some schoolkid burst from her door. I'll ask her was anything nicked.'

'But Ada, why would she tell a stranger?'

'Why? So we can compare descriptions of course!'

They made to go on their way. When they were about twenty yards on, I called out, 'What did you think of the verse?'

She paused, gave an indifferent shrug. Did I have her at a disadvantage? 'You… don't read German?'

She turned square about and raised facetious eyebrows. 'I don't read anything, Guido Hayek!'

I blushed, dug my nails into my palms until they hurt. 'B-but,' I stammered. 'That day in the park. You were reading a book!'

She tossed her hair lightly. 'Simpleton,' she laughed. Then, arm in arm, the two turned a corner.

So she'd been faking it, that day in the park! It had all been a part of the act. Holding an unintelligible book, to give colour to her sitting there alone. She couldn't read! That put a different complexion on everything.

And such a fool I'd been, to try to win her with poems!

But then, if she couldn't read, that also meant that that little display she'd put on in Meisel's window, tearing up my letter and letting it fall about her, was a mockery aimed at herself as much as it was at me. What Katya had intuited was true. She struck out because I had seen her weakness.

I couldn't wait to get to the hospital to share my news with Katya.

The next day, a Saturday, I was crossing a bridge over Čertovka, not far from the watermill, when I once again saw Leah Meisel in company with the youth she'd called Zak. Whether this was a shortened form of Izsak or Zakary, short for a surname, or something else entirely, I didn't know. They were seated at a table outside a café – it's an area popular with weekend strollers. Today he was bareheaded, his hair oiled and parted in the middle. She wore a light summer frock of buttercup yellow, very becoming. They might have been any couple out enjoying the weather. Seeing me, she waved.

'So it's true then,' she twirled an imaginary ring about her ring finger. 'You really did take that little something.'

I flushed with manly pride.

'Join us. Sit.' Confused, ridiculously happy, I pulled over a chair. 'Now. Tell Zak here how you carried it off, the way you explained it to Ada.' I glanced at her companion, who was sizing me up superciliously. Then, taking elaborate care I couldn't be overheard by any of the other tables, I recounted again the details of my bungling raid on the little jewellers. I was surprised to see him taking my account seriously.

'I see,' he said. 'Very good.' He made a little signal to the waiter, held up three fingers.

'How old are you, Orlando?' he asked.

'Fifteen.'

'You look more. That's good, too.' At this moment, the waiter returned with three glasses of schnapps. *'Na zdraví,'* said Zak, raising his toward the centre of our little triangle. I lifted mine, the three glasses chinked. *'Na zdraví,'* we both repeated. The schnapps went down with a potent sweetness. It was my first time trying anything stronger than wine, and I was relieved not to have coughed.

'Ok,' said Zak. 'Do you know this little game?' He reached into his breast pocket and pulled out three playing cards, fanning them out. The Queen of Spades, and two numbered cards. I hadn't noticed he had such slender fingers. They were flexible as a pianists. 'I want you to keep your eye on the Queen of Spades. You understand?'

'Sure,' I shrugged, and with an attempt at nonchalance added, 'I've seen gypsies do this trick with shells and a pea.'

'Very good. Now, watch.' Two cards he sustained between thumb and middle-finger of his right hand, one similarly in his left hand. He allowed me to see which was which. He then executed a little flick, and they danced into a row on the table. 'Ok, where is she?'

I tapped on the card to the far right.

'You're sure? You don't want to change?'

I shook my head, tapped it again.

'Very good!' he said, flipping over the card. Sure enough, it was the Queen. He and Leah exchanged a good-humoured glance. 'Now go again.' This time, as he showed the faces of the cards, his fingers danced in a sort of showy figure of eight, his eyebrows executed a comical hop and skip, Leah said, 'Zaki, I think…' as the cards fell into a row of three. His open hand invited me to choose.

It was the middle one. That, or the far left. The right, the two of clubs, he'd dropped directly from his left hand. This time, I tapped the middle one. Eyebrows hoisted, he turned it. The seven of diamonds.

'Try again,' he said. Just two remained to choose from. I tapped the far left. The two of clubs. I shook my head, grinned in admiration. 'You see what was different this time?'

'No.'

'This time, there was a little distraction. The tiniest thing.

The moral of the story, always have a distraction. In the jewellers shop you were lucky. That old battleship complaining about the engraving was a distraction. You understand?'

'Sure,' I said.

'Lesson number two.' All three cards were now face up on the table. He picked up the Queen with his left, the two and seven with his right, which he then butterflied over the back of his left hand. When he turned up the left, it was now holding the seven of diamonds. 'The Queen never stays in the hand that lifted it. You understand?'

I understood. He meant the little package, dropped into Leah's laundry.

He swept up the three cards, replaced them into his breast pocket. Then he tousled my head. 'He's a clever little bourgeois.' He motioned again to the waiter, three more. The waiter had been watching the card trick with suspicion. He had no time for sharps or conmen at any of his tables. A stubby finger singled me out. 'He's too young.'

'That's our nephew,' smiled Leah, all sweetness. 'We're taking him out to celebrate. Today he turns eighteen, don't you Daniel?' She pushed her fingers affectionately through my hair.

'You're eighteen?' he closed one eye. I beamed up at him. 'Ok. But it's the last one you people get at this place, see.'

XIII

Chess Pieces

Katya was to be discharged from hospital. I stood by the window, watching out for Papa's car. There wasn't much change in her that I could see. The arm still stuck out from her body like a plaster girder, her head and ribs were still swathed in bandages, and her breathing was still hoarse and laboured. And there was a new concern. She'd experienced a couple of seizures. The doctor said it was by no means unknown in cases of what he termed 'trauma to the head', though it was too early to say if they were of an epileptic nature. The tests were inconclusive.

Her left eye had cleared. That was about the only improvement that I could see.

'Our friend isn't still out there?'

'Rasputin? Not today. He's to return to Yugoslavia. He told me.' I turned to face her. 'Did you know he's a Muslim?'

'*Ivan?*'

'Yeah. He told me himself.'

'No way!'

'Yesterday when I was leaving, he asked what he could do

for you, before he left. I asked would he not go up to see you, to say goodbye. "You tell her goodbye!" So then I suggested, maybe pray for her? So then he shakes his locks, you know how he is. "Maybe I pray to wrong god." That's when he told me. He's a Muslim, from Banja Luka.'

'I thought all Serbs were supposed to be Orthodox.'

'Yeah. Same. I guess we never asked him.' I sat on the bed. 'Papa says none of the others have been to see you.'

'He's mistaken. Sandu and Mihaela came.'

'Who?'

'Hansel and Gretel. But it was really awkward. I couldn't think of a single thing to say. I don't blame them for not coming back.'

'What about Václav?'

'He sent flowers.'

'Big deal!'

'His parents are rich folk. I think they were horrified when it came out in the papers. Then they realised the kind of riff-raff he'd been hanging out with.'

'So much for Trotsky! I never warmed to him you know.'

'No?' She fought a smile. 'It was Brunhilda brought out his little bunch of flowers. Now *that* was awkward.'

'I don't doubt it.' I stood, checked back out the window. 'Still no sign of Papa.'

'So Orlando, what will your next move be, now you know your Rosalind doesn't read?'

'Hunh?' I'd told Katya nothing whatsoever about the little raid on Lowenthal's jewellers. For that matter, I hadn't said a word to Father Kaufmann about it either. Nor that I'd agreed to meet them the following Saturday. If it was a mortal sin, then I was a damned soul, a *poète maudit* who would write my verse in reckless deeds. That was the sort of verse that Leah Meisel would understand. Ridiculous, looking back on it after so many long months. But I was fifteen then, and caught in the full flow of my first infatuation.

'How much progress are you making with Jan?' This was Papa. We were making our way across the Karluv Bridge early the following Thursday.

'If you mean the lathe, I'm doing ok I guess. If you mean am I making any progress with Jan as a person... yeah right!'

'Don't mind that. Jan is prickly as a frozen hedgehog.'

'Papa, he's convinced you want me to skill up so eventually I can take his place.'

'He need have no fear of that! I've seen how you handle that machine.'

'It's not easy, when he begrudges every word of instruction. You know he doesn't let me touch any of the tools he has marked out on the wall? I have to use your old stuff out of the toolbox.'

'They were good enough for me. No. What you need is a project to work on. Something that will inspire your interest.'

'Fat chance of that!'

'Don't sulk, boy.'

'I wasn't.'

'No? Then here's what I propose. Make a chess set. You know all that spare wood we have out the back? Well, select one type of wood for the light pieces, and one for the dark. You're free to design the pieces yourself. Just so they're all of a set. The same dimensions. The same design, you follow me? You can think of it as a trial piece. Once you finish it, if it's up to scratch, we'll put our arrangements on a more formal footing.'

'And what about the knights?'

'Very good. That's a different set of skills entirely. As I'm sure Jan will tell you in good time, there's woodturning, and there's wood joining. They're chalk and cheese. Woodturning you'll learn Tuesdays and Thursdays. Wood joining, Wednesdays and Fridays.'

I stopped. Papa turned. 'You want me at the gallery four days a week?'

'The boy can count.'

I was more than pleased. It was another step toward adulthood. So I broached the first doubt. 'What does Maman have to say about it?'

'Leave Maman to me. With the summer auction coming up, I could use an extra pair of hands about the place.'

That was certainly true. The *U Černého Slunce* held four auctions annually, one at the end of each season. It's when most of the business was concluded. If the spring and autumn auctions were given over to trends in continental painting – constructivism, say, or futurism – the summer and winter auctions were almost exclusively Czech affairs. Although viewings for the summer auction weren't scheduled to take place until the final week of August, as early as June the organisational work began. Letters had to be written and sent out to look for consignors to fill the various spaces. There were three floors to the gallery, with the main exhibition space on the first floor. But during the seasonal auctions, every inch of wall space was taken up. Even the stairwells were closely hung.

So, in the run up, it was always all hands on deck, writing to consignors, compiling addresses, cataloguing, gathering information for the catalogue, sending out invitations, wrapping, unwrapping, hanging, re-hanging. 'What about Jan? I still say Jan isn't going to like it one bit.'

'I'm the boss of the gallery so far as I'm aware. It's my name on the stationery. And listen,' he winked, 'as soon as he goes home, you can use any tool that you see fit. Just be sure to put it back up in its correct place afterwards so he doesn't cop on.'

I loved the idea. 'Papa, maybe I could present the chess set to Father Kaufmann.'

'Of course. But only if it's good enough, Guy. You're old enough now to know. You can't pass off shoddy workmanship any longer.'

Was there a barb in this? I wasn't sure. Papa was beginning to think of me as an adult, and that made me walk taller. I'd show him that when it came to something like a chess set for Father Kaufmann, I meant business. Besides, I felt guilty in regard to my spiritual advisor. There was a whole area of my soul that I was keeping hidden from him, as the moon keeps one face always dark to the earth.

'If you're serious, Jan will need to show you the basics of marquetry too. How to inlay. That's a skill in itself. You can't very well present Hans with chess pieces and no board to put them on!'

My mind was floating high over the city roofs by this juncture. 'He's bound to complain how I'm taking up too much time on the lathe, working on a project for Hans.' Had Papa noticed I'd slipped in the Christian name, the first time I'd ever referred to the Jesuit as anything but Father Kaufmann?

He put his fist to my chin and pushed hard, as though he were tiring of my doubts. 'Jan is not going to know. What I'm proposing, you go on with your instruction in the morning, when he's there. It's in the afternoons, after he's gone, that I suggest you work on your little project.' A rough hand tousled my hair, though I was a good two inches taller than him. 'One other thing. Don't call me Papa. It makes you sound like you're still in short pants. Who in their right mind would buy a painting off someone who calls their father Papa?'

'Ok, uhm,' I hesitated, not at all sure what I was supposed to call him. But he'd already set off, was already ten yards ahead of me. He called without looking back, 'And leave Maman to me. I don't want to risk you making a pig's arse of things at home.'

XIV

Apprenticeship

Throughout that long summer of '38, I led a double life. It was a long hot summer for Czechoslovakia too, a time when the future hung perilously in the balance. We were a small country surrounded by enemies. Not just the German Reich, with its growing demands for the Sudeten Mountains. Poland was eyeing up the territory around Český Těšín, Hungary had an appetite for great swathes of Slovakia, the Ruthenians to the east were making separatist noises, even the Slovaks were restless. Who could Beneš look to, with so many wolves circling? Romania was weak. Daladier was miles away, sitting pretty behind his Maginot Line. The Soviets? But could Russian wolves be trusted any more than German wolves? As for Mr Chamberlain, he'd dispatched a sheep named Runciman to council Beneš to simply allow the wolves into the fold.

It was a time of anxiety. The dread was palpable. Every news broadcast deepened the sense of ineluctable disaster. And yet there was a sort of recklessness abroad. Life should go on as though that future might never arrive. There was a defiant gaiety or a gay defiance, the hysterical jauntiness of the condemned prisoner. Papa determined that the *U Černého Slunce* summer catalogue should be the thickest yet, though who in their right mind buys art with a catastrophe looming? Gold, perhaps, but contemporary Czech painting? In Nerudova Street, preparations continued apace for the society wedding of Lt Niklaus Hayek, or Mikuláš as he now styled himself, to Eva Špotáková that was to take place in September. Both families agreed that the shouting of Henlein's SdP ruffians should not be allowed to drown out the big day. Quite the opposite! The wedding should be all the more opulent in the face of impending disaster. It was a patriotic duty.

Maman was in her element, drawing up plans for the wedding. By rights that should have been the concern of the bride's family, but Mrs Špotáková was in the latter stages of throat cancer and was quite content to allow Maman to assume the responsibility, to say nothing of sharing the costs. Špotákov was a wine importer, and not short of a few koruna himself. Naturally, the ceremony was to take place in the Church of St Niklaus, with Father Kaufmann one of three priests officiating. For the reception, nothing less than the Art Deco splendour of the Hotel Imperial on Na Poříčí would serve.

The guest list itself was something to behold. Klaus would appear in full military regalia. As early as March, even before the mobilisation had been called, he'd enlisted in the Signal Corps, his Olympic connections and years as a reservist shortening his cadetship and easing his passage to a full lieutenancy. Eva Špotáková loved the idea. With his athletic build, Klaus really did make quite the dashing officer. Her cousin Tadeusz, an air force pilot, would be best man. How well the two uniforms would look, side by side. And how appropriate, too, with so much sabre rattling going on. To represent the Hayeks and balance the three bridesmaids, my only cousin, Rudi, would be groomsman. A customs officer, he too would look resplendent in uniform

I'd always fancied Eva Špotáková with that adolescent fascination that can't quite believe such beings are mortal. When Klaus had first brought her to dinner in Nerudova Street, I'd have been thirteen. Girls my own age were absolutely unknown to me. And here, contemplating me with not unpleasant irony was a female creature whose proportions and white teeth seemed perfection. It was as though a being had stepped down from a Leni Riefenstahl movie and assumed three dimensions. It was quite literally unimaginable what she and Klaus got up to when they were alone together.

I say all this to differentiate my feelings for Leah Meisel, which from the start were complicated, to say the least. When Father Kaufmann talked of raising a mortal up onto a pedestal, he might have been describing my reaction to Miss Špotáková's arrival in the hallway. He'd said something interesting. Attractiveness is not the same as beauty. Eva Špotáková may well have been the more beautiful of the two. But for my money, Leah was the more attractive. Two years had passed, I'd fallen under the sway of the dark-haired orphan, and now, although Klaus' fiancée had lost none of her glamour, she had no longer any claim on my erotic imagination.

While Maman busied herself with wedding preparations and Klaus learned the rudiments of signalling and army discipline, the rest of us threw ourselves into readying the gallery for the summer auction. In previous years, Katya had taken care of the catalogue. This year she'd need help. Besides everything else, she was unable to type with her right arm stuck out like a signpost. 'And that's down to you, Guy, since you're about the only one round here she doesn't appear to be mortally mortified with.'

I was never busier. And I was never happier. Piece by piece, the chessboard filled up. Page by page, the catalogue. Katya lent me her box camera, an Etsy, though she insisted on looking over my shoulder and checking apertures and exposures. Even Jan begrudgingly acknowledged my faltering progress at both turning and joining, setting me trial pieces with which he'd invariably find fault, but with less hostility than in former times. And all the while, unbeknownst, I was leading my double life.

That first Sunday I went to meet them by arrangement, it was like I'd fallen into an Aladdin's cave. The cave was a disused warehouse over a wharf by the Štefánikuv Bridge, where Josefov meets Florenc. At some point, they'd filled one wall with crates of old clothes and accessories, and even a vanity unit with a cracked, liver-spotted mirror. There was a coat-rack such as you might find in a clothes-shop from which various costumes hung, so that that corner resembled nothing so much as a dressing-room in a rundown music hall.

Ada inspected me. 'Tsst, he's still so much a boy.' She sat me on the wreck of a barber's chair by the vanity unit, angled my head this way and that. 'Come back in a half hour,' she said. Beneath the surface of the mirror's dirty pond I watched Leah Meisel and the one she called Zak set off into the daylight.

Alone with her, I couldn't think of a word to say. But she carried on a banter as she worked that took away any need. First she tucked a towel about my neck, then daubed at my face with what felt like the damp corner of a sponge. She wasn't gentle. She pushed, rubbed, poked. Working around my blinking eyes with a charcoal stick she taunted my timidity. Occasionally her breasts would brush against my arm and I'd experience a giddy thrill at the contact, as though she were electrically charged. The contact and thrill were so persistent that I folded my hands over my crotch, to cover and curb my enthusiasm.

At length the other pair returned with a couple of street kids in tow, a girl of perhaps eight with knee-length straggly hair and a five year old boy in flat-cap and waistcoat who looked the perfect miniature of an adult. Just before they returned, her face so close to mine that her eyes were slightly crossed, Ada dabbed glue across my upper lip and with two fingers pushed a pencil moustache into place. 'There,' she said. 'Now to dress the character.'

The face in the dirty mirror looked to me like something out of a Yiddish vaudeville. My eyebrows had been darkened, my eyes lined with charcoal. She'd oiled and flattened my hair. There was a duskiness to the complexion, too, which didn't appear to be all down to the filthy glass. I stood and looked to Leah, who was flicking through various coat-hangers. 'Here,' she extended toward Ada a cravat, 'put this on him.' 'And this,' said Zak, though it was he himself who slapped onto my head a homburg and tilted it by the brim. He then pulled from a box a silver-handled cane, brandishing it as though it were a sword. 'On guard!' He tossed it toward me, and in my clumsiness I fumbled and let it clatter across the floor.

'Well, he no longer looks fifteen.'

'No. Seventeen maybe.'

'Seventeen won't be any good for a boyfriend or fiancé.'

'How about a little brother?'

'A fine Aryan type like him, *my* brother?!'

'I wouldn't say I was Aryan, Leah.'

'Don't call me Leah!'

'No? Why ever…'

'Don't *ever* call me Leah,' she snapped, turning.

All at once I understood. No real names. 'What should I call you then?'

'If you have to call her anything,' said Ada, whose real name was anything but Ada, 'call her Becca.'

'Becca,' I nodded. 'Got it.'

What we did for the remainder of the afternoon was practise what they called 'scenarios'. All of these scenarios had three elements. The set up. The decoy. The switch. That was drummed into me again and again. Set up. Decoy. Switch. For the set up, we were paired up in every conceivable permutation. Sometimes I'd be strolling with Ada. Sometimes with 'Becca'. Sometimes I'd be alone, and they'd be together. Or Zak would take one of these parts. One or another of the street kids might even play the part of a child of one or another of the adults. Before the day was out, I too was invited to dream up a scenario.

The decoy could take many forms. Perhaps in my carelessness I'd left a wallet momentarily on the counter, and in a flash, one of the street kids made off with it – for the purpose, they gave me a finely tooled wallet fat with twenty kroner notes. Or better, the shop assistant would see the kid slide the wallet from my pocket. Perhaps whichever of the girls I was accompanying would suddenly throw a strop at my meanness, or perhaps it was the child that would throw a strop.

The point was, in that instant, 'the hit', as they termed it, was made. Almost instantaneously, the extra element, the person who had not been involved in the scenario to date and ideally had not even been inside the target premises, would casually brush past whoever it was who had made 'the hit' – that day it was invariably Zak. This last pass was the most crucial. 'Under no circumstance does the Queen of Spades remain in the same hand,' he reminded. It was also trickier than you might think. You had to contrive a pretext for passing the shopfront precisely at the moment that Zak was erupting from it. Sometimes, a slight bump or jostle might occur, sometimes a hand was briefly thrust into your pocket. Twice, I fumbled the pass. It was not an acceptable statistic.

'And where do these scenarios take place? Always in a jewellers?'

Leah, or I should say Becca, shook her head, grinning. 'He's still such an innocent.'

'Come on,' said Ada, tugging the moustache lightly from my lip. 'Sit! Let's get you back to what you were. We don't want you to frighten your mama.'

I stooped before the mirror and wiped my face and hair vigorously with a rag. When I was back to an approximation of what I had been, I searched out Leah's reflection and boldly addressed it. 'So when do we try out one of the scenarios in the real world?'

It was Zak who replied. 'When we're ready, we'll be in contact.'

I turned to face him. 'But you don't know where I live.'

His joined eyebrows, a crow as a child might draw it, twitched. 'Everyone knows the fine house on Nerudova Street where Emil Hayek lives.'

For the first time, I felt a pang of foreboding. If anything went amiss, it might come back to my home to haunt me. These characters knew where I lived.

XV

Exodus

The following Tuesday, when I arrived home for lunch, I was met by Maman in the hallway. She had an agitated look, far more pronounced than her habitual concern. 'Run up, Guido. Throw your head in to see what's going on in your sister's studio.'

'Katya? Why?'

'There are a couple of very peculiar characters gone up there to see her.' She shook her grey head. 'I don't know who comes and goes here any more.'

I experienced a somersault of dread. But as I mounted the stairs, I thought, it's far too early to be worried about anything. What can they possibly be doing here? It's not as if any crime has been committed. It's not as if anything has actually been stolen. And if they were here to bring me out on a scenario, I couldn't go. I had work to do in the gallery.

I paused at the foot of the final flight of stairs. It struck me that Katya must have had her phonograph replaced, because I could hear a faint strain of music emanating from the attic – a tremolo voice, female, singing in a language I didn't know.

Magyar, perhaps, or Roma gypsy. I hesitated to knock, let the song run its course. I listened, barely breathing. To judge from the air and tone, it was a song of unrequited love. When it ended there was a pause, then two pairs of hands applauded. I tapped at the door and stuck my head around.

At first I didn't recognise the girl by the music stand. She was colourfully dressed, her hair wrapped in a headscarf from which dangled coins or medals. It was only when I looked to the bed and saw who was sitting on it beside Katya that I realised who they were.

'Guido! What are…? You know Sandu and Mihaela…'

'Of course,' I said. Hansel and Gretel. I made straight for the bed and extended my hand. Sandu, dressed in a wide-brimmed hat and particoloured waistcoat, shook the hand vigorously. With Mihaela I wasn't certain what form my greeting should take, so I took her fingers, clicked heels, and brushed her knuckles with my lips. She laughed at the gesture.

'They dropped in to say goodbye,' sighed Katya. Her arm by this time was in a sling, which greatly eased her movements. 'They're leaving us, it seems.'

'Oh yeah? Ivan is to leave, too.'

'He already has! We saw him off at the railway station on Sunday.'

'I see. Gone already.' We smiled at one other, nodding, each trying to think of something to say. 'Did you guys realise he's Muslim?'

A shrug. 'Sure.'

'I didn't know Muslims were allowed to drink alcohol.'

Mihaela moved away from the music stand. 'We didn't know Christians were allowed to murder and rob and hate.'

'A fair point.' Once more, silence. Smiles. I noticed that, under one eye, Sandu bore the discolouration of a recent beating. For a while I considered relating how the Serb had stood sentinel outside Katya's hospital. But it seemed a betrayal of a piety. 'So where to? Back to Dresden?'

'I don't think so,' snorted Mihaela.

'Did we ever tell you why we left Dresden? No? After all it's one of the most beautiful cities in the world. Not like Prague. More... I don't know. Think the Brothers Grimm. The Pied Piper of Hamlyn. Or the musicians of Bremen. A Germanic kind of beauty. Nuremberg has it, too. Of course, we didn't live in Dresden itself. Not in the city, proper. It was an encampment, further along the Elbe...'

Mihaela picked up the story. 'Then one night the fairy tale turned dark. We had a visit from the S.A. Clubs and flaming torches. It wasn't long after Hitler became chancellor. These guys felt no need to cover up their faces. I still remember those faces. They weren't human. They were lit by bestial glee.'

'Not bestial,' corrected Sandu, 'No beast would take such pleasure in inflicting pain.'

'Demonic, then. *Kraft durch Freude*. A mindless fury. They smashed in the windows, set fire to the caravans, then beat anyone unmercifully who tried to escape. To this day I hear the screams of those of us who were trapped inside.'

'That's how our father died.'

'And *bunică*. Grandmother. So you see, we're in no hurry to go back to Dresden, for all that it's a fairy tale city.'

'But that kind of thing could never happen here, I'm certain.'

'I wouldn't be so certain.'

'Let's just say we're tired of the jeers and stares and fists. Only today, as we crossed Malostranské Square, Mihaela was spat upon.'

'That's only the start of it. How do you think it'll be when the SdP get their way? How long before Prague goes the way of Vienna?'

'That'll never happen!'

'No?'

'Nobody would risk war. Not after the last one. Papa said things got so bad toward the end that people ate cats, and rats were sold on the street.'

'They went to war in 1914 over one dead aristocrat. I don't see what's so different this time round.'

'Because this time, everyone knows just how bad it would be. Back then they had no idea what was in store for them.'

'You really think man is so rational?'

That comment led to a stalemate. We were all still smiling, but the atmosphere in the room had darkened. 'So where will you go?' I asked.

'We're not sure. East. The farther east, the better.'

'It's not so bad, really. Sandu and I were born to a nomad's life.'

'And have you any family?'

'We're gypsies. We'll always find family.'

I noticed Katya was looking at me interrogatively. In a flash it came to me what was on her mind. She'd been present that May evening when Klaus had said that Old Meisel was readying travel documents. It was a cataclysm that I kept to the back of my mind just as the Czech people kept to the back of their minds the prospect of imminent invasion. But then, there wasn't the slightest sign as yet that Ezra Meisel was making preparations to leave.

Time enough to tell that to Katya after the brother and sister had taken their leave.

XVI

Scenarios

That Friday at supper, the phone rang. Maman answered it.

'Yes, he is.' From the drawing room door she looked toward me, her brow furrowed. 'Who will I say...?' A pause. A deeper frown. 'He may know who you are. But I don't know who you are.' Another pause. No one at the table had taken another bite. 'Very well.'

Slowly, magisterially, Maman returned into the dining room. 'Guido. There's an 'Ada' on the phone who wants a word with you. Try not to let your dinner go cold.'

Papa watched me with mild raillery. Katya and Eva exchanged significant looks. When Klaus was away on manoeuvres, she often dined with us now. Surely, Katya wouldn't have betrayed me to her? My cheeks aflame, I rose.

The phone-call was very short. I scarcely spoke. When I returned, the atmosphere about the table was one of surface normality. 'Guido, who was that?' asked Maman, casually.

'Leave the boy alone, can't you. Don't you realise he's old enough to have secrets?'

'Emil, I'd like to know who's ringing up my son in our

own home. Is that so unreasonable?'

'He's a working boy now. He's entitled to a little privacy! You mollycoddle him, Mia. You always have.'

'Do *you* know who this person is? This "Ada"?'

'Not the foggiest.' He winked toward Eva Špotáková. 'If it comes to that, I'm far easier knowing Guy is chasing after a bit of skirt. It's not before time!'

'Don't be vulgar in front of our guest.'

'Eva, my apologies. Your future father-in-law is a rough diamond.'

'I don't mind, Mr Hayek.'

'Please. "Emil."'

'I don't mind. Really.'

'I suppose you're all laughing at me.' Maman laid her napkin across her plate. 'I'm just one big joke in this house, yes?'

'No one's laughing at you, Mia.'

'Please, Maman.' This last interjection was from Katya. She spoke so seldom it had the desired effect, though to my mind everyone finished their supper with scant appetite.

At precisely ten the following morning, just as the skeleton began to pull the chord on the great Astronomical Clock, a hand was laid on my shoulder. I turned to find Zak, recently bearded and eyes enlarged behind a gilt pince-nez. 'Come,' he said. We made along Celetná Street, not yet busy with Saturday shoppers, stopping about halfway along. 'That's this morning's target.' This morning's target was a family business retailing quality leather merchandise. 'Go in,' he said. 'Familiarise yourself with the layout.'

'What if someone asks why I'm there?'

'Use your imagination. Aren't you poets supposed to have imagination?'

I had no idea what I was meant to be looking out for. Still, I didn't want to burden him with questions. If I'm honest about it, this Zak character made me feel uncomfortable to the point of being a little frightened of him. So I entered, wandered a little, casually fingered a couple of bags, flipped through a finely tooled wallet. When a salesman approached, I smiled weakly and left, blinking into the sunlight. Zak had continued on, and was idling not far from the Powder Gate. Barely waiting for me to catch up he passed under it and turned up Revoluční Street, continuing until he had entered the old disused warehouse by Štefánikuv Bridge. Leah, Ada and the two street kids were waiting for us. The girls were luxuriantly turned out. Leah Meisel had become Becca, in a gorgeous dress of Prussian blue with a parasol that didn't quite match, Ada in marzipan green with a little hat perched to one side of a great column of red hair. Each wore elbow-length gloves.

Ada sat me into the old barber's chair and set to work, darkening my eyebrows, oiling down my hair, dabbing the pencil moustache into place. Though I wasn't to be directly involved in the 'hit', it wouldn't do for anyone to recognise me. Once more, each time her breasts brushed my arm, I felt a giddy thrill. It was less pronounced though. Probably, I was too nervous to feel their full erotic charge. The seven year old girl had a dirty smock and a bunch of violets. She was to pester me to buy one until I lost the rag with her and flung them to the floor. At that she'd burst into tears. That was the diversion. Whatever items Ada and Becca were examining, one at least would be slipped under a bodice, then passed to Zak as they exited. He'd be casually passing the shop hand in hand with his little boy, the five year old. Several times we practised the scenario in that dusty interior before blinking into the sunlight. Then we set out in three different directions, to converge on the shop at twenty past the hour. It wouldn't do for us to arrive on Celetná Street as a party.

The plan went off precisely as planned. In fact it was over in a blink of an eye. I felt my trousers tugged, the violets were thrust up, I pushed them away, the girl persisted, I threw them to the floor. As I saw the blue and pistachio dresses swish out of the shop, I was left squatting on the parquet floor, gathering the violets for the teary beggar girl while suffering the opprobrium of a pair of Carmelite nuns.

It had gone off without a hitch on Celetná Street. Now it was time to try it over the river. We set off on two different trams to rendezvous down in Nové Město. This time the target was a merchant of fancy goods. Once again, the routine worked. It was all done so effortlessly it appeared that all the stores of Prague were at our disposal. All that was necessary was to select one. A perfumery in Vinohrady was our final target that Saturday in June. They were family affairs, all three of them. All this was some months before the grand opening of the White Swan on Na Poříčí, just in time to become the foremost department store of Herr Hitler's *Protektorat Böhmen und Mähren.*

By four o'clock our day's work was done. Once again taking separate trams, we converged on the warehouse by Štefánikuv Bridge. I had no idea what had been achieved, what precise trophies the girls had taken. All I knew was that

I was one of the gang. They'd looked at me with amused but approving eyes. And that was enough for me.

XVII

Reckonings

Thus passed July. Gradually, the crude plywood chessboard I'd sketched out and tucked behind Papa's desk away from Jan's narrow eye began to fill with pieces. The production rate wasn't quite as slow as I'd anticipated. Sometimes, out of a single piece of wood, I might be able to turn three or even four pawns. True, the knights still looked crude and uneven, and the kings' high crowns and rooks' castellations required finer attention. But piece by piece we were getting there. Or so I believed.

The day came when I presented it to Papa for inspection. It was a Thursday, not long after Jan had signed off. Perhaps I'd been too eager to get it finished. To win Papa's approval. Perhaps I'd been distracted by my secret life. One way or another, it seems I'd taken my eye off the ball. For a while Papa said nothing. He lifted the pieces individually, sniffed, hummed, tutted. One of the bishops he laid his thumb against, and pressed, hard. The thumb whitened, its tip crimsoned, it shook briefly, then the bishop snapped. He shook his head. 'This is shoddy work, Guy.'

'Yeah?'

'Did you check the materials you used for dry rot? For woodworm?' Helplessly, I shook my head. 'Didn't Jan teach you that? That should have been the first thing he taught you. But he shouldn't have had to. You should have asked. And look at those pawns. Are they all the same height? The same diameter?' He lifted a knight, and snorted. Then he took up the board, walked to one of the bins, and allowed the lot to slide in. 'That's shoddy work, Guy. You're not a child any more.'

In my parallel life, we ventured wide. It was a rule not to strike the same street twice, nor the same neighbourhood more than once on the same outing. There was always a chance that a random shopper or passer-by would recognise the routine. We struck a camera-shop in Mala Strana, a purveyor of silverware in Nové Město, and of watches in Florenc. The only quarter out of bounds was Josefov. 'One doesn't fleece one's own'. Besides, the girls were too well known there.

It would be a mistake to think that hitting shops was the stock and trade of the gang I'd fallen in with. The more I knew of them, the more these scenarios resembled days out, excursions to exercise their talents and have fun dressing up. The bread and butter came from the three card trick and shell game which Zak played on an upturned soap-box at markets and fairs, and for Sunday strollers in the parks. That, and pickpocketing. It was only the first of these I was permitted to be party to. My role was to enact the casual stroller, fascinated by the dexterity of the play. I'd watch, consider, and at length chance my fifty koruna. Invariably I'd win. I'd repeat the trick. I'd win a second time. If one of the girls was on my arm, this is where she'd grow uneasy and pull me away, but not until I'd ventured and won a third time. By this juncture a small crowd of onlookers would have gathered about the soap-box.

It was no harm to have a winner who looked innocent and Aryan. Whatever about innocent, to my mind I looked more Slavic than Aryan. True I was blond, but I had the high cheekbones and slightly slant eyes of the true Slav. Maman may have been from Turin, but her people were from Slovenia by way of the Tyrol.

I wasn't permitted to join in the pickpocketing. I was far too clumsy. And perhaps that was no harm. I still had qualms of conscience, and pickpocketing was too directly theft, too brazen a breach of the seventh commandment. But I was intrigued on the occasions I was allowed to observe. The three phase rule still applied. There had to be the decoy, the hit, and the switch. Tourists and those self-evidently from out of town were the preferred target. Anyone with an open street-map or a Baedeker was fair game. One of the girls, or both of them, might approach and sweetly offer help. But they were standing in a thoroughfare, how unthinking. The arrangement was an obstruction. Hurrying by, a gentleman in a hat might bump into the party. It was done in a flash. And in a flash, one or other of the street kids would pass by in the opposite direction, holding a balloon.

One of the favourite routines was what they called 'the packed tram'. There was another, occasional member of the group. Goran, they called him, a disreputable old rogue. His head was crowned with a wild wreath of white hair, and his stubble was like hoar-frost. He had a wall eye, so that as Zak put it, while one eye looked at you, the other looked for you.

The routine was this. During the busy hour when crowds rushed to or from work, just at the moment there was a general surge onto a packed tram, Goran would already have taken up position with an old sack or two, blocking the passageway. Impervious to the imprecations of the jostling passengers, he'd hold his position, hands in plain sight on either pole, aloof, deaf or simply heedless. Perhaps he'd been drinking? Excuse me, could you let me pass? Could you stand aside, please? Perhaps he's German. *Enschuldigen Sie bitte.* Foolish old man. Look at the wandering eye, is he touched or what?

By the time he alighted at the next stop, several wallets had gone missing from the squashed commuters. But how could that be? His hands were clearly visible all the time. I kept my eye on them because I smelled a rat. Then why didn't you speak up? What about that guy? He's very quiet. Zak would pat his breast pocket, mine is gone too! The rogue! And even if they searched him, which they never did, his pockets were empty. And who would dream of searching the pregnant girl who was seated over to the side? How could she have passed among them, squashed in like sardines as they were?

The end of July came. It was Saturday, two days after Papa had binned the shoddy chess set. After an unexpectedly profitable raid on a numismatists in Nové Město, we convened back at the warehouse by Štefánikuv Bridge, where I exchanged a pinstripe suit for my regular clothes. Just as I was making to leave, Zak thrust a bundle into my hand. It was a roll of notes, twenties and fifties. 'What's this?' I asked.

'Your cut.'

'We divvy up at the end of every month,' said Ada, who was at that moment shimmying out of her pistachio dress so that beneath her shift one could have gazed at the swing of her pendulous breasts. I reddened. But it wasn't on account of her immodesty. Strange as it may seem, I'd never expected to receive any monetary reward from our adventures. I was in it for the adrenaline. I was in it because I was hungry to grow up. I was in it because Leah Meisel was mistress of my imagination. On the rare occasions the scenario would cast us as lovers and we'd walk arm in arm, my body, overcome with her musk, would be charged as though with static. There was even one scenario, in a covered market in Nové Město, where we pushed a pram before us. Where they'd borrowed the infant remains a mystery to me. It remained largely oblivious to the bundles of contraband that shared its bedding; any time it did make to squall, a finger from Leah immediately pacified it (how I envied that gummy mouth then!)

These brief moments became the springboard for many a fantasy. I didn't actually want money. This money was tainted! But what was I to do? If I were to refuse it, to return the bundle, she would likely laugh at me. Ada too. So, with guilty heart, I tucked the roll deep into my trousers without deigning to count it. That night, I scarcely slept. It seemed to me that the biscuit tin to the back of the wardrobe was emanating some sort of maleficent glow.

I once asked Father Kaufmann if he believed in the Devil. It was shortly after my raid on the jewellers, when my spirits oscillated between dread and bravado.

'Of course,' he'd replied. 'I realise my view is somewhat out of fashion, much as the medieval view of Hell is out of fashion. But the Devil exists, alright. And I daresay Hell exists too.'

'Oh yeah? What makes you sure?'

'You only have to listen, to hear his urgings. I don't say I believe in a creature with batwings and lizard's tail. No. The Devil I believe in dwells in each of us. He is the arch-rationalist. You must remember, he was first and foremost the Bearer of Light. His urgings are subtle. Not the tempter, saying to Eve *Do wrong, and you will be like unto God*. Rather, the voice of low reason. The voice of 'yes, but...' The voice that whispers in the counterfeiter's ear, *If I make a forgery so perfect it is never discovered, whom do I cheat*? The voice that goads the adulterer, *If my spouse were not so possessive, I wouldn't be driven to this pass*. It whispers, *In this special case, for this particular circumstance, this is no sin*. But the reasoning of the Devil is tainted. More correctly, it's rationalisation. Sophistry. To follow it is to act in bad faith.'

'But how is one to distinguish, Father?'

'Because we are given conscience.' He wetted a finger and ran it around the rim of his brandy glass, coaxing a hesitant resonance that gradually condensed into a pure note. 'The ring of conscience is never mistaken. It doesn't require argument. It only requires you quiet the Devil's babble to hear it.'

A giddy impulse tempted me to come clean, to confess my raid into the jewellers. But he'd require restitution, to return what was stolen. How Leah Meisel would despise me if I asked for the ring back! Instead, a tiny imp whispered in my ear. I gave it voice. 'You know Papa says you're an atheist? His word for this sort of reasoning is Jesuitry.'

The old priest nodded, smiling. 'Emil tries so hard to be an atheist! Your father,' he pronounced, 'is a good man.'

Sealing that roll of ill-gotten banknotes inside the biscuit-tin, this all came back to me. Was it the Devil who whispered, *At least you haven't pickpocketed anyone?* Was it at his urging I made a vow not to spend it? Not unless some disaster came to pass. If the Germans were to invade, say, before Leah Meisel had got away to Odessa. Then I might use it, and whatever else had accrued in the interim, to obtain documents for her on the black market. I'd escort her to safety over the border. In my adolescent imaginings, I actually craved some such disaster, anything which might make her reappraise my insignificance.

July had one final card to play. Sunday 31st was a lazy day of intermittent sunshine. Leah's bare shoulders pushed resplendent from her summer frock of buttercup yellow. We spent the afternoon operating the shell-game up around the Observation Tower in Petřín Park. In place of Zak, Goran was with us that day. Where Zak's fingers were slender and elegant, his were stubby. Nevertheless he was as skilful a prestidigitator as ever I'd seen, and could make the pea disappear and reappear as though it were on an invisible thread. Pickings were so lush we even had the leisure to get lost for a time in the Maze, where for ten glorious minutes I trotted hand in hand with Leah into dead end after dead end. Her lameness at such times was scarcely noticeable. About four or five, we convened back at the warehouse.

This time, as I was about to leave, Ada and Leah stood either side of me, and each took an elbow. Ada's cheek brushed my ear. 'I've been thinking, Becca,' she whispered, 'we can't very well have our fancy man played by a virgin. Can we?'

Leah made a show of sniffing the air around my face. 'He does smell of virginity.'

'What should we do?'

'Let's bring him to Nana Levy's! I think I know how we can get rid of that smell.'

And so, arm in arm between the two belles dames and aware of the different perfumes to either side of me, the one sweet, the other musk, I was walked out of the warehouse and into the sunlight. We took a right, then a left, away from the river. I moved in a trance, nervous, but sick with desire. I dared not think. I dared not imagine. Soon, we came to a closed door. Leah jingled the bell-pull.

After quite an interval, the door opened unto a dark passageway. A woman of about fifty who looked like a vaudeville drag queen blinked at us. 'Is Nana Levy up and about?' asked Ada.

'Phhh! So early?'

'Can we use one of the rooms?'

The woman shrugged, indifferent, then stood aside to let us pass. I was giddy, my gut filled with as much dread as anticipation. Ada remained on the ground floor. Leah mounted a narrow staircase ahead of me. In a trance I followed the spoor of musk and the hesitant flick of her yellow frock.

We entered a small room. It was bare except for a sort of iron cot beneath a rust-stained mattress, and a chipped enamel basin on a stool by the window. A yellowed net curtain was drawn across the window, which was itself so small and begrimed it hardly required the curtain to taint the daylight a tobacco shade. 'Wait here,' said Leah, manoeuvring me onto the cot. 'Two minutes.'

For what seemed an age I sat, listening. But all I could hear was my own breathing. Was Leah taking off her leg brace? Or had they already left, the whole thing a big joke? My heart hammered madly. I was torn between expectation and a desire to run for it.

I was about to rise when the door opened. A girl entered. I think she was no more than my age, but infinitely older in experience. She was barefoot, her skinny body clad only in a shift. In a trice she was sitting on my knee. She smelt of salt, and something vaguely sour. I still remember that smell. Unsmiling, she draped her left arm about my neck. When I did nothing, she took my hand and slid it inside her shift. She was flat-chested, but I could feel the fatness of her nipple. I'd never touched a girl before.

She moved her hand down to my flies. But I was mortified. This was not right. I felt my erection soften. My imagination went blank. This was all wrong. It was Leah I wanted. Not this girl, who smelled sour and salt, and who looked at me with unsmiling eyes. 'No,' I said. 'Please.'

She shushed me. Her fingers still fumbled about my flies. I stood, sliding her from my knee. 'I can't do this,' I said.

'You don't like me?'

'Sure. Yes. You're...' I stared at the bare floorboards. 'Look...'

She came to me, put one arm about either side of my neck. Her eyes serious beyond her years, she tried to press a kiss on me. My lips remained clammed shut. 'Tsst,' she said.

I moved her to the cot. I made her sit. 'Look,' I croaked, my mouth dry and sore, 'I have to go. Really. It's not that I don't...' She watched me in solemn silence. I tried to think of something else to say. Something to finish the sentence. I could think of nothing.

As I hesitated at the door, she whispered, 'Say to Nana Levy that you liked me.'

XVIII

The Letter

August drew to a tumultuous close as the Sudeten crisis came rapidly to a head. The viewings for the summer auction were upon us. One evening, as we were shutting up shop after a day of hanging and altering and re-hanging, Papa asked me to step out the back. I'd rarely heard such seriousness in his tone. My throat contracted, and cement set in my gut. Somehow, he'd got wind of my misadventures! Yet part of me felt relief, the relief that the accused feels when the jury hands down its guilty verdict and the dreadful suspense is ended.

'This came,' he said. He reached into his inside pocket and pulled out an envelope, addressed and stamped. But I couldn't make either out. My vision was blurred. The world tilted before my eyes, which I now closed. I was close to fainting in anticipation of what that letter might contain.

I felt him push the envelope into my hand. 'A couple of days ago,' he added. When I at length opened my eyes, he'd left me alone.

Heart high at my throat, I examined the envelope.

p. Emil Hayek
Nerudova ulice 37
Mala Strana
Praha
Czechoslovakia.

The three stamps were United States Postage. Ridiculously, my first thought was how well they'd sit in my stamp collection. I pulled out two closely written pages. *Vážený Pane* the letter began, which seemed somewhat formal for what was to follow.

Vážený Pane
You have not heard from me in the better part of two decades. It was a condition you laid down at the time of Elsa Mörschel's funeral. Probably, you will not have heard about me either. And that's as it should be. You probably are thinking, and why should I read this through now? Why shouldn't I throw this letter into the bin unread? I appeal to you not to do that. This letter does not concern me. It is not an appeal for forgiveness, nor reconciliation. All I ask of you is that you read it through to the end. Then decide.

I need to go back to that summer, the summer you found out that Elsa was to have a baby, and that that baby wasn't yours. I know she told you, that same night, that she'd be leaving you. Also, that we could not take our baby with us. And she told me how you reacted. How reasonable you were. The wronged man – for that's how the world saw you. You were the wronged man. You'd invited me into your house, and I'd betrayed your trust. To an extent there's truth in that. Now is not the time to rehearse all the mistresses you kept throughout Europe. I don't expect you to forgive me. I don't ask it.

You knew about her stomach cancer. I know this because Elsa told me she'd informed you of that last diagnosis. And that was why, maybe, you didn't hate her, or hit her, or threaten her. And of course you knew how much she was drinking. The whole of Prague knew about Elsa's drinking. But what you didn't know, what I don't think you knew, was how heavily she'd come to rely on the laudanum. Of course, Niklaus' birth had not been easy. And it was for that that she'd been prescribed the accursed opiate in the first place. Before ever I set foot inside Nerudova Street, she was already a dope fiend. She said you weren't aware, not fully. But how could you not have been aware? You were never a stupid man, Emil.

We could not take our daughter with us. Graciously, you assured Elsa you'd raise the girl as though she were your own. Me, you'd long since thrown out. And so we left Prague as exiles. The rest you know. At the end of seven miserable years, she was dead. They said it was an overdose. Death by misadventure. Nothing will ever convince me that that overdose wasn't deliberate. She couldn't stand the pain of her condition. She couldn't stand the ugliness of it. You brought her body from Bratislava to Prague, and only suffered my presence at the graveside on condition I agreed never once to make any attempt to contact you again. That I never once ask how our Katerina was faring.

And I haven't. To this day, I haven't. You will have to grant me that.

Which brings us to the purpose of this letter. Who can foresee the future? After Elsa's death, I spent several unsatisfactory years in Prague. But life at the Rudolfinum wasn't the same. There were those who blamed me for Elsa Mörschel's death. So talented a singer! So once again, I became a wanderer. Vienna. Salzburg. Then Munich. It was while in Munich that the vehemence of the new hatred was made manifest. And so, in 1935, I set sail for New York.

My sister, Golda, moved here in 1919. Her husband works for the INS, which is the Immigration and Naturalisation Service. This fact greatly facilitated my entry into the country, and can be useful again. It has taken me three years to become established. But now I am respected here. I have clients, some of them well known. Most are exiles like me from a Europe that daily grows darker. Several of them are of my own race. I say this only to give an idea of how tolerant the society is here toward the European Jew. I'm not rich, but I make a good living.

From my apartment in Brooklyn, I've been watching what has been happening in Central Europe. All those mixed up lands of hatred and jealousy. And so to the purpose of this letter. I lived in Munich for four years. I've seen the future play out on the Munich streets. And the future for the European Jew is black. Ask yourself, Emil. Will France go to war to save Czechoslovakia? Will Britain go to war to save Czechoslovakia? And when they don't, and Bohemia becomes a province of the Third Reich, what future can Katerina have there? I can tell you she would be safe, here in America. Here in New York, where there are even neighbourhoods where Yiddish is spoken.

I realise she's never met me. I've never seen our daughter. Even as an infant. It was forbidden me. And so I appeal to you directly, rather than to her. Besides, I made a solemn vow at that graveyard that never would I try to contact Katerina without your knowledge and your permission. And to me, a vow is sacred. I appeal to you, as the father who raised her even as his own child. Would you see her bullied and spat upon? Would you see her ghettoised, her citizenship removed? No father would.

Send her to me, Emil. While there is still time. Because the door is closing.

You will say I forfeited my rights as Katerina's father. You'll say that, once long ago, I betrayed such trust as you placed in me. But we both know how things had become strained between you and Elsa long before I arrived upon the scene. So let the past be buried alongside her emaciated body. It's Katerina I'm thinking of, and only Katerina.

I live alone, but I have a spare room. It can be hers. A safe haven, in a safe country. I include my address. I appeal to you to act without delay.

S pozdravem,
Mordecai Gans

I folded the letter back into the envelope. The courtyard was empty. It had grown cold.

XIX

On the Bridge

Nothing was said, not so much as a word, before we passed under the Bridge Tower and onto the river. Far too much was going around in my head. And yet I had the distinct feeling that Papa wanted me to speak. About a third of the way across, he stepped over to a parapet and leaned over, waiting. 'Have you shown the letter to Katya?' I asked.

He shook his head.

'To Maman?'

'No, Guido. I wanted to show it to you first.'

'Why to me?'

He examined me. The crow's feet, so usually couching a sort of mischief, seemed old in the evening light. 'I wanted you to find out what kind of a man your old man is. You've never really known.'

'I've never known much about Katya's mother.' It was my turn to lean my elbows on the parapet. 'Klaus' mother,' I added.

'No. I never spoke to you about her. I never spoke to anyone about her. You know it's curious, Klaus has never

138

asked. Katya I can understand. She never knew the first thing about Elsa. It was as if she was a foundling. And besides, she's so reticent there are times I think she might just as well have been born mute. But Klaus? Klaus I can't understand for the life of me! His own mother?'

'I always had the impression he blamed her for abandoning him.'

'It was me she abandoned. It wasn't him.' He met my eye directly. 'She was my great love. You only really have one love, you know. She was it. That's why I'm trying to make up for lost time with you, Guido.'

'I don't understand.'

'You see, after she left, after she ran away with that Jew, leaving me to raise Katya, I did something very unfair. I brought Maria Tedesco out of her natural home, transplanted her here, where she didn't know a single word of the language. Even today, twenty years on, her accent is like that of a chambermaid. What's worse, I knew perfectly well how unfair I was being.'

'You needed someone to raise the girl,' I tried.

'It wasn't so much that. I could have employed a nanny. But I wanted Elsa to know, if she gave a damn any more, that I was doing ok. That there was life after Elsa Mörschel. Your mother was what people sometimes call a rebound. It's never fair.'

'Then you never loved Maman?'

He considered. 'I loved her father. You're too young to remember him.'

'I remember his funeral.'

He looked at me. Then looked away. 'To make up for my

unfairness, and because she knew so few people here, I allowed her to have her way with you. Where you were concerned, she could do pretty much as she pleased. She named you for your Uncle Guido you know. The seminarian. I think she's always planned you might one day replace him. And because I felt sorry for her, and because it was the path of least resistance, I let her have her way. And for that I can never be forgiven. I don't ask you to forgive me, Guy...'

'But Papa, I don't...'

His raised palm cut me off. 'I don't expect you to understand. Not as yet. Perhaps when you're older.'

'You make it sound like I'm a total failure!'

'If you are,' he said, 'it's down to me. Blame your old man.' I examined his features for raillery, but if there was any, it was strained. 'I have every hope it's not too late.'

'Jesus,' I laughed. 'It's not like I've terminal cancer!'

'You'll come good. I don't doubt it, Guy. Look. There's something else I want you to know.' He took a long time, staring down into the flowing river, before continuing. 'What I did, taking that home job directing munition trains while both my brothers did the manly thing, that's what came between Elsa and me. Never mind that it was her own family who'd found me the post. Never mind that it was precisely the fear of losing her through death or mutilation that held me from joining up in the first place. It's ironic. One thing you'll find as you grow older, Guy, is that fate delights in ironies.

'So, with every month that went by, with every bulletin from the front – and believe me, for the Austro-Hungarians the bulletins were always bad – for every new draft that called up yet more of the able-bodied and for every trainload of broken men that came back, a little more of me died. I could no longer hold my head up. I was no longer a man. Elsa knew it. She never taunted me, nor took me to task. Never openly. But Elsa was a part of why it happened. By the time Klaus was born, with all the complications and the immense agony she was in, things were pretty much over between myself and Elsa Mörschel.

'Gans wasn't the first. Not by a long chalk. By this time she was drinking. Not heavily, but steadily. And badly. Nastily. It brought out the worst in her. She became mean when she drank. To protect myself, I took mistresses, though not so openly. None in Prague.

'Her voice was affected. Her dependability. Concerts were cancelled. To try to remedy the situation, to try to rescue the woman who, despite everything, I still loved, I engaged Mordecai Gans. Irony again. Can't you hear fate, having its laugh? Gans was the most expensive. The most renowned. I was desperate, and would try anything to have the old Elsa back.

'Of course it failed. I wasn't even particularly heartbroken that it was the Jew she left with, finally. He'd always seemed such a wimp to me, in comparison to some of the others.'

'And raising his child?'

He examined me. The squint suggested that it had been an acute question. 'A child is innocent. A child is always innocent. Besides everything else, she was all that was left to me of Elsa Mörschel. The one proviso, Mordecai Gans must disappear as completely as her mother had.' A moment passed. 'I told her he was dead. You remember that?' He looked away from me. 'So now you know.'

141

'So what will you do? Will you show her the letter?'

'So she can despise me, too?'

I stood, rigid. I was taken aback. 'I don't despise you, Papa! How could you ever think that?'

'No? When I never loved your mother? When I abandoned you to her whims?'

'No!' I made to hug him, but it was an awkward gesture. I was awkward. 'Will you tell Maman? About the letter?'

'I haven't decided. I think a part of her wouldn't be at all sad to see Katya out of the house. They've never really understood one another.'

'She's always been closer to Klaus.'

'At least Klaus has some of my blood. That's the way your mother looks on the whole thing. She never understood my decision to raise another man's child. Or that's wrong! I think she understood perfectly. And she resented it.' He stood tall, put one hand on either of my shoulders. 'There's another reason I showed you that letter, Guido. Can't you guess?'

I racked my brains. I could think of nothing.

'Let's just imagine that everything this Mordecai Gans writes comes to pass. Let's say they fumble the ball over the Sudetenland, and carve up Czechoslovakia. Let's say the best thing, the only thing, would be for Katya to take up this man's offer. A safe room. A safe haven. And after all, he is her natural father. Are you with me?'

'Sure,' I shrugged.

'Now suppose I were to show the letter to Katya. What do you think she'd say? Do you think she'd be prepared to sail to New York, to a man she never met? To a life she never knew? With not so much as a word of English?'

'I guess not.'

'I guess not.' He pushed himself away from the parapet. 'That's where you come in, Guy.'

I shook my head. I had no idea where this was going.

'I'll leave it with you. You're not a child any more. Come on. Let's get home. I'm hungry as a hunter.' Invigorated, though not entirely, he set off for the Mala Strana side.

XX

September 1938

The summer auction was a disaster. Numbers passing through the gallery during the viewings were down on previous years. But it wasn't so much the numbers that had Papa concerned. It was what he was overhearing. On the night of the auction itself, fewer than half of the exhibits made their reserve price, and for those that did, the bidding was subdued. Even the one or two 'bankers', the Kupka, say, or the Preisler, disappointed. When the accounts were totted up over the following days, they turned out to be the worst set of results in a decade. Not since the crash of '29 and the hard couple of years that followed had the Czech art market experienced such a reversal.

Papa was worried. Between them, Maman and Lorenz Špotákov had laid out quite a sum on wedding preparations. With the big day less than three weeks away, as the political clouds darkened, payment of bills up front was increasingly demanded. Credit dried up, debts were called in. Papa was forced to sell a number of government bonds at considerable discount. Suddenly, the whole world was in a scramble for cash and movables. But if Papa was worried, he was also pig-headed. Along with the rest of the Czechoslovakian army, Lt Mikuláš Hayek – he insisted on the Czech form of his name – was placed on standby, all leave cancelled, so that the honeymoon trip to Venice, though largely paid for, would have to be deferred. As if to compensate, the guest list for the wedding breakfast at the Hotel Imperial continued to swell. For every name and business colleague that Špotákov, the celebrated vintner added, Papa insisted the Hayeks must find a counterpart, and since neither he nor Maman had living siblings, his list searched far and wide. It was a kind of madness. Even Maman said so. Already, Papa's bill was running to tens of thousands. For the wine alone, which after much heated argument was to be the gift of Špotákov, no less than three thousand koruna had been set aside.

I had my own concerns. For the first time, Meisel's van was gone for upward of a week. Word was that he was scouring a couple of big estates in eastern Bohemia for bargains – distressed sales of those wishing to leave the country in anticipation of his own big sell-up. I couldn't get a word out of Leah Meisel on the subject, and Papa was too pre-occupied to allow my enquiries any but the most cursory of replies. Ezra Meisel had been invited to the wedding, perhaps I could ask him then, if he deigned to concelebrate with Gentiles. 'Time to forget about that little Jew girl,' he growled, one morning when I persisted. And I resented him for it. It was a curious sensation. Never before had I been angry at Papa.

I could no longer imagine that the black day would never arrive. It seemed certain Old Meisel was making final preparations to leave. It seemed no less uncertain he'd take away with him the orphan he'd raised as a granddaughter.

Then I'd never see her again, never get lost in a maze with her again, never hold hands again and act out the role of a lover. The prospect was a dismal one. But it was, as it were, in eclipse. Like all Czechs, I was under the shadow of the looming conference. Everyone sensed the betrayal that was imminent. It might be a quarrel in a faraway country between people of whom he know nothing, nevertheless Chamberlain had argued that the German claims were just. Edward Beneš would be hung out to dry. Already, the Poles and Hungarians were sharpening their knives, salivating over whatever parts of the carcass the Germans allowed them.

Then another bombshell burst. On a Sunday afternoon, with less than a fortnight to go before the wedding, Eva Špotáková asked me would I go up to talk to Katya. It seemed she no longer wanted to be one of the bridesmaids. 'You talk to her, Guido,' said Maman. 'She listens to you.' 'Would it be such a disaster?' I asked. Maman shut her eyes, the strain of the last few months clearly marked. 'Just go, Guido.'

'For me?' added Eva. And I have to admit I was flattered.

We'd talked, briefly, about the letter Papa had received from America. Katya hadn't seemed at all surprised that Papa had shown the letter to me. 'What do you think?' I'd asked.

'About?'

'If things got bad here.'

'Phhh! You know I think Papa actually wants me to go.'

'If he does, he's only thinking of your safety, Katya. He's worried about you.'

'I know I've been a disappointment to him.'

'What are you, nuts? Papa's crazy for you. After you were attacked, he practically bit my head off for leaving you on your own to face them. You know what's funny? I still haven't the balls to tell him about his broken Carlos Gardel records!'

'And Django Reinhart!'

'Really? Oh Jesus!' We were smiling at one another. 'He's quite a guy, Papa.'

'He is that.'

'So what do you think? I mean if things get really bad here.'

'Would I leave? No. Never! What would I do in New York? My life is here, Guy. My family is here. My mother is dead, buried in the Olšany cemetery. I've only one father. That father is Papa. It always has been, and it always will be.' She shook her head reproachfully. 'How could you even ask, Guy?'

Ten days had passed since that exchange. If nothing else, it had set my mind at ease as to Papa's injunction. *I'll leave it with you. You're not a child any more.* Well, whatever Papa may have had in mind, Katya had her mind made up. So that was that. Matter closed.

I held out little prospect of convincing Katya to be bridesmaid. Several times already she'd tried to back out of it. True, her hair had regrown somewhat, and if it looked boyish, it was not unattractive. But her right arm wouldn't fully straighten – it seemed now it might never straighten – and her birthmark, of which she was so self-conscious, was entirely visible. There were no plans for a veil or even a net that might in some way disguise it. To make matters worse, Eva's sisters Terésa and Eliška, who were to be the other bridesmaids, were beauties with complexions clear as water.

I found her dressed in her bridesmaid's rig-out, a gorgeous

147

concoction in kingfisher blue. She was standing near the mirror, watching the open doorway as though she were expecting me. 'So what's this all about?' I tried, the jaunty tone not quite coming off. As if in answer, she turned a profile, her hands bunched over her tummy as though to hold a bouquet. 'You've Maman close to hysterics you know.'

'I'm sure she'll get over it. What does Eva want with three bridesmaids anyway? It's not as if Klaus asked you to be a groomsman. His own brother!'

'Half-brother,' I corrected. 'I wouldn't want to be one. Besides, I don't have a military uniform. I don't even have a customs uniform, like cousin Rudi.'

'Such bullshit!'

'But why back out now, when Maman has her heart set on it?' I readied my trump card. 'Papa, too. He'll want a Hayek for every Špotákov.'

'And be on show in front of everyone? Really, are you sure that's what they'd want?' She was firing me a 'significant' look. A 'come on, you're not stupid' look. But I remained stupid. 'Fuck sake, Guido! Haven't you guessed?' A perceptible spasm ran down her arms, and her bunched fists, resting on her belly, gave a tiny jump. All at once it came to me, what she was implying.

'Jesus, Katya! How long have you known?'

She shrugged. 'Couple of months.'

'A couple of months! Does Papa know? Maman?'

'I haven't told anyone.'

'But are you sure?'

In place of answering she moved over to the bedstead and sat, her hands still folded on her tummy. All the while her dark eyes remained on mine.

'Who…' I began. 'Was it that Václav guy?'

'I don't see who else it could have been, short of an immaculate conception.'

'And does he know? Have you told him?'

'I told you, Guy. I haven't told anyone. You're the only one who knows.'

'Jesus, Katya.'

'Yeah.'

'So when will it…?'

'I'm not sure. February, I think. Or March.'

'But you'll have to tell him. Václav. You'll have to let him know.'

'Not for anything! He's never going to know.'

'You're not thinking of…' My hands thrashed about. I wasn't sure how to finish.

'Of finding some old crone with a knitting needle? No, Guido. I'm not.'

I sat beside her. My head was reeling. I took her hand. 'You'll have to tell Papa. Maman, too. You can't very well not tell them.'

'I daresay they'll all find out soon enough, without me telling any of them.'

Ok, I thought. Ok. Papa was a reasonable man. After all, I'd been born out of wedlock. It had taken them several years to regularise that arrangement. 'And for the time being?'

'The world goes on turning.'

I gave her hand a squeeze. 'Stand up! Let me see.'

She did so, turned to the left, then the right.

'But there's nothing on show. Not a thing. I mean, so

149

far as I know, it's six or seven months before anyone would notice. Especially when it's a first child.'

'Huh! The expert!'

'Father Kaufmann told me.' I reddened. 'He's told me lots of things, actually.'

She snorted. 'I'm sure he has!' Then she turned again to the mirror. 'And you think I should go through with this wedding thing?'

'Of course you should go through with it! This is all in your head, Katya. No one's going to have the faintest idea.'

There was one final bombshell in the run up to that wedding. The ceremony was to take place on Friday 30th of September, an infamous day if ever there was one. Fate having its ironic snicker, as Papa might have put it. On Saturday 24th, he found me out the back of the gallery, working on the pawns for the new chess set. 'Here,' he said, 'this came for you.'

It was a note, hastily scribbled on the inside of a torn cigarette packet. 'Meet, soon as you can, the den.' The den was the disused warehouse by Štefánikuv Bridge. But who had written it? Not Leah, anyhow. 'Who left it in, Papa?'

'She didn't say. Redhead.' Then he quipped, unsmiling, 'Looked like a streetwalker.'

I hid the chagrin. 'Can I take the rest of the morning?'

'Do what you like.'

I removed the apron, swept up hastily the shavings from the floor.

'Guido. I've been giving you your head. In trying to make up for lost time, perhaps I've been too free. I thought you'd find out people your own age. What I'm telling you, you need to be careful who you fall in with.'

'Ok,' I said. Now wasn't the time to engage in an argument.

I hastened to the warehouse. There, I found Leah. She looked distraught, more distraught than I'd ever seen her. 'What is it? What's happened?'

It was Ada who answered. 'They've got Zak.'

'Zak? When? *How?*'

'This morning. Doing 'the packed tram'. There was this bunch of tourists. From Bavaria. Only thing, turns out they were a bunch of off-duty S.A. They caught him redhanded, fingers in one of their pockets. Gave him one hell of a beating once they pulled him from the tram.'

'But where is he?'

'Arrested. If the gendarmes hadn't interfered, they might have beaten him to death. As it was they snapped back every finger in both hands.'

An image of the slender fingers executing their comical dance over the three cards came to me. 'Jesus Christ!' I looked from one of them to the other. Leah was watching me intently, as though she were waiting for me to say something. 'So what happens now?'

'Now?' This was Leah. Her eyes were spitfires. 'On Monday he'll be dragged up before the magistrate. That's what happens now.'

'For sentencing?'

'Tsst!' she spat, exasperated by my naivety.

'It's just an initial hearing, to formally charge him' said Ada. 'They'll set a date for the trial, if it's to go that far. They'll take details, set bail conditions. Assign legal counsel. It might go easier if he admits everything.'

Leah made an animal sound, somewhere between a hiss and a growl. 'He's no lacky! He'll never plead guilty!'

'If they've found out his real name, he won't be in for an easy ride.'

I looked back to Leah, who was glowering at the floor. 'What can I do?' I asked.

Instantly, she sized me up. 'You can say you were on the tram.'

The suggestion hit me with the force of a slap.

'You could! You could tell them they got hold of the wrong hand. It'd be your word against a bunch of Germans probably here to spy on us. Say that you saw who'd actually picked out the wallet. Maybe a street kid did it. There was a street kid, I remember there was.'

'You'll be saying it too, then?'

'I can't. It'd do no good. I'm a known accomplice. But you...'

I nodded. Me with my respectable address. Me with my Aryan-Slavic looks. I needed time to think, but bravado and something else, some form of recklessness, some streak of anger against my father, made me short-circuit the time needed. 'Tell me about the tram.'

'You see,' called Leah, triumphant. 'I told you we could rely on him.'

XXI

Witness

The following afternoon we reconvened in the warehouse. I'd scarcely slept. All morning, my mind was alive with possibilities. My heart raced. Perjury was a biting insect that I kept clear of. A scorpion, scuttling at the back of consciousness. 'I told you we could rely on him,' she'd said. For the longest time I'd dreamed of some danger Leah might be in, and I able to prove to her my worth. Here at last was my chance to impress her. To impress all of them. Even Zak would have to see I was no mere adolescent bourgeois. I'd played the tram scene so often in my imagination I could actually see the crush of bodies, the street kid's fingers picking the wallet, the wrong hand grabbed for its unlucky proximity. As the Štefánikuv Bridge came into view, my spirits soared.

I was surprised to find Hookworm was there, bald head and frown and leather coat. He was seated in the barber's chair facing toward the mirror and watching my entry in its murky depths, hands thrust deep in his coat pockets so that the coattails enfolded his legs like the wings of a bat. Perhaps I shouldn't have been so entirely surprised at his presence. The gang had occasional dealings with Hookworm. He'd act as fence for the more valuable items of merchandise. I've no idea what sort of a cut he took.

Ada met me at the door, in her pistachio green dress and lurid eyeshadow. Now that Papa had pronounced the word, it was hard not to think of her as a streetwalker. Leah was in a plain smock, tatty and creased, her black mass of hair dishevelled and dark rings under her eyes. When she saw me it was as if she briefly lit up. I thought her hauntingly beautiful.

The barber's chair swung about and Hookworm took me in directly. Without rising, he called out, 'So this is our star witness! Come! Enter!' I did so.

'So,' he said, rising, his hands still deep in either pocket, 'you were on the tram, eh?'

'I was.'

'What tram? Tell us.'

'The 8:35. Down along Masarykovo nábřeží.'

'I see. And what were you doing, on the 8:35 tram down along Masarykovo nábřeží?'

I hesitated.

'Come, you must have been doing something!'

'I was running an errand for my father.'

'Running an errand for your father! Ah! What errand?'

Again I hesitated. I glanced about to the girls.

'It's not a difficult question. You were running an errand for your father. What errand?'

'I was delivering a bill. A demand for immediate payment.'

'Oh. To whom?'

'To the Minerva Gallery. It's in Vyšehrad.'

'Ok. So at 8:35 on the tram on Masarykovo nábřeží, what

was it that you saw?'

'There were a party of Bavarian tourists.'

'Ba-*varian*. How do you know they were Bavarian?'

'The accent. The type of German they spoke.'

'Well? And so?'

'I saw a child, picking a pocket. And I saw a man being mistakenly accused of that theft.' I awaited the next question. He waited for me to go on. 'They dragged him off the tram, this man. They started to give him a beating.'

'What was he wearing, this man?' I pivoted about toward the girls. 'Don't look at them. Look at me. What was he wearing, this man you saw beaten?'

I shrugged. 'A suit? A *hat?* No. No hat.'

'You're sure? No hat. I'll make a note of that. A grey suit? A blue suit? A candy-striped suit?' I remained silent. 'And these Bavarians, this party of tourists, how were they dressed?' Still I remained silent. I could feel my cheeks aflame. 'Lederhosen and Alpine hats?' I shrugged, helpless. Ashamed. 'And tell me, if you saw that it was a street kid who took the wallet, why didn't you say anything at the time? Why didn't you try to stop an innocent man getting beaten? Why wait until now?'

'I was in a hurry. I had to drop off the bill in Vyšehrad and get back to my father's gallery.'

'You were in too much of a hurry to stop an innocent man from being dragged off a tram and getting beaten? You must be in mortal fear of your father! Ok. So let's say that's true. Your father is a bastard. Tell us. What else did you see on this tram? Describe it for us.'

'Just before Karluv Bridge, there was a mad scramble to get on.'

'You were already on the tram?'

My eyes fixed on the chevron of his odious brow. I tried to see where the trap was, but couldn't. 'Yes,' I said.

'And yet you say you were on an errand from your father's gallery on Karluva Street to the Minerva Gallery in Vyšehrad. How came you to be already on the tram?'

'What I meant, I got onto the tram before the general push. Before the group of Bavarians.'

'Ah. I see. Did you notice this lady on the tram?'

I followed his finger. He was indicating Leah, whose eyes were intently on me.

'No,' I began. But then I vacillated. 'Or, maybe.' Could she have decided to corroborate my story. 'Maybe she was on the tram.'

'She was or she wasn't. Which?'

I begged her with my eyes for a hint. None came. 'Yes,' I said. 'I think she was. Seated already. By the window.'

'Seated by the window. Well? And what then?'

'There was this guy. Blocking the way.'

'Was there? Can you describe him for us?'

My blush deepened so much that my face ached. I knew I was making a balls of the whole thing. And still the inquisition went on.

'Just a guy.'

'Just a guy?'

'An old guy. He was blocking the passage. With bags.'

'Would you know 'this guy' if you saw him again?'

Helpless, I shrugged.

'Look around. Do you see 'this guy' anywhere in the courtroom?'

Timidly, ashamedly, I pivoted about. Just inside the door stood Goran, wild white hair and crazy eyes. Hookworm collapsed back into the barber's chair, waving the batwings of his coat. 'And then you ask me why we can't trust this boy on the witness stand!'

It was a humiliation, from start to finish. The only thing they would allow me to do, in fact they asked me to do it, was to attend the magistrate's hearing on the following day. It was open to the public, they said. But it wouldn't do at all for any of them to be seen there. They were known accomplices, all of them.

I was to find out everything I could. That he would be refused bail and remanded in custody was a foregone conclusion. But what name did they use? Was there any mention of previous convictions? How did he look? How was his morale? What was the date of the next hearing? Before what magistrate? In short, glean anything and everything I could.

The hearing itself, one of about two dozen that morning, was so brief I was amazed. Zak, or Simon Aaron Rosenthal as he was addressed, was a mess. His fingers stuck out in splints like a parody pair of hands, something you might see on a scarecrow or snowman, and he gazed mournfully at them, as a child might. His face was bruised, one eye with a duck egg underneath it. In fact he rather called to mind Lizaveta after her beating, except that where her battered face showed defiance, his shoulders were slumped in defeat.

'Bail refused,' I told them. 'Legal counsel provided by the state. The hearing is set for three weeks tomorrow. The magistrate is called Jänecke.'

'That's not good. A right bastard if ever there was one. He'll have to throw himself on the mercy of the court.'

'Plead guilty!' Leah was outraged.

'He doesn't stand a rat's chance in a trap. They know who he is. Si Rosenthal will have to plead mitigating circumstances. He was driven to do it. On account of his children. He couldn't simply watch them starve. Even a bastard like Jänecke will have to cut him some slack if they're in the court for sentencing.'

His *children*? It came to me that the two street kids we operated with might well be his. Now it had been said, the young boy did resemble him somewhat. A sort of three foot miniature of the adult Si Rosenthal, or Zak as I had known him. He even had a hint of the eyebrow. Hookworm turned to Ada. 'Put them on half rations. Make them look the part.'

'Is there a mother?' I asked, in my gauche way.

'She's mad!' hissed Leah. 'She's certified crazy!'

'It'll have to count for something. Taking the guilty plea and the mitigating circumstance into consideration, he might be looking at three years. Four, with the final one suspended.'

'Three years,' groaned Leah.

'He's an old jailbird, Si is. He can whistle away three years. He fights them on this, he's going down for maybe seven.'

'And that's what you'll tell him to do. Plead guilty.'

'That's what I'll tell him to do.'

Leah had drawn back a hand as though to scratch her hair, and now tried to smash it across Hookworm's face. But he was too quick for her. He seized it. 'Careful, alley-cat! I bite back.' She stared fire at him, then spat a cobra-spit onto his face.

Instantly his free hand grabbed her about the neck and he flung her to the ground. My fists clenched, I stepped up. As I did my hair was grabbed and tugged backwards and an open blade thrust side-on against my naked throat. I was overwhelmed by his body odour, felt his hot breath on my face. 'Touch me, it'll be the last thing you ever touch! You're out of your depth here, boy.'

Panting hard, itching to hit his pig-eyed face, I glanced to Leah. She was rising awkwardly on her lame leg, brushing herself down. 'Leave him be,' she said. 'Go home. Run! It's finished, here.'

XXII

The Carve-up

The Friday of the wedding was a surreal one. Prague was a city in suspended animation, as though some natural disaster had been visited upon it. In every café, in every bar and betting-shop, crowds clustered around the wireless sets as though they were household gods. Oracles handing down sentence from the ether. From the kitchens of the Hotel Imperial, grim-faced waiters imparted amongst the three hundred wedding guests, along with the seven courses and bottles of Hermitage Gran Cru, the latest bulletins from Munich. Rumours circulated like an undercurrent under the clack of a thousand oyster shells.

Earlier, the ceremony itself had not escaped the unreality. In the weeks leading up to the Munich Conference, there was a wave of resentment against Prague's German-speakers. Ugly graffiti appeared, reports of commuters pulled from trams. Windows of business premises that had been respectable for decades were smashed. A number of guests with German surnames, judging discretion the better part of valour, sent their regrets. In such a fevered atmosphere, the question arose as to whether Johannes Kaufmann SJ was the right choice to celebrate the wedding. To give him his due it was Klaus – he who had once declared that three million Sudetens might be removed 'at gunpoint if necessary' – who was most vociferous in insisting it must be Father Kaufmann. 'For as long as I remember he's been our family padre. He's stood by us. If he was good enough to marry you and Maman, it would be shameful if we sidelined him now.'

A guard of honour stood on the steps of the great Church of St Niklaus – the Kostel Sv Mikuláše – and came to attention as the groom and best man arrived. The altar itself had been decked out in patriotic bouquets of blue, white and red. From the pulpit, Father Kaufmann asked the congregation to pray for Czechoslovakia in her hour of need. Then, just before bride and groom turned to exit down the aisle, an impromptu rendition of the national anthem rose to the vaults, led by three powerful pews of officers from the various branches of the military, some Klaus' age, others beribboned veterans of the Great War.

We were met in the foyer of the Hotel Imperial by a string quartet playing decidedly patriotic music – Janáček and Dvořák and Smetana. Maman was in her element, gliding about the parties of wedding guests she scarcely knew and greeting them in her execrable Czech as though she were some visiting foreign dignitary. Papa, his hair curled tight, might have been a Roman patrician. All the while we awaited the arrival of the bride and groom I hung back, awkward as any adolescent in adult company, exchanging mortified glances with the unfortunate Katya. Though she mightn't have thought it, the boyish haircut suited her. Besides Katya, the only adult in whose company I was comfortable was Father Kaufmann, but he was much in demand.

Around eight o'clock, the tables were cleared away to one side. A gypsy trio brought in especially from Český Krumlov struck up some Hungarian folk-tunes, and the notables of Prague society took to the dancefloor in tuxedos and gorgeous dresses, reflected to infinity in the high facing mirrors. Looking about the gilded colonnades and mouldings, the coloured stucco, the fittings and glasswork in the Art Deco style, I had the curious sensation we were on a great ocean liner, doomed to collide with the fatal iceberg and waltzing in the face of that inevitability.

To one side, a group of figures had gathered who I knew by sight. These were some of Papa's guests, a collection of art dealers who styled themselves *Zlatou Ruku*, the 'Golden Hand'. Including Papa, who was the youngest of them by at least a decade, there were five in all, and together they'd pretty much cornered the art market of Prague. There was Kovak, who ran a boutique gallery up behind the castle in Hradčany and another in Bratislava; Sumilov, whose Minerva Gallery down in Vyšehrad had come to my aid while I was being cross-examined by Hookworm; Černý, who had a great warehouse somewhere south of Prague but whose city premises fronted onto Václav Square; and Solomons, who had three city galleries. Each had his own speciality, so that although they often ran into each other at viewings and auctions – in the back room of Meisel's place for instance – they tended where possible to avoid bidding directly, one against the other. It was good business not to tread on one another's toes. I probably would have paid them no heed except that, in passing, I twice heard the name of Old Meisel bandied about.

Ezra Meisel cut an impressive figure. I was sorry he had declined the wedding invitation, and not merely because of his connection to Leah – though I had dearly longed for her to witness this show of elegance. Somehow, he'd fired my imagination before ever I'd clapped eyes on the orphan. He was a tall man, and though he had become gaunt in latter years, he was imposing for all that. He had a spare, bony face, high cheek-boned, with jade-coloured eyes set wide apart under severe, Old Testament eyebrows that curved up like owl wings. Outside the shop he wore knee-length boots, an astrakhan coat heavily furred at cuffs and sleeves, and a sort of Cossack hat that made me think of the Circassians out of *Taras Bulba*. I could well imagine those jade eyes peering out from the prow of a privateer sailing the Caspian Sea. He'd arrived back from his ten days' peregrination a couple of days previously – at least, the green van had reappeared outside the shop on Bilkova Street on the Wednesday. But as Papa had said, perhaps he didn't care to feast with Gentiles.

From the little I caught of the conversation, Old Meisel had made quite a killing on this last foray into the Bohemian countryside. He'd laid out pretty much everything he had, put it all on the line, but from what any of them had heard, he'd struck gold. In particular, there was an oil by Giorgione that could be worth a packet if it was restored and properly accredited. For some reason, Papa's name was mentioned in relation to the Giorgione. This surprised me. Now, Papa did occasionally restore an old painting. But that was usually as a favour to a client. As a dealer, his area of expertise was contemporary art. Several times, Maman had asked him why, 'when all the great art was painted centuries ago.'

'All very well my dear, but you see, with your contemporary painter, you know where you stand. A living painter is someone you can shake by the hand. If you have a mind to, you can watch him at work. You travel back to the age of the old masters, and everything comes down to provenance. Can you show an unbroken chain of paperwork from the artist's studio to the easel standing before you? All very well to say it looks like a Titian. Alter an 'attributed to' to a 'school of', the value plummets a hundred-fold. A hundred-fold, think of that! I prefer to leave that sort of detective work to those who have a taste for it. All that class of pettifoggery, I happily commend to Čermák, our castle mole.'

Now I thought of it, it was curious that Jaroslav Čermák wasn't here now. He was in charge of the National Art Collection up in Prague Castle, and had been a colleague of Papa's for years. They'd even been in the Gymnasium together, way back when. I was certain I'd seen him at the church, unmistakable in his dove-grey homburg and gloves, lugubrious brown eyes behind bottle-thick spectacles. Very much the castle mole, and yet he had quite the sarcastic humour. Probably he'd left, the minute the tables had been cleared away. I couldn't imagine his stoop-shouldered shuffle gracing the dancefloor.

The conversation about Old Meisel's haul was interrupted by a horrendous squeal of feedback. The best man had risen – Eva's cousin Tadeusz Špotákov in his elegant air corps uniform – and had moved to the microphone. He tapped it several times. *'Vážené dámy a pánové,'* he began, the voice echoing metallically about the high room. 'Today has been a momentous day. Let me first and foremost invite you all to join me in a toast. To the bride and groom!'

'To the bride and groom!' resounded about the ballroom. It was my third glass of champagne, but I wasn't feeling the least light-headed. It had been a long day.

The best man gave a signal with his index finger at which the waiters began to refill the champagne flutes. 'It has been a momentous day, not just for the bride and groom. For Mikuláš and for my dear cousin, Eva. It has been a momentous day, not just for the illustrious families of Hayek and Špotákov. My friends, today has also been a momentous day for the entire Czech nation.' He paused, allowed the moment of his words to sink in. 'By this time, you will all have heard the news from Munich. Our allies have abandoned us. Our friends, so called, have betrayed us. In short, they have seen fit to throw us to the wolves.'

There were stamps and whistles and jeers. A slow hand clap did the rounds, slowly subsiding.

'Our country, my friends, is to be carved up. The Sudeten Mountains, so long the very bastion of our defences, are to be handed over to our enemies. I don't say this to take the shine away from the sacred and special union of Mikuláš and Eva. I've spoken to them about it. I understand how they, too, feel about it. How we all feel. But what I do say is this. And let them hear it in Paris and London and Berlin.'

He paused, took a drink. There was scarcely a sound in the entire room.

'The Czech people have been abandoned. But the Czech people have not been defeated. In Plzeň and in Mladá Boleslav, the great Škoda plants produce the finest tanks in the world. I was there just last week. And I can tell you, as an airman, the air corps will not go down without one hell of a scrap. We may have been thrown to the wolves. But my friends. *Vážené dámy a pánové*. Just because you've been thrown to the wolves, that does not make you a sheep. So I invite you all to drink with me a second toast. To the eternal glory of the Czech nation! Long may she stand, alone!'

'Long may she stand, alone!' cried one and all. Loudest were the various officers of his and Klaus' age. The veterans, medalled and bewhiskered, were more circumspect. Papa now stood, tipsily. 'And that no lesser toast be drunk from it!' he cried, holding the flute aloft as though he were a red-cheeked Statue of Liberty, then dashing it to the floor.

There was a hush like a gasp. Then one and all, the entire company followed suit. It was a thrilling moment. As waiters frowned, the gypsy band struck up the anthem. By God, I thought, I'll join up! I'll lie about my age. I'll lie about my faulty heart. And if they won't have me, then by God I'll join the partisans.

At fifteen years of age, I meant every word of it.

XXIII

Bloodlines

Eight days later, the oil painting was delivered to the *U Černého Slunce* Gallery. Papa brought it into the back workshop, where he unwrapped it, angled it to the light. It was smaller than I'd imagined when I'd overheard the four dealers mention it, perhaps two foot by three, though elaborately framed. It sheened dismally, the figures subdued under layers of yellowed varnish spider-webbed with fine cracks. To the top right-hand side the varnish was blistered and hazed over with the milky blue of an old man's cataract.

To the bottom of the ornate gilt frame, a wreathed legend read:

"Susanna e gli Anziani"
di Giorgio da Castelfranco
detto "Giorgione"

He touch-flicked one of the blisters with the ball of his thumb. 'Water damage,' he muttered, as though to himself. Reverently, as if it were a religious artefact, he placed it on the easel. He then stood back and contemplated it, one cheek cupped in the palm of his right hand.

It came to his notice that I was standing there, observing him. 'Giorgio da Castelfranco. Venetian School. Died around 1510, scarcely thirty years of age. Known to posterity as Big George. What do you think? Is it his?'

'I don't know, Papa.' Try as I might, I couldn't bring myself to call my father Emil.

'If it is his, if it's *definitively* his, then it's one of only six or seven that can be firmly attributed to Big George. Think of that, Guido.' He shook his head. 'Think of that.'

'Do you think it could be?'

'Phhh! Who knows? We'll see what we can see.' He was on the point of draping a towel over it when he eyed me merrily. 'What do you think of it, Guido Salvatore, detto "Guidone"? As a composition, I mean. You like it?'

I shrugged. Then I stood beside him and angled my head, scratching at the first hairs that had begun to down my chin. The central figure was a nude, recumbent, the corner of a sheet coyly touching her crotch, languorous in the way that Renaissance nudes are usually languorous. Behind her, through partly drawn crimson curtains, one could make out the heads of two, no, three lascivious old men. There was also a coloured maid beneath what appeared to be an ostrich feather, pouring water into an enamel basin standing to the left of the reclining figure. But the whole thing was so yellowed, so gloomy, that it was hard to judge the effect. 'Not sure. I sort of prefer the nudes you keep hidden in the prints cabinet.'

He flicked me painfully with the towel. 'Get the hell out of here, you dirty scamp!'

The episode provided a little light relief from what

was troubling my mind. Zak's hearing was almost upon us. When I'd informed them of the date, Hookworm had snorted, 'They're not hanging about.' That had surprised me. It seemed to me that three weeks in custody with bail denied while awaiting even an initial hearing must be an intolerable delay. But those weeks had flown. Now the hearing was upon us.

I'd heard nothing, not a word, from any of them since that day when Leah Meisel had told me, 'Go home. Run! It's finished, here.' All the same, the Saturday before that, she'd asked me to watch this hearing, too, from the public gallery, and to report back. I'd no reason to think she'd changed her mind on that one. Would Zak, or Si Rosenthal as was his legal name, enter a guilty plea? Throw himself on the mercy of the court citing starving children, as Hookworm might counsel him? Or would he make a fight of it, and have the case go to trial? In short, might I yet be called up to bear false witness?

The very thought of it made me feel sick. That first Saturday night, when I'd imagined myself riding to the rescue of my Rosalind, I'd buried the word 'perjury' somewhere in the murk of consciousness. Now it had returned, and like all buried things loomed ugly and large. Worse, I'd been so discomfited by Hookworm's exposure of my story that the thought of the witness box filled me with repugnance. For a while I played with the idea of coming clean to Father Kaufmann about how far things had gone. Lilith, he'd called her. Now Lilith had said, 'It's finished, here.' And I sensed it was. For me, in any event. Besides, how long could it be, now, before Old Meisel took her away, and for ever?

But suppose Hookworm tried to reach me. To threaten me somehow. Even blackmail me. I could smell again his body odour, see the metallic glint of his grin, feel again the blade at my throat and the stale breath on my face. Zak had said that everyone knew the house on Nerudova Street where the art dealer Hayek lived. I lived in dull dread, the way one imagines a debtor lives. So, finally, after days spent equivocating, on the very eve of the hearing, I decided to bare my soul to Katya.

I hadn't seen her in quite a number of days. Not since the wedding, if one discounted the family meals at which she was usually a silent spectator. Now that the big day was over, these were taciturn affairs. Gloomy. Haunted by the dismal results of the summer auction and the bills that still had to be met. With the annexation, the bottom had entirely fallen out of the art market, at least the contemporary Czech art market. As moveable wealth, the old masters were as sought after as ever, but not the work the gallery dealt in. Reluctantly, Papa told Jan he was letting him go. 'I'm sorry about this, Jan. Truly I am. If there's anything I can ever do for you. References?' To my dying day I'll be haunted by the basilisk stare he gave me as he left the gallery that morning, as though I had somehow usurped him. He took with him all his tools, and for months the outlines he'd painted on the wall were the ghosts of the veteran's methodology. In fact, the only employee whose position I usurped was Darja the cleaning woman's. From now on it was down to me to make the premises respectable before the doors were opened to a public that increasingly failed to come.

The autumn auction at the gallery, a surrealism retrospective that seemed to follow hard on the disastrous summer auction, was another damp squib. The appetite for government bonds, in which Papa had always trusted, was gone, and they were being sold for a fraction of what they'd been worth a year before. 'A diminished value,' he declared, 'for a diminished people.' And that pretty much summed up how the city felt. Klaus was off on manoeuvres somewhere with the Signal Corps; Eva had returned to the Špotákov household. Father Kaufmann was a seldom visitor, up to his eyes with the refugees that had begun to stream into Prague from the occupied territories.

I didn't broach the subject straight away but let her talk. 'So, you'll never guess who I ran into,' she snorted. 'There yesterday when I was coming out of physio.' I shook my head. 'Leon Trotsky,' she groaned.

'No! Did you speak to him?'

'He sort of nodded and grinned, like a marionette. He was with his mother. At least, I suppose it was his mother. A spherical woman in furs with a bulldog scowl. I wasn't about to go over and make my introductions.'

'Was he still wearing that preposterous army coat?'

'Oh no! And the goatee is gone. He looked more like a bank clerk or something.'

'Václav… what was his surname?'

'He never let on.'

'Hunh! What's the betting it's German?'

'What's the betting it was Schicklgruber or something.'

'Hey, Václav probably wasn't even his real first name.'

'That was probably Adolphus! What's the betting?'

'Ha! I love it! All the same, it'd be easy to find out both. Wasn't that cafeteria on Hybernska his uncle's or something?'

'Would I want to find out?'

'You could tell him about you know what. Send him a

little anonymous note. I'd love to see the look on his puss…'

'It might be worth it, just for that. But Guy, suppose he wanted… you know. Custody, or something.'

'I doubt very much he'd have it in him. That milksop?'

'It's not a chance I'm willing to take.'

'I can't say I blame you.'

Her features darkened. 'You know Papa was at me again, to think about New York.'

'You know his philosophy. Every mouse should have two boltholes.' She wasn't in a mood to smile. 'When was this?'

'A couple of times. Ever since the annexation. He reckons that's just the start, that Hitler won't rest easy until he has the whole country and half of Poland annexed.' In this my father was prescient. What he'd underestimated was the Führer's insatiable demand for Lebensraum, and the Allies' belated realisation of the fact.

'Even saying that doesn't happen, Guy, he says things could get very rough, here. Particularly for a Jew.'

'Come on! You're a Jew, now? You were raised Catholic like the rest of us. You did your Holy Communion. You went to a boarding school run by nuns, for God's sake.'

'A Catholic! Look at me, Guido.'

'Father Kaufmann says that according to Jewish law, Jewishness is passed down through the mother's side of the family, not the father's.'

'You think people like that will make a distinction?'

'Ok. So whose name is on the birth cert? Papa told me. It's him and Elsa Mörschel. That's right! And you can't exactly get any more Aryan than Elsa Mörschel. I've seen the pictures.'

'My father is Mordecai Gans. You can't get much less

Aryan than that.'

'But who's to say he was your father? Who's to tell them?'

'Papa says we have enemies.'

'Enemies! I don't buy that.' I was pacing up and down, not liking at all the turn the conversation had taken. 'So you are thinking about New York.'

'What would I do there? I don't speak a word of English.'

'Gans writes there are entire neighbourhoods which speak Yiddish.'

'Wonderful! I don't speak Yiddish either. I might just as well go to a Russian neighbourhood where I don't speak Russian!'

'At least you'd be safe.' I hesitated to add, 'Your baby would be safe.'

'I'm not going, Guy. Even saying there is a war. Even saying we do become part of the Third Reich. This is where my home is.'

'If we ever do become part of the Third Reich, I'll take Papa's hunting rifle and join the partisans!'

'Oh, Guy. You sound just like Klaus now…'

'Well what are we supposed to do? Roll over and take it?'

'I can just see the look on Maman's face if her Guido Salvatore told her he was setting off to join the partisans!'

'Don't make fun of me Katya. I'm serious.'

'I know you are.' She pushed a hand through my hair. Was she mocking me? At that moment, all thought of confiding in her the pickle I was in with Leah Meisel's gang evaporated.

Perhaps she'd picked up on my dismay. 'My place is here, so I can fight them too.'

'You, fight them?' My eyes were on her belly. 'How?'

'I'm not so helpless. I have my weapons.'

'Yeah?'

'Leaflets. Posters. Broadsides. Lampoons.' She saw me smirk. 'Whatever it takes.'

'Jesus! You think you're going to stop a tank with a lampoon?'

'Why, do you think you're going to stop a tank with Papa's hunting rifle? Listen, Guy. These people... here. Now. Nevermind the Germans. Last week there was a boy beaten to death on Slovanský Ostrov, just because he was homosexual.'

'I don't see your point.'

'Because the fascists can't stand deviants of any kind. You remember that word they scrawled up on the wall, *Degenerate*? That's what drives them crazy, Guy. They can't stand anyone that deviates from their ideal. You don't stop that with a gun! That's just the sort of fight they're spoiling for. What they can't take is ridicule.'

Her face was lit by something almost preternatural.

'If you're right, Katya, you'd be in all sorts of danger. I'd be worried sick for you.'

'And I wouldn't be worried, if you joined the partisans?'

'I guess.'

She was staring strangely. Then she sat, erect, and her features became set. Her eyelids flickered. 'Katya, what's up?'

Something like an animal groan emanated from her. Her eyes rolled back, white. Then she slid from the cot and onto the floorboards, her limbs rigid but shivering as though electricity were flowing through her frame. Her dress had ridden up over her thighs.

I'd never seen one of her fits, or 'seizures' as Maman

insisted. Her head had begun to thrash about. The first thing to be done was to place a pillow beneath it. As I did so, I noticed a puddle had begun to spread over the boards between her thighs. For a crazy second I thought her waters might have broken. When I realised what it was, I moved her to one side and towelled it with a bedsheet. I arranged her dress back below her knees, a strange sensation rushing through me to know my hands were so near to new life. I then looked to find the bandaged spoon that I knew must be placed between her teeth, to prevent her biting her tongue in her spasms.

On such occasions, the slumber that followed on a seizure might last for hours. All the same I hastened to leave her, lying as she was like a child in deep sleep. I was afraid she might wake and realise how I'd seen her.

XXIV

Susannah and the Elders

At the hearing the next day, Si Rosenthal, who also went by the name of Zakary Grau, entered a guilty plea. The judge was not minded to take into account the mitigating circumstances – the two starvelings that stood in rags in the gallery. Taking into consideration, rather, a string of previous convictions running back to his time as a juvenile, at the sentencing three days later Jänecke handed down five years, with a recommendation that parole be refused. In Prague, in 1938, that was a death sentence for any Jew. The accused heard the dreadful judgement with bowed head. When she heard it pronounced, Leah Meisel had to be dragged shrieking like a harpy from the public gallery. I followed her exit, to see if she was ok. Her eyes were dead. It was as though she failed to recognise me.

In Nerudova Street we lived alongside the castle. Under its shadow, as it were. Several times I'd been inside its gates with Papa to view the art collection in the Klášter Sv Jiří. I still recall the thrill, on the first occasion, of passing between the giant clubbed figures that stand sentinel, then skirting the great, dizzying tower of St Vitus' Cathedral and watching the clouds skit over it until it seemed the masonry was teetering. I'd have been seven. All the family were there on that occasion, even Katya. It must have been during the summer vacation. Papa's old school colleague, Jaroslav Čermák, gave us a rundown of the collection's highlights. 'Now those, Emil, are masterpieces,' opined Maman. 'That is true art.' Klaus was inclined to agree with her.

Čermák wasn't the first visitor who came to the gallery on Karluva Street to view the oil painting. Not long after Papa had set it on the easel with a view to slowly removing the layers of yellowed varnish – excavating, as he dubbed the process – we had a visit from three of the *Zlatou Ruku* art dealers: Kovak, Černý, and Solomons. 'Like the adoration of the Magi,' said Papa, pulling the towel from the exhibit like a conjurer, 'Behold, a child is born unto us this day!' About a third of the surface had been cleaned by this juncture, the portion containing the coloured maid and ostrich feather. Now, the highlight on the cracked enamel bowl winked delightfully.

'Guido, go and see if the little green fairy is home.'

I returned with the bottle of absinthe and a tray of four glasses to find the three dealers gathered and peering and clucking about the nude, to my mind the very incarnation of the three ancients who peeped from the parted curtain at the voluptuously reclining Susannah. Removed from the gilt frame, she looked more naked than ever. 'Get a fifth glass, boy!' said Papa. I hastened to do so. He placed a sugar cube half dissolved in water on the absinthe spoon, then dribbled the spirit through it until he had five glasses of a jade coloured liquid. 'Gentlemen,' he said. All took one, I too, and sipped. To

Papa's merriment, I coughed and sputtered.

The three dealers returned to the examination. *'Susanna e gli Anziani,'* read Moisés Solomons, whose *Staré Město* Gallery specialised in Renaissance art. 'Perhaps. Who knows? But what's to say this isn't a Venetian brothel scene, the customers being invited to view the wares before purchasing.'

'Well, Guido? How do you answer that?'

I blushed. My one experience of a brothel scene had been a sorry affair at the edge of Josefov with a skinny, reluctant teenager. Or it was I who'd been reluctant.

'Who's to say what anything is that Big George of Venice paints?' said Papa.

'Very nice,' said Kovak. 'Very fine. All the same, that hand of hers.' He hovered a finger over the model's hand which coyly held a drape over her modesty. 'Those fingers. Clumsy for the old master, I would have said.'

'I'm inclined to agree with you, Pavel. All the same, I've a hunch that area's been retouched. A piece of hackwork. Perhaps we'll find out when I clean it up.'

Černý said little. He just frowned and nodded. But then, his expertise, like Papa's, was for contemporary art. Back in 1934, after the Nazis shut down the Bauhaus school in Dessau, he and Papa had together curated an exhibition of graphic prints by Paul Klee, Wassily Kandinsky, Kurt Schwitters and László Moholy-Nagy at which the last two put in an appearance, along with Herbert Bayer, a former director who, as a Jew, had been dismissed from the post. He still had a photo of the five of them at the opening of that exhibition behind the counter on the gallery wall. It was as near to a political gesture as he'd ever made in his long career as an art dealer.

After they'd left, Papa returned to the meticulous process. I loved to watch him. It was like watching an archaeological dig, like watching tiny circles of dirt polished away from a Roman mosaic. 'What will happen,' I asked, 'when you finish? Do you get a percentage, if it turns out to be genuine?'

'Ha!' said Papa. Tongue peeping between teeth, he was working an area just shy of the model's face, and was taking the utmost precaution about it. 'I'm doing this as a favour to the Old Jew. No fee.'

'Then *why*?' I was taken aback. 'You're right, I don't understand.'

'We agreed if I bought it from him, he'd discount the work from the price.'

'But if it's a genuine Giorgione, what then?'

He looked up at me, one eye squeezing the jeweller's monocle. 'What do you mean?'

'How will you ever afford it?'

'Hunh! Well. That's to be seen.'

'I mean, won't those guys bid against you for it?'

'No, Guido. No they won't. In the first place, it won't turn out to be a genuine Giorgione. Have you any idea how rare a genuine Giorgione is? And in the second place, they're not going to bid against me.' He returned to his close examination. 'It's a wedding present.'

'A wedding present!' My head swam. How could that be? No one knew how much the painting was worth. Until it was properly cleaned and Jaroslav Čermák had properly assessed it and it had gone to auction, who could say how much it might end up costing. But I could see from Papa's features he was at a critical point in the process, so I held my tongue.

Another ten days passed before Jaroslav Čermák, the castle mole with trademark attaché case and bottle-thick glasses, dove-grey homburg and matching gloves, paid the gallery a visit. By this time the restoration was largely complete. It had been painstaking, fiddly labour. In particular, the area that had hazed over like an old man's cataract had caused Papa much grief. Because of the water damage, it was difficult in the extreme to prevent tiny grains of the original paint from flaking away, powdering the sill of the easel. Many times I'd been the butt of Papa's short temper. One of the few areas he'd left pretty much untouched was the hand that held the drape, the one Kovak had said was clumsy. That omission, I couldn't fathom.

On this occasion there was no getting out the green fairy. Not that Čermák wasn't partial to a drink, on the occasions he'd been a dinner guest at the house on Nerudova Street. When he was on duty, as he called it, sobriety was his watchword. He was a meticulous man. Nor did Papa want me hanging about, that day. With a flick of his head, he gestured that I should step out to the main gallery while the examination took place. Twenty minutes later, folding up his attaché case as he was leaving, the castle mole declared, 'There's no mention of a "Susannah and the Elders" by Giorgione in Vasari. Nor in the notes of Marcantonio Michiel, the Venetian collector.'

'Precisely so,' said Papa.

'Have we any idea how much Old Meisel laid out for it?'

'Hard to say. Kovak tells me he paid somewhere shy of a quarter of a million for the entire lot. And there's no doubt at all what the jewel in the crown is.'

'No doubt at all.' He flipped shut the attaché case and

nodded toward me, his lugubrious eyes enlarged by the lenses. 'Good day, gentlemen.'

'It is that,' said Papa.

XXV

Suspicions

When was it that I began to grow uneasy? That I first began to suspect that all was not as it should be? Not, I think, on that day in early November when I accompanied Papa to deliver the restored painting to the shop on Bilkova Street. It was my first time to visit the shop, or even to pass by it, since things had gone so badly awry. With every step my trepidation grew. It was a phase of my life that I'd hoped I'd escaped unscathed.

Not that I'd stopped thinking about Leah Meisel. No day went by without her at some point colonising my thoughts. I'd reasoned that she was set to leave. That I'd never see her again, and would soon have to deal with that separation. She'd never noticed me, I reasoned, not in a way I craved. I'd dodged a bullet – Zak's fate could well have been mine. But as Father Kaufmann would say, the heart has its reasons that reason knows nothing of. And Leah Meisel was imprinted in my senses. A whiff on the street of the musk she wore was enough to short-circuit memory. Scent will do that. My pulse would race, then, as though I were in her actual presence. Or her cavernous absence. The sight of a girl strolling past the gallery, whose massed black hair might have been hers, made my gut turn a somersault.

And there were daydreams. Once, she'd dared me to steal a ring. Once, to falsify testimony. Now, as I worked in the gallery, I'd let my imagination dream up new scenarios in which I might come to her rescue. In one, I stood up to Hookworm, twisted the blade from his hand. In another, the Germans had overwhelmed the country. In this new scenario, we lived out in the wilds, Leah Meisel, Katya and the baby. I wasn't a partisan, all the same they relied on me. To hunt. To gather. Gradually, Leah would come to realise I wasn't merely the clumsy adolescent she took me for.

All the same, as we approached the shop, it was with a deepening sense of dread.

There could be no doubt now but that Ezra Meisel was preparing to sell up shop. Fliers and posters pasted about the door and the nearby lampposts declared as much. Inside, all was bustle. From what Papa had gleaned from Pavel Kovak, the bulk of the lots he had gathered from the dissolution of the Hradnařece Estate, which had belonged to a branch of the Lobkowicz family, consisted of ancient weapons, globes, silverware, great porcelain vases, assorted antiques and antique furniture. Many of these were already wrapped and labelled and awaiting dispatch. Had he really 'lain out just shy of half a million' in the hope of a quick profit? How much had he already recuperated? I had no idea. The world of fine arts and antiques was as arcane to me as the astrology of Tadeáš Hájek z Hájku.

I dreaded running into any of the old gang. So of course one of the first things I encountered, on entering the dim interior, was the glitter of Hookworm's three gold teeth. Today he was out of his leather coat, his shirtsleeves rolled up past the elbows. I was instantly mortified, and tried to avoid his glance in the childish hope that he then wouldn't see me. Would he dare say a word to Papa, or indicate by a familiar nod or a leer what had transpired between us? The other nephew, the one that drove the van, was beside the till, running through a checklist on a clipboard. He motioned to Papa with a flick of the head that we should bring the precious cargo into the interior.

Meisel himself met my father as we entered the rear room. He was as imposing as ever, half a head taller than either of us, though gaunt out of his astrakhan. Beneath the owl's wing eyebrows the verdigris eyes were restless, the jaw continually moving as though working up instructions. About this space were displayed a couple of tapestries so faded that only the yellow and blue survived and their hunting scenes could scarcely be made out; an antique map of Bohemia; a family tree of gorgeous heraldry; and a gallery consisting of: a pair of still-lifes – one of fruits, the other of game; a moonlit landscape by Vavřinec Reiner which included a castle; two mythological allegories, unattributed; and a half-dozen family portraits, passably executed by, "A Follower of Jan Kupecký". In the centre of the room, dressed like a merchant prince, sat Moisés Solomons, hands complacently on his belly as though he were proprietor of all that he surveyed. Without rising from his seat, he too greeted Papa. Although it was I who carried the precious load, I may as well have been invisible. I coughed. 'Where shall I put it?'

Meisel turned to face me. I hadn't seen him in a number of months. There was something decidedly skeletal about him now, as though Death were already imprinting its image upon him in readiness for the harvest. He motioned a bony hand toward an empty easel to the centre-right of the display.

Carefully, I placed the draped oil-painting, back once more in its ornate frame, then stood aside to allow Papa to unveil the masterpiece. 'See how eagerly they wait,' pronounced Solomons, his eyes half-closed, 'as Priam's refuse sons, when the fates borrowed Hector. Isn't that it?' It appeared to be a quote.

'Very good,' nodded Ezra Meisel, his body doubled at the waist to take in the restored painting. 'Very good.'

'If it turns out to be the real thing,' said my father.

'There is a doubt?'

'Čermák says the provenance isn't entirely clear. He's still making enquiries. Awaiting a reply from some authority in Venice. Oh, he also took away a few tiny samples of the paint that had flaked away.'

'Why?'

'To conduct some sort of chemical analysis, he said. There was some question about the pigment used in the curtain. The precise tint of alizarin crimson. He wanted to be sure the pigment was available at the time it was supposedly painted.'

The old man's features darkened, the owl wings lowering onto the perch of his brow. 'Why wouldn't it have been available?'

'It may have incorporated cochineal, a dye from the Americas made from beetles. If it does, that would date it several decades after Giorgione's death.'

The old man emitted a strange sound, something like a tyre deflating. 'When will we hear from him?'

'You know Jaroslav. How meticulous he is. A week? Perhaps ten days.'

The old man shook his head, the eyebrows alighting and perching. His bony fingers scratched his chin to aid the calculus. 'We must postpone the auction.' He moved toward the door from where he called out toward the two nephews. 'You hear? We must postpone the auction!'

Hookworm appeared, his eyes sly and grinning gormlessly. 'Postpone?' he shook his bald head, not understanding. The pig eyes took me in, as though he thought that I might be in some way behind the delay. Once again I was in dread that he might implicate me before Papa.

'You heard me,' growled Meisel. The underworld figure held no terrors for him.

'All the same,' nodded Moisés Solomons, rising wheezily, 'a fine picture. Very fine.' An index finger rose. 'You've done a fine job restoring it, Emil.'

As we made to leave, Leah Meisel appeared, behind the very counter where I'd seen her that first day. It seemed like a lifetime ago, now. Medusa haired, her eyes glinted in the dim light. She was staring straight at me. It wasn't quite an interrogation. It wasn't an accusation, either. I wondered, not for the first time, was there a touch of madness in her.

I was walking ahead of Papa. As we left, I raised a hand in salutation.

'I thought I asked you to steer clear of those people.' We had barely taken a couple of steps outside, so that I was mortified any one of 'those people' might have heard him.

'I have,' I stammered. 'I haven't been next to or near them in months.' This was an exaggeration. But indignation gave it the ring of truth. At the moment I spoke it I believed the assertion.

'Ok,' he said. 'I'll believe you. But on another subject. Have you thought any more about what I said about your sister?'

'Katya?'

'How many sisters do you have?'

'You mean about America?'

'The boy is quick.'

'Papa, she doesn't want to go.'

'Doesn't *want* to?'

'She's not a bit keen on the idea.'

'I know that. I think I know that, Guido. What I'm asking, have you spoken to her about it? Tried to convince her.'

'I think you overestimate any influence I'd have over Katya! When her mind's made up, that's pretty much it.' We walked on a couple of streets in silence. 'You really think she's in so much danger here?'

'That day the fascists set upon her at the exhibition. Why do you suppose they did that?'

'Because it was unpatriotic.' It sounded lame. 'Even Klaus said it was unpatriotic.'

'Unpatriotic.' He stopped. I turned to face him. 'Guido. Why do you suppose she was the only one that they put into hospital that day? There were three of them there, so far as I'm aware.'

I could feel my fingernails digging into my palms. 'Because she's a Jew.'

'Because she's a Jew. Right. And lest there be any doubt, you remember the *Židé* and the Star of David they scrawled up on the wall?'

I nodded.

'Think it through, Guido. What I'm asking of you. What your duty is.'

'Ok Papa,' I said, turning. But I said it as much to shut down the conversation as anything else. I had a horrible suspicion he was on the point of spelling out what he was asking me to consider doing. It was not something I was prepared to consider.

XXVI

Endgame

Things were getting very ugly for the German-speakers of Prague. I heard Papa say more than once that the Czech nation was sensitive as a mollusc whose shell had been ripped from it. And that's how it felt. As it lay quivering and vulnerable, in its pain it turned on itself. Families who had been settled here for decades, for centuries, were set upon for the Germanic ring of the family name. Shop windows were smashed, premises looted. Angry crowds turned on respectable burghers, beat them and spat at them. Even their children were openly taunted. They left the chaotic city in droves, on the very trains which daily brought in thousands of Czech-speaking refugees from the distant Sudeten Mountains. And Father Kaufmann was in the thick of it.

For weeks on end we barely saw him. Word was that the old Jesuit was to be transferred to Rome after Christmas. This was not so much on account of his outspoken Marxist tendencies or even his German name. He was increasingly hard of hearing, and though his efforts with the refugees of whatever ethnic background were indefatigable, his deafness lent him a new irritability. He was becoming unsuited to public service.

In the back of the gallery, the chess set's ranks slowly began to fill. Before Jan had been let go, I'd learned from him the skill of gauging which wood was flawed or knotted, which sound to its heart. I'd mastered the callipers and the screw-gauge, and if nothing else, the figures I'd produced to date were uniform. I was determined that, for Christmas, I'd be able to present the set to my old friend.

Papa dropped in occasionally, to pick up a piece, to assure himself of my seriousness. As often as not, the examination and grunt he'd give were a pretext for broaching another subject. November came, November went. The board was just shy of a couple of black knights.

Twice more, Old Meisel had been forced to postpone the auction, though all was ready for his departure for the east. His and Leah Meisel's departure. There were unavoidable delays. Unforeseen delays. Jaroslav Čermák had established from castle correspondence that Prinz Theobald Lobkowicz had been in Venice during the summer of 1542, the year the painting had been purchased from a certain Gianfranco Maldini. The bill of sale declared as much, but it was important to place him there. But 'Giorgio da Castelfranco detto Giorgione' had died in 1510, and while there was a passing mention of a 'Susannah and the Elders' by a Florentine merchant who had visited the painter's studio the same year he died, who was to say it was the same 'Susannah and the Elders'? Where was the paper evidence? A lot can happen in thirty-two years! The authority in Venice to whom Čermák had written obviously didn't prioritise a Prague enquiry as to a painting's provenance just because it had originally belonged to a Prinz of the Lobkowicz line. Hadn't the Czechoslovakian government voted to abolish their aristocracy?

Any day now, the definitive reply was expected. Any day now.

And then, the results of the chemical analysis weren't forthcoming, either. Traditionally it was Čermák's close colleague, the chemist Konrad Webern of Prague University who carried out such analysis for the National Collection's art expert. But Dr Webern had abandoned Prague for Leipzig some months before the Munich deal would have made the transfer desirable. As the new appointee was still finding his feet in the Science Faculty, Čermák had dispatched the sample to the University of Leipzig for analysis. So with all due respect, we're no further along than we were six weeks ago.

'And what would happen if the auction went ahead without authentication?'

'Are you crazy? With so many doubts in the air, the old man couldn't hope to recuperate the tenth part of what he laid out. Not the tenth part. I told him it was madness on his part to lay out so much in the first place in the hope of a quick killing.' He replaced the white knight on the board with an approving nod. 'That's fine work, Guido. Fine work. I also told him, if he's so keen to get away from Prague before the year is out, I'm prepared to go twenty thousand on it. As a favour.'

'*Twenty* thousand?'

'It's a fair offer, considering.'

'When he spent over a hundred thousand.'

'I told you, Guy, the old man was crazy to do that on trust. If he knew anything about Giorgione, he'd never have done it. The man died at thirty years of age. Some of the few masterpieces they actually attribute to him were finished off by other hands. There was even a flourishing trade in supposed Giorgiones for a full century after his death.'

'Then why offer twenty thousand?'

'Because I feel sorry for the old Jew. Because there's still the chance it might be worth something, even if it is a collaboration. Meisel's trouble is that he's in such a hurry to leave.'

At one time I would have been desperate to hear that the move had been postponed. Now I wanted to see him safe and settled, so long as it was anywhere but here. 'Then can't he simply take the painting with him, when he goes away? Sell it in Odessa when the word finally comes through.'

'Ah, but you see, Guy,' Papa grinned, his eyes sly, 'until such time as there's a decision either way, he won't be permitted. If it proves to be worthless, then sure, he's welcome to take it with him. But would he want to? The problem is, at this time, the painting may still be valuable. Far too valuable to allow an export permit. And that's the exquisite bind in which the old Jew finds himself.'

I didn't like that grin. Not one little bit.

The following day Papa again picked up the identical knight. He again replaced it. No grunt of approval on this occasion. 'I've been thinking. Your friend Hans Kaufmann mightn't be the only one who's facing a transfer after Christmas.'

'How do you mean?'

'I've asked you to think about Katya. To think about her situation. To take her seriously'

I nodded, avoiding his eye.

'So? Have you?'

I shrugged, immensely interested in a splinter that was dangling from the bridle of the final black knight.

'Do you know she's expecting? Don't answer that. You might be tempted to lie about it. I know that she told you. What I can't understand, Guido, is why you didn't see fit to tell me about it.'

God, I thought, here it comes. For weeks, I'd known that this particular wave would have to break. 'She asked me not to. She said you'd all find out, in time.'

'That's great, Guido. I'm trying to help you become an adult here. An adult isn't a matter of running about with God knows who. First and foremost it's a matter of responsibilities. Loyalties. And this is how you repay me?'

I looked back at the rows of white pieces, but his hand gripped my jaw and he forced my face to face his. 'Look at me when I'm talking to you, boy. I don't suppose you've any idea who the father is? No. I thought not. She didn't seem to know, either. I have to say that surprised me. When I heard that. I mean, I can't imagine that Katya was exactly besieged by would-be lovers. Well never mind. Who the father may be is beside the point. The point is this.' He let go my jaw, which he'd clamped hard. Angrily, I rubbed it with my fingers. 'The point is, now more than ever it becomes imperative that she take up this man's offer. Gans. Her father. You must see that?'

I continued to rub my jaw. I could see that. 'And if she won't?'

'If she won't, it's down to you to convince her.'

I stood, walked as far as the sink. My heart was hammering.

I had a foreboding of what was coming. But I could no longer escape it. I no longer had the stomach to escape it. 'And how do you suppose I do that?'

'Simple,' said my father. 'You tell her you're going with her.'

That evening at the dinner table, the atmosphere was tense. Neither of my parents would look at the other. Conversation was limited to the 'Pass the salt' variety. As Jula, the maid, cleared away the soup bowls, 'Guido, Katya,' said Maman, 'you're excused.'

We looked at each other. The main course had not as yet been served.

'Go,' said Papa. 'Go!'

We slid back our chairs, dropped our napkins, stood. Tureen still in hand, the maid hovered at the door uncertainly, such was the palpable tension in the room.

I followed Katya up toward the attic. For the remainder of the evening we sat on the final flight of stairs before the door, still as eavesdroppers. Though the studio was two flights up from the dining-room, Maman's more impassioned fragments reached us. When Papa was angry and resolved, his voice dropped.

Like scolded children we held hands, squeezing when a more choice fragment penetrated, whispering in between.

'JESUS CHRIST, EMIL! OVER MY DEAD BODY!'

('When did you tell him?')

('I didn't tell him. Maman told him.')

('Maman? How did she find out?')

('She worked it out from the laundry, I think. Your mother

194

is no fool.')
('Far from it.')
'THAT'S BRILLIANT! AT FIFTEEN YEARS OF AGE
HE'S SUPPOSED TO…'
('Sixteen.')
('Sixteen next February.')
'HE DOESN'T HAVE A WORD OF ENGLISH!'
('She has a point there.')
('Well neither do you.')
('"How do you do?"')
('That'll get you far!')
('I'm not going anywhere.')
('So how did he take it? Was he angry?')
('He was very reasonable, actually. He just saw it as one
more reason I should pack my bags is all.')
('He's worried. Even more so, now.')
('I'm still not going.')
'OH YOU'D LOVE THAT, WOULDN'T YOU!'
('He wants me to go with you, you know.')
('No!')
('He does. He asked me. Today.')
('I don't believe you, Guy!')
('In fact, he practically told me I was going.')
'BAD ENOUGH THE CROWD YOU LET HIM RUN
AROUND WITH. I'M NOT BLIND. OR STUPID.'
('And what did you say?')
('I said no way. What would I do in America?')
She gave my hand a heavy squeeze. We were allies.

XXVII

Through the Looking Glass

The following morning, in the dark since winter was upon us, as we made our way across the Karluv Bridge, Papa again picked up the subject. Once more, we took our place in an alcove watched over by statues.

'Your mother and I had words last night. I expect you heard.'

'She doesn't think I should go.'

'Of course she doesn't. You're her boy.'

'Maman doesn't want me to go. I don't want to go. Katya doesn't want to go. Papa, why are you persisting in this?'

'Listen to me, Guido. The world is about to go up in flames. You're too young to remember. But I saw it once before. I lived through it. Twenty million died. One hundred thousand Czech soldiers never returned. Thirty thousand civilians starved to death here.'

'As many died afterwards in the flu epidemic.'

'This is no joke, Guido. This is no time for idle comparisons. Listen, I wouldn't ask this of you if there were any other way. The whole world is about to go up in flames. When it does, things will go badly for the Jews. For anyone with any taint of Jewishness in their blood. The Nuremberg race laws make no secret of it. What do you suppose their *Kristallnacht* was about? For God's sake, that maniac spells it out in *Mein Kampf!*'

'But on Katya's birth certificate, it says that you are the father.'

'Guido, for Christ's sake! This is no time to quibble. Do you think those psychopaths are going to worry about what it says on a birth certificate? Perhaps you think they'll have a qualm of conscience when they see that she's with child? Listen to me! The door is closing. In another few months it may be too late. You've got to get her out. And soon. You've got to convince her, Guido. I'm counting on you.'

'But Papa…'

'And it's not as if we're talking about forever. This war won't be like the last one. There'll be no trenches. No stalemates. This will be a war fought from the air. When cities can be bombed into submission, like they did in Spain last year, who do you think is going to hold out? There's no defence against that. The next war will be over in a matter of weeks. Three months. A year, at the most. Then we'll see how the world stands, once the dust has settled.'

'And we're a German province! Do you think that Katya could come back then, to such a world? If as you say, these psychopaths are bent on exterminating anyone with a taint of Jewish blood.'

'Maybe not. But you could. You could, Guido. By then, you see, she'd be established in New York. She'd be living with her natural father. These things matter. These things count for something. She'd be raising her own child in safety.'

'Maybe.'

'Here is certain death for that child.'

We sat on in silence, clenched against the cold. The sky to the east was beginning to lighten. He reached into a pocket, pulled out a small packet, and passed it into my hands.

'What's this?'

'Open it.'

I did so. It was a pocket dictionary. Czech-English. It was so incongruous I guffawed.

'Promise me you'll at least think about it Guido.'

I stood. 'Ok,' I said, slipping the book into my own pocket. 'I promise.'

That afternoon, Papa took out a business card with the black sun on it and scribbled down a sum on its reverse side. Kč 30,000. 'Go around to Meisel's place,' he said. 'Tell him, if he throws in the six portraits, I'll raise the offer to thirty thousand.'

'Are they worth ten thousand?'

'"Follower of Jan Kupecký." What do *you* think, Guy?'

'Then why offer him so much?'

'I want to make it possible for him to leave. He knows well enough they're not worth the half of that.'

I pulled on my coat and cap. As I was stepping out the door, he added, 'Don't say a word of that to Meisel. I wouldn't want him to think your old man had taken leave of his senses, or gone soft on him.'

Had I been unfair to Papa? Had I misjudged his motives? As I made my way to Birkova Street, it did come to me that, according to his way of viewing the world, with Leah Meisel on her way to Odessa, I'd have one less reason to stay on in Prague.

It was a topsy-turvy city I walked through that afternoon. Bilkova Street is not far removed from either Masarykovo or Hlavní Railway. Since September the entire area in the vicinity of these termini had been turned into a shanty-town of refugees. Families wandered dazed, their entire belongings in suitcases and prams and pushcarts. In the green spaces along Opletalova and the side streets bordering Josefov, makeshift shelters had been put up, shacks and tents and lean-tos. Quite a number of shops had been boarded up, particularly those with anything resembling a Germanic surname. Many of these may have been Yiddish, probably were in all likelihood, but this was not a time for nice distinctions.

I took a diversion to the area because I hoped to run into Father Kaufmann. Anywhere there were refugees, he was sure to be in the thick of it. My head was so muddled in relation to what to do about Katya that I needed to talk to someone outside the immediate family. Above all I needed a dispassionate assessment, and who better than the worldly Jesuit? He'd told me once that poverty has a smell. Here, I was finding that hopelessness, too, has its odour. It was a mixture of wood-smoke and incontinence and wet cloth and acrid perspiration. It had sapped everyone I encountered. Aged them. Even the children seemed old.

Was it really possible that, one day soon, Katya and I might figure among their number? If you discount the trip to Turin for my grandfather's funeral when I was five, the farthest I'd ever been was on overnights to Hradec Kralove and Český Krumlov. On these occasions, it had been Papa who'd taken care of all the arrangements, and they'd occurred in more innocent times. True, Katya had been abroad, on a trip with the convent to the Austrian Alps. A pregnant twenty-one year old prone to seizures and a teenager not yet sixteen, and Papa was talking about a journey to the New World? It was too fantastic. Surely Father Kaufmann would back me up.

Where, amongst all this despair, might I find the old priest? Having wandered pointlessly through this netherworld for the better part of an hour, I tried to find someone I might ask. In several places long queues had formed, listless affairs characterised by the general aura of fatigue, occasionally bursting into brief, violent squabbles. Though the people taking details or stamping forms or doling out clothes and steaming mugs had armbands and caps and an aura of officialdom about them, I was loath to be seen as a queue skipper. After about another half-hour I gave up the search.

Meisel's shop had been largely cleared out. Most of the merchandise that I'd seen wrapped and labelled on the previous visit had been dispatched. Much of what remained was the sort of thing I'd heard him refer to as *drek*. It always filled me with apprehension, stepping into that interior. Would Hookworm – his real name I'd discovered was Chaim Grossman – be there? Would Leah Meisel?

At first I didn't see her. I was about to step into the back room when she spoke up. 'Don't go in there.' I turned. She stood by the counter, skin more luminous than I'd remembered, eyes of pitch. In that second, three months were short-circuited. Since Zak had been taken, I'd succeeded largely in blocking the memory of her. The infatuation. But this vision was as charged as anything I'd ever fantasised. My entire body felt weak.

'Is your grandfather back there?'

'He's with someone.'

'Ok,' I nodded. She was looking at me strangely. She was looking at me as though I might be an emissary of some kind. A bringer of news from the court. I wasn't sure what to make of it. In order not to allow silence the chance to settle, I asked, 'Any word on Zak?'

Immediately, something changed in her. It's hard to quantify what. It was as if I no longer existed.

'I mean Si. Si Rosenthal.'

She looked at me as though my mentioning the name had sullied it. 'I haven't seen him.'

'Really?'

'What would be the point?'

Ok, I thought. Ok. This might be the final conversation you ever have with this strange girl, Guido Salvatore, and though you feel light-headed and though your heart is fluttering at your throat, by God you're going to speak to her. 'Will you go, when your grandfather goes?'

'What's to keep me here, now?'

I mattered less than nothing, then. I'd always known I hadn't mattered to her. She might have been just a little more diplomatic, all the same. My next question was out before I had the chance to consider what I was saying. If there was intuition I've no idea where that intuition came from. 'You're carrying his child, aren't you? Si Rosenthal's child?'

In place of answering, her hands folded over her belly and she glanced downwards. It was a form of confirmation.

I've often thought about that moment. That intuition, if intuition it was. I think it may have been this. Somewhere, in the recess of my mind, I'd noticed a bizarre, imperfect symmetry at work. Fate, not delighting in irony this time, but in riddles. Leah Meisel was the illegitimate daughter of a wayward artist's model, Dinah Jacobs. Katya was the illegitimate daughter of Elsa Mörschel, the soprano. Both mothers had died, soon after. Both daughters had been taken in and raised by a man with no claim of blood. Both were in danger, because of their Jewishness, and destined perhaps to eat the bitter bread of exile. So if Katya was pregnant, why not Leah? Of course Katya was no thief, far from it. And where she was an accomplished artist and musician, Leah was illiterate. Might she be a dark twin, then, a Lilith to Katya's Eve? The whole thing was fantastic. Irrational. But in the topsy-turvy looking-glass world that Prague had entered that winter of 1938, it was just the kind of logic that might operate.

At that moment the door to the rear area opened, and Pavel Kovak stepped out. His presence took me by surprise. But if it did, what transpired as he left the shop bothered me far more. He threw me a wink. That in itself might have been alright. But it was the kind of wink he threw that discomfited. A conspiratorial wink. A *we-both-know-tee-hee* wink. And what was worse, I was sure that Leah Meisel had seen it.

Embarrassed, I made for the back room. The entire galley of paintings was still there on display, everything but the two faded tapestries and the landscape by Vavřinec Reiner. Ezra Meisel was slumped on the chair upon which Moisés Solomons had sat on the previous occasion. The astrakhan coat was draped loosely about him. Somehow, his frame now appeared too frail to fill it.

The old man looked up at me as I entered, fixed me with his jade eyes. The eyebrows asked, 'What have you come here for, boy.' Then he stood, slowly.

'I've brought this,' I said, proffering toward him the business card with the black sun logo. 'From my father.'

His head flicked, the way a horse's head might. 'What does he say, your father?'

'He'll increase the bid to thirty thousand. If you'll throw in the six portraits.'

'Does he indeed?' said the merchant. He examined the card. 'Thirty thousand. Does he indeed?'

'What should I tell him?'

The old Jew nodded. He looked at me, his eyes half a head above mine, then he nodded again, slowly. 'Tell him this,' he declared. Then, demonstratively, he held the card aloft and tore it in two, then in two again. He took my hand in fingers cold as marble, and folded it over the fragments.

XXVIII

Complicity

Papa wasn't the man to hang about. That weekend, Maman was away on a religious retreat to the Church of All Saints in Kutná Hora, to pray for the salvation of the Czech people. On Saturday morning, myself and Katya were summoned to the study. By the desk stood a woman in a tweed tailored suit, her long hair threaded with silver. Papa was seated, a pocket book open before him. 'This is Miss Ivors,' he said.

I shook her cold hand. Katya gave her a small curtsy.

'Miss Ivors is from Liverpool. For the time being, she has kindly agreed to act as your English tutor. You'll take classes three afternoons a week. Mondays, Thursdays and Saturdays. Starting today. Isn't that what we agreed, Miss Ivors?' Miss Ivors nodded, offering us an efficient smile.

'Here?' I asked, exchanging glances with Katya. We both knew that Maman would throw a fit when she found out.

'Here, or the gallery. Leave the logistics to me.'

'And what about the winter auction?' We'd sent out the usual mailshot in mid-November looking for consignors, and I'd already begun compiling a list of works that we'd find room to exhibit. 'Aren't we to put together a...'

A raised hand forestalled us. 'Leave the winter auction to me. I've decided against a brochure for this year. Good. Now, Katerina. I took it upon myself, a number of weeks ago, to write to Mr Gans, to thank him for his very generous offer.'

'You haven't told him I've agreed to go! I haven't agreed anything!'

'...to thank him for his very generous offer,' continued Papa. 'I felt it was important to establish contact. Good. Now, what I'd like you to do, Katerina, is write to him... to your father... and thank him for his offer. Tell him a little bit about yourself. Maybe include a photo. Yes, I think he'd appreciate a photo. Don't you agree, Miss Ivors? Perhaps that one that was taken at your twenty-first. I've always liked that one.'

Katya was staring daggers. 'You haven't told him about...'

'I haven't told him anything. Merely that you're doing very well. That you've established yourself as something of an artist here in Prague, with a reputation as an *enfant terrible*. That you've always known all about the circumstances of your birth.'

'But I already told you, Papa. I have *not* agreed to go.'

'I know. I know that, Katya.' Papa stood, and smiled at Miss Ivors. 'What is it your Bard says? "The readiness is all." I hope I have it right?'

Miss Ivors nodded, her smile for Papa far sweeter.

'That's settled then,' he declared. 'I'll leave you three to get acquainted.' And without further ado, he departed the study.

When is it that we become complicit? When is it the decision is made to go along with a scheme? Up to this point I'd made no attempt to convince Katya to go to New York. I'd given no intimation that I might be prepared to undertake the journey with her. Of that I'm quite sure. Quite the opposite, in fact. Yet somehow, it now appeared to be accepted that, early in the New Year, we'd set sail for an unknown life. The matter had been decided. Such was the force of Papa's will.

Dutifully, Katya wrote this man she'd never met the letter that he'd suggested. She decided to come clean from the first about her condition. Perhaps she was thinking that he might then reject the idea out of hand. But I'm not sure that was it. By that Thursday, the third of our English lessons with Miss Ivors, we'd both simply come to accept that the journey was going to occur. The lessons took place in the *U Černého Slunce* Gallery, but that was just for form's sake. Maman knew well enough what was going on.

That Thursday evening, I went up to Katya's room to go over the day's lesson. She was making very slow progress, said she found the language bizarre. Unlike Katya, who'd spent her childhood at a boarding school, I'd been raised trilingually, and though English had little enough in common with Italian or German, and nothing at all with Czech, that early experience seemed to have opened my mind to all languages.

The door was slightly ajar and as I tapped on it, it opened further. The room was unlit, but for the streetlight through fogged up glass. 'Come in!' she called. But I froze. She was standing side-on to the mirror in her underclothes, holding a little bump that protruded above her hips. Turning her head toward me, 'Come in,' she said again. Still I hesitated, eyes firmly on the floor and colour pounding at my face. I'd never before seen a girl in bra and panties. But there was something about how she looked at me, with such innocent wonder, that all prudery evaporated. I entered.

The scene will always stay with me. Snow was falling outside, and against the condensation of the windowpanes, the flakes drifted by like slow, soft shadows. 'Come over, Guy,' she smiled. I did so. She took my hand, placed it on her belly. 'You feel it?' What I felt was warmth, intense warmth. 'It's moving!' she said. Unable to look directly at her face, we were too close for that, I watched her expression in the mirror. Pure wonder, her eyes large and hormonal, her face and bare shoulders dappled by the moving shadows of the snowflakes.

'Kneel down,' she said. With no will of my own, I did so. She took my head in her hands, and placed one of my ears against her hot belly. 'Listen!'

What did I hear? Fluids. A gurgle. Was there a heartbeat? If there was, it was my own, amplified. Or Katya's. Her fingers moved through my hair, as though I were a child. I'm quite sure this was an innocent gesture on her part. A mark of affection. I was also aware of the first, queasy stirring of arousal. Was this because I imagined her to be Leah Meisel, even then carrying a child of some six months? Or was it a dim awareness that this girl and I shared not a drop of blood, she the daughter of Mordecai Gans and Elsa Mörschel, I of Emil Hayek and Maria Teresa Tedesco?

Looking back, I think it was simply because I was fifteen, and was in such close proximity to the heat of a girl's body. I had little time to consider what was at the root of it. All at once, I was aware that we were being watched. In the depth of the mirror, framed in the doorway, stood Maman. To this day I recall the expression on her face. But I can't describe it. Perhaps my father had seen it, if Maman had ever walked in upon him when he was with a mistress. For a moment I thought she was about to scream. Clumsily, I stood. But by the time I turned to face the doorway, Maman was gone.

When is it we first become complicit? When is it that I first became aware my father was actively trying to cheat Ezra Meisel?

Certainly, I'd had my suspicions. When, during the wedding reception, I'd first overheard the members of the Golden Hand mention Papa's name in relation to an Old Master, I'd cocked an ear. Then there was talk of the painting as a wedding present, and the visit of Kovak, Černý, and Solomons to the gallery to view it. Was the wedding present simply that they would forbear to bid against him, or was there more to it? And then there was the business of the model's hand. The three visitors had agreed with Papa that it looked like a clumsy restoration. Why then had Papa not tried to remove the overpaint? Why precisely had my father asked Jaroslav Čermák to question the painting's provenance, and to raise doubts as to the chemistry of the paints? Was it simply caution on his part? But if so, why offer twenty thousand koruna, at a time when money was so scarce? Why raise it now to thirty thousand? And what was the meaning of that odious wink that Pavel Kovak had fired me as he left Meisel's shop.

I can't say precisely when I first suspected it. But I can say with accuracy when my suspicions were confirmed. It was the Thursday immediately before Christmas, Thursday the twenty-second of December. I know this because we were winding down from another lacklustre auction, and preparing for one final, desperate Christmas push. Papa was at the upstairs gallery, repackaging unsold paintings, when he sent me down to the front counter to find an invoice. As I searched through the stack of papers, my attention was drawn to a manila envelope. I can't say why. There was nothing particularly unusual about it. What was odd was that it was addressed to Dott. J Čermák, Curatore, Obrazarna Prazskeho Hradu, Praga, Cecoslovacchia. The stamps were Italian, the postmark dated some five weeks before. With a quick glance toward the stairs, I slid from the inside a single sheet of paper with an embossed card affixed with a paperclip.

The sheet was a facsimile. What drew my attention initially was the logo to the top of the card: the winged lion of San Marco, and beneath it the Latin words: *Venetiarum Respublica*. From my stamp collection, I knew there hadn't been a *Repubblica di Venezia* or even a *Republica Veneta* in decades, certainly not since Italy became a unified country in 1871. The facsimile to which the card was appended appeared to be a page out of some kind of register or ledger. One entry in particular had been circled in red pen. There was a date: *primo giugno del AD MDXI*. Partly because the entries were hand-written, partly because they were in a dialect of Italian closer to that of Petrarch or Dante than to the Italian I'd been raised on, it took me some minutes to decipher.

By the time I was back upstairs with the invoice my heart was pounding. I was unable to speak. For how many weeks had my father been in possession of the missing years of the painting's provenance? Because of one thing there could be no doubt whatsoever. The entry referred to a 1511 purchase, by one Gianfranco Maldini, of a *"Susanna e gli Anziani" di*

Giorgio da Castelfranco detto "Giorgione".

I'll hold off, I said. I'll wait until we close up shop. Until we return home. I'll have it out with him, then. But it wasn't to be. What met us on our return to Nerudova Street was a house in turmoil. An ambulance was pulled up outside the door.

XXIX

Showdown

It's a curious sensation, turning onto one's native street and seeing a parked ambulance. Our house was about two-thirds the way up the hill, on the castle side. As we ascended, our pace slowly picked up, but it was as much a case of wondering which of the neighbours it had called for as any real apprehension. It was only when we were inside the last thirty yards that it became certain at which door it had pulled up. We ran those final thirty yards.

My first thought was that it was there for Katya. She'd had another seizure, and had fallen. Banged her head. Perhaps it had brought on a miscarriage. But no! There was Katya, standing just inside our hallway. Could it be Maman? She'd been acting very strangely ever since that evening she and Papa had had their altercation. Perhaps she'd been taken ill? Or could it be that she'd once more tried to take her life? Once, many years ago, she'd taken an overdose of sleeping-pills, and had had to have her stomach pumped.

The mystery was soon solved. It seemed there had been some sort of a fracas the evening before, in the vicinity of

Vacláv Square. A group of Sudeten refugees had tried to storm a fabric shop bearing the provocative name of *Steinitz & Söhne*. A riot had ensued. Somehow, Father Kaufmann had got caught up in the midst of it, striving to usher the cloth-merchant and his family to safety. A cobble had struck him on the brow.

All this Katya told us, as we stood in the hallway. At this point, Maman appeared at the head of the stairs, descending them in company with a paramedic. 'Maria Teresa? What's going on?' called Papa.

'Would you keep it quiet, please. You're disturbing Johannes.'

'I asked you what's going on.'

At the mezzanine she halted, looking down at us imperiously. I verily believe she only deigned to answer for appearances sake, so that the paramedic wouldn't see how frosty relations had become on Nerudova Street.

'Father Kaufmann – Johannes – is upstairs, in the guest room. He was discharged this morning. He spent last night on a gurney in a corridor, which I find disgraceful. A man of his age. A servant of God, all his life. They said that, since his injuries were not life-threatening, they couldn't find him a bed. A man who's spent all his life dedicated to this city.' She nodded to the paramedic and offered him her fingers, a gesture of dismissal. 'I arranged for him to be brought here.'

'But see here Mia! Who's to look after him?'

'He's not in any danger. All the same, I've arranged for a Sister Agatha to stay with him. Sister Agatha is a Sister of Mercy. I've had a cot placed in the room for her.'

Aware of the value that Maman placed on dignity, Papa waited for the paramedic to depart before he replied. 'I think you might have let me know.' Maman, from her vantage on the mezzanine, turned to go. 'I do think you might have informed me, Maria.'

She paused and shook her head determinedly, her lips pursed. 'I don't know what's happening in this house any more.' Briefly, she turned her gaze on me. 'I don't know my own son any more.' Then she ascended to the first floor in the manner of a Duchess.

I kept my eyes on the floorboards, afraid to glance at Katya. I wasn't sure if she'd been aware of Maman's horrified gaze, fixed upon us from the doorway of the attic studio all those evenings before. Because there was no doubt in my mind, that was the incident Maman was referring to. What she thought we were up to, I didn't dare imagine. Surely she couldn't harbour any doubt as to the paternity of the child? I couldn't speak to her about it. It had never been our way. But perhaps, through her old confidante Johannes, I could at least put her mind at rest on that score.

This wasn't the time to broach my father on the subject of what I'd recently discovered in the gallery. There'd be time enough for that. My first thought, a selfish one, was that at long last I'd be able to have that long discussion with my old tutor. What would he have to say about Papa's plan to pack us off to the New World? Never mind that neither of us spoke the language nor had any great enthusiasm for the move, if it was the case it was the only chance for the safety of her unborn child, should Katya take it regardless of her personal wishes? But if it was right for him to insist on sending her to safety, how could it be right if it was at the cost of preventing another pregnant girl the same opportunity? For surely Ezra Meisel would have been long gone if only my father would offer a fair price. How could it be right for one, but not the other?

And where did my duty lie? If, as Papa believed, Katya would only consent to go if I accompanied her, would it be wrong of me to refuse? Or was it rather cowardice to fly Czechoslovakia, when the country faced such imminent danger? And what about Papa? What would the priest make of what I had to tell him on that score? At least he'd help me get my facts straight, of that I had little doubt.

But that evening he was to be left to rest. I looked in the door, saw from a distance the head bound in bandages propped up on a bank of pillows. Sister Agatha, a kindly faced woman who wore half-moon glasses on a fine silver chain, shooed me from the door. My heart thumping, I waited impatiently the chance to talk to my old friend and confessor.

That Friday I had to return to the gallery. Sales had been so dismal that Papa planned to open the premises even on Christmas Eve, to catch the last of the seasonal business. There were a couple of canvases that needed framing, and besides, I wanted to put the final touches on Father Kaufmann's chess set. With any luck my father and I might remain in separate rooms for most of the day. I had little appetite for the impending confrontation, and wanted at least the chance to talk to Father Kaufmann to set my thoughts in battle order.

Although there were only two canvases to be framed up, I planned that this might take up most of the morning. I wasn't bad on the lathe by this time, but the finer points of wood joining still eluded me. This wasn't only down to my clumsy fingers. Jan, suspicious of my father's intentions, had begrudged me any hint and instruction he passed down. He'd also taken away with him all the finer tools. It was just as well we'd stockpiled so many lengths of prepared wood. I might be able to cobble together a passable frame, but working the lengths of raw wood into finely chiselled and bevelled lengths was not within my rudimentary skill-set.

After lunch I set out the thirty-two pieces on the parquet board I'd made. By this time they'd been measured and tested and finely sanded, and waited only a final varnish, the one side light, the other with a tinted lacquer. I was about to finish the final rook when Papa entered. He stood a while in silence. 'That's fine work, Guido.' He lifted several pieces, examined, hummed. Usually this would have been a time of pride and mild trepidation. Today all I felt was discomfort. He replaced the black king. 'Very fine.'

'Listen, Guy,' he scratched the back of his head. 'I want you to run back over to that old Jew. Tell him I have another offer.' He fished out a business-card with the black sun logo. 'A final offer, tell him.'

I took the card, flipped it over. On it, in pencil, was scribbled the sum Kč 15,000.

'I don't understand,' I said. 'Is this a mistake?' It was some sort of joke, perhaps.

'It's no joke,' he smiled. 'I've been playing out the line long enough. It's time that old miser was brought to the shore.'

I felt my eyes blur with dry heat; my throat hammer. 'I won't do it,' I said.

'You won't?'

'I won't go.'

'Oh?'

'It's not a fair price.'

'Isn't it?' He turned from me. His voice, when he spoke, was very measured. 'And you know so much about the value of Renaissance paintings. Tell me. What would be a fair price, do you think?'

I flushed red. I stared hard at the floorboards, dug my nails painfully into my palms.

'You can't answer that, can you?' He stepped back into the front room, his head bowed in thought. 'Go home Guido. Go. Take your chess set.'

Hurriedly, clumsily, I swept up the pieces, put them along with the board into my knapsack. I pulled on my coat and hat, hesitated, looked about the work station. It was as though I had an intuition that this would be the last time I would see it.

I moved quickly through the show room, hesitated at the door. It seemed impossible to set off without saying something, even if it was only 'Goodbye.'

'And Guido,' said my father, not looking up from the register, 'don't bother coming in tomorrow.'

The next morning, before dawn, I heard him pottering about the kitchen. It was the first time in a long time that I wasn't setting off with him. It made me feel like a schoolboy being admonished. Maman too was to go out, in the company of Marta, the cook. Father Kaufmann and Sister Agatha were to be guests at the Christmas Eve dinner. Along with Maman and Papa, myself and Katya, Klaus and Eva, that made eight for the traditional fish dinner. Several days earlier, when Papa had mentioned that Miss Ivors was destined to spend a joyless Christmas on her own, an indignant Maman put her foot down. He'd conceded the point. He was prepared for a tactical defeat, so long as he kept his eye on the campaign itself.

By ten o'clock, I pretty much had the house to myself. This suited me. After breakfast, I tapped gently on the guest's bedroom. Sister Agatha opened the door, her smile framed by her wimple. Father Kaufmann was awake, his eyes closed, but as I lay my palm on his brow, he looked at me. With the large eyes in the desiccated, equine face, today more than ever he recalled the Knight of the Doleful Countenance. With the bandaged head, he might have been Quixote after the episode with the Yangüeses.

'How are you feeling today?' I asked.

'When one has attained the biblical span of three score and ten, one is grateful *that* one feels, never mind *how* one feels.'

'Don't mind him,' the Sister of Mercy tutted, mildly. 'Like every Jesuit, he has a vocation to be a martyr.'

'Do not be taken in by Sister Agatha's lovely smile,' frowned the patient, his eyes closing. 'Under her wimple she appears so saintly.' He looked up at me with exaggerated dolefulness. 'But when it comes to cigarettes, that woman has the heart of a Gestapo operative.'

'I'm amazed your Father Provincial didn't want you back with them. Wouldn't Sister Agatha be allowed to visit a priest in his cell?'

'Of course, but you're reckoning without Maria Teresa. Maria Teresa can be most persuasive when she has a mind to be. She wouldn't hear of me spending Christmas anywhere but here. Our unfortunate Father Provincial didn't stand a chance.'

'I suppose not.' It wasn't lost on me that Maman's insistence was a direct consequence of Papa having his way here in other regards. 'I come bearing gifts,' I said. 'Not cigarettes, I'm afraid.' I'd selected some half dozen chess-pieces, and these I now unwrapped and set on the bedside table.

He lifted the knight, the king. 'The traditional gift would be gold, frankincense or myrrh.'

'I made a full set. In the workshop of the gallery. It'll be under the tree for you, later on.' I looked at the Sister of Mercy. 'Don't let on I gave you both a preview.'

'Your secret is safe,' she beamed.

'Very nice. Really. They're very fine. I'll treasure them from the Curia, in Rome. They'll always remind me of my time in Prague.' Father Kaufmann replaced the pieces. 'I enjoyed our games, Guido.'

'That's because you always beat me, Except when you let me win.'

'I thought I was being subtle! I understand you too may soon be undertaking a voyage.'

'Who told you that?'

'Maria Teresa.'

'It hasn't been decided.'

'Oh? I understood it had been decided.'

'No. Papa asked myself and Katya to consider the possibility. That's all.' I wasn't being entirely truthful, and I was concerned that he sensed it. 'Actually, that's what I want to talk to you about. Did Maman tell you? About... Katya?' I let the inference hang, not sure how freely I should speak before the Sister. Father Kaufmann had never been slow at picking up a hint.

'That Katerina is, as they say, "with child"?'

'Papa's of the opinion it'd be crazy for her to bring a baby into the world here, with the way things are going.'

'And Katerina is unwilling to leave everything she knows for a life in a strange city with a father she's never met.'

'She's shy at the best of times.'

'Which is where you come in.'

'Apparently. Papa is of the opinion that if I agree to go with her, it'd decide Katya's mind for her. I'm not so sure. Besides, Maman hates the whole idea.'

'I think you'll find Maria Teresa may be becoming reconciled to the idea. She hates the thought of separation, naturally. From her only son, and the apple of her eye. What mother wouldn't? But then, as I understand it, whatever about Katerina staying on with her father, your move there wouldn't be on a permanent basis.'

'Papa says the next war will be so terrible that it can't last long.'

'All over by Christmas, isn't that the old saying? There's no doubt it will be a terrible affair, with the weapons they have today. Entire cities destroyed from the air.'

'What I want to ask you, Father. Would it not be cowardice, to run away? Haven't I a duty to stay here? To fight evil, if needs be?'

'The theory of the just war. Certainly, there's an argument for it.'

'But then, don't I also have a duty to Katya? And to Katya's baby?'

'Of course. But you would wish me to tell you which duty is the more imperative.'

'I'm confused.'

'What Hegel memorably terms the clash of right against right. No one said that being a Christian is easy. What do you say, Sister Agatha?'

In place of answering, the nun looked at me with beneficent sympathy.

'There's something else, Father. About Papa. Can we…?' I flashed a semaphore which I knew he'd understand. His eyes closed once more. It appeared to hurt him to keep them open. 'Sister Agatha,' he said. 'Would you be an Angel of Mercy? Would you fetch an old invalid a mug of beef tea?'

She shook her wimple. Then she left us alone.

XXX

Christmas Eve

That evening, despite the best efforts of the newlyweds, the traditional carp dinner was a subdued affair. Maman and Papa were studiously polite to one another, just as studiously they avoided all eye-contact, as though their gazes were like poles of two magnets. Father Kaufmann was tired, though he did his best to hold up his end of such tattered conversation as emerged. Katya and I were silent, Sister Agatha a stranger, so it fell to the newlyweds to regale the company with their plans for married life, 'once things begin to calm down', as Lt Hayek, in officer's uniform, put it. In place of the abandoned Venetian honeymoon, a ski-holiday beckoned, perhaps in the Tatras Mountains.

There was a good reason that myself and Katya were silent. I can't speak for her, but my guts were in turmoil all through dinner, in anticipation of the scene that was now inevitable. In previous years, in between the courses, Ježíšek would arrive to place the presents under the Christmas tree. Back in the days that Klaus used to call me Kašpárek, that task had usually fallen to me. This year, Papa had broken with the tradition. A little before we all gathered at the table, he'd asked the two of us to step into his study. There, he presented us with a pair of envelopes. Each contained an ocean-liner ticket:

La Stella di Oriente; da Genova a New York; 18:25
venerdi il 6 gennaio.

Maman must have known all about it. No sooner had the table been cleared than she rose and invited the ladies to withdraw. 'Do you play a hand of whist, Sister Agatha?' she asked, forcing a horizontal smile.

'I'm happy to try.'

'Don't listen to her, Maria Teresa!' growled the priest. 'And be sure to keep the stakes small. In the convent that one's quite well known as a card-sharp.'

The ladies – Maman, Eva, Katya and the Sister of Mercy, withdrew. This time there was no concession on Maman's part to open the partition between the rooms.

Klaus walked slowly to the drinks cabinet and returned with three balloons and a brandy decanter. 'Bring one for the boy,' said Papa. 'Who knows when we might all be sitting around this table again.'

'It's all arranged then?' asked Klaus, pouring the three balloons and sliding one of them to me with a wink before returning to the cabinet for a fourth glass.

'I picked up the tickets on Thursday. The *vapore* sails from Genoa on January sixth.'

'The Feast of the Epiphany,' put in Father Kaufmann, savouring the alcoholic fumes. 'An auspicious day for journeys.'

'You'd enjoy a cigar with your cognac, Hans?'

'I would murder for a cigar with my cognac, Emil.'

Papa opened the sandalwood box he'd had sent from Havana and selected two, squeaking them beside his ear before clipping the ends. Klaus was still hovering by the drinks cabinet. 'Does Maman know?' he asked.

'Of course. I couldn't very well not tell Maman.'

'What do you say, Kašpárek? A voyage to the New World, eh?'

With Papa's eyes upon me, I flashed Klaus a noncommittal, watery smile.

'And what does Katya make of it all?' he asked. 'Is she in any way excited by the prospect?'

'Who knows?' Papa spoke gruffly, inhaling rapid puffs in order to light his cigar. 'Does anyone ever know what Katya makes of anything?'

'I think I do,' I said. I hadn't touched the brandy glass. On any other day, I might have been delighted at this mark of inclusion. I wasn't yet sixteen. But all through dinner my insides had been hollowed out in dread of the scene I knew was drawing closer with each forkful.

'Oh?' Papa looked at each of us in turn.

'I think she feels pretty much the same about it as I do, actually.'

'And what's that?'

'That it'd be wrong to go.'

'*Wrong?*'

'This,' I said, pulling out with trembling fingers the envelope containing the boat ticket. 'You've booked us a cabin, I see. I imagine that can't have come cheap.'

'That's not your affair.'

'Isn't it? What is my affair, Papa?'

'Your affair… your *business* is to see your sister to safety. I should have thought that much was obvious.' He eyed the Jesuit. 'What do you say, Hans?'

Father Kaufmann was wreathed in smoke. His eyes, rimmed in red, were watering and he rocked with a cough. 'I say this is a very fine cigar, Emil. I'm not used to such richness.'

'Father Kaufmann,' I said. 'You remember that parable, the one about the man who finds treasure in a field, then sells everything to buy that field.'

'Matthew. The Kingdom of Heaven is like unto that man. In his *seeking*, you see. That's what's intended by the parable.'

'But before he bought the field, he first hid that treasure. You remember you told me that? He hid the treasure, and deceived the owner.'

'Our Saviour doesn't say it in so many words…'

'Where are you going with this, Guy?' The question was from Klaus, who was still on his feet. I had to pivot about to face him. But it was Papa who answered. 'Guido thinks that I'm not offering Ezra Meisel a fair price for his old painting.'

'Susannah and the Elders?'

'Guido feels that fifteen thousand koruna is not a fair price.'

'Then let the old Jew get a fair price somewhere else!'

'Ah, but you see, Guido knows that the old miser is desperate to leave Prague. Like Belshazzar, he has seen the writing on the wall. And Guido is afraid he is about to take his pretty little granddaughter with him. What Guido doesn't, perhaps, know is that Old Meisel's shop is no longer Old Meisel's shop. It was bought some weeks ago by our friend Moisés Solomons. So you see, it's perfectly true. The Meisels are staying on here on borrowed time. But tell me, Guido. Since you're a judge of such things. Would you say Moisés Solomons gave Ezra Meisel a fair price for his shop? Yes? No? I'll tell you. His offer was scarcely half the market value. One of his own tribe. Think on that.'

My ears were burning, my heart skipping. 'Does that make it right to cheat someone?'

'Cheat is a strong word, Guido. An ugly word. As Klaus pointed out, no one is compelling the Jew to accept my offer.'

'But you said yourself that he'd never get a permit to take the painting with him!' I'd begun to shake. It wasn't anger. It wasn't nervousness. But my hands became so palsied that I had to sit on them. 'I heard you say that.'

It was Klaus who now took up the argument. Father Kaufmann watched us from red-rimmed eyes, the eyes of an old man. Earlier, I'd tired him out. 'Guy. Do you suppose Ezra Meisel paid what you'd call a fair price for that piece? Or for any other painting, for that matter? All his life, he's made his fortune living off other people's misfortunes. Auctions. Distressed sales. He sniffs them out. He's like a carrion crow, descending onto the corpse to snap up what he can. Do you suppose he *ever* paid a fair price in his entire life?'

'You sound like a Goebbels propaganda film.'

'Why? Because he happens to be a Jew? I'd say the same if he was a Czech or a Slovak.'

'Would you?' I was on my feet. My throat had tightened and my heart, in double-beat, was hammering against it. To stop my hands from trembling, I pressed my fingers hard onto the table. I wanted to cry out, 'Then why can't you say it about Papa?' but it jammed in my throat.

My father was watching me with cool eyes.

'I've seen how the game is played,' I went on. "Nice painting," says Černý, "such a pity about the hands." Then Kovak takes up the song. "Such a beautiful work. It could really be a genuine Giorgione, if it weren't for those hands." All the other viewers and bidders begin to back away. But Papa still isn't satisfied. Suppose one of them knows how to remove a shoddy piece of overpainting? He needs to open up another front. Another set of doubts. So he brings in Čermák, the castle mole.'

'Careful, Guido.'

My face ached for lack of blood. My heart was skipping crazily. "'Tut-tut," says the mole. "You see those beautiful curtains? Such beautiful curtains! Such a lovely shade of crimson. I wonder if that could possibly be alizarin crimson…"'

'You ungrateful brat! You'll apologise to Papa, or I'll…'

'No, Klaus. Let him finish.'

"'Alizarin crimson,"' I repeated. "'A particular pigment of alizarin crimson that, I suspect, incorporates cochineal from the Americas. Common enough in Venetian dyes, but only later on. How to make sure? Chemical analysis! But you see Dr Webern has abandoned Prague University for Leipzig. What can be taking him so long to reply? *Es tut mir leid, aber die Analyse ist sehr schwierig.*"' The room was tilting. My heart galloped, mad and ineffectual. My face ached for want of blood. "What else, Jaroslav?" says Papa. "You seem, if I may say, *doubly* doubtful." "Where's the bill of sale to say this is the same 'Susannah and the Elders' that Gianfranco Maldini purchased, hmm? These Venetians! Why won't they reply? *Scusi, Dottore, ma non si trova questa fattura di vendita...*" I teetered, pushed on the table to recover my balance.

'Have you finished?'

'Are you all right?' This was Father Kaufmann. 'Is the boy all right?'

But I wasn't all right.

Everything had become preternaturally bright. The room had begun to pulse. There was a sound like a rapid percussion behind my left ear. A presence, of evil. I was seized with panic at it.

In my agitation I upset the brandy balloon. It tipped over, rolled a mocking, slow arc about the table-top. I lurched for it, but only succeeded in knocking it to the floor, where it shivered into fragments.

I stooped to collect them. Then I rose, too rapidly. The table pivoted up to the vertical several times in rapid succession. Then the floor did so, once.

XXXI

Christmas Truce

I don't know how long I was unconscious. When I came to, it was dark. I was in my bed.

I felt my brow, which smarted. There was a bump covered with sticking-plaster where I must have caught the table on the way down.

This was not the first fainting fit I'd had. Soon after I'd turned fourteen, I was on a stepladder, helping Maman and Jula, the maid, put up winter blankets toward the top of the linen-cupboard. I looked down too rapidly. The room became preternaturally bright, the percussion drummed at my left ear and the floor began to tilt, once, twice. I'd barely had time to drop from the ladder before it seized.

On that occasion, Maman had brought me to hospital for the full barrage of tests. No, it was not epilepsy, thank God. Exhaustion. Anaemia. The several inches I'd grown. The arrhythmia I was prone to. Turning too quickly. The same basic precautions were repeated. Not to get overtired, not to get dehydrated. No sudden or prolonged exertions. No sudden turns. Beware of stress.

I lay still and listened to the silence of the house.

The next several days were an unreal time in Nerudova Street. I came to think of them as a Christmas truce, a domestic version of the hiatus between the September annexation and the full invasion of Bohemia and Moravia the following March.

Any doubt as to whether my diatribe had carried beyond the dining-room was dispelled by Katya, who visited me on Christmas morning. 'You really had a go at Papa,' she said. 'Where did that come from?'

'You heard it all?'

'You were pretty loud, Guy.'

'Maman, too?'

She nodded.

'How did she take it?'

'She put her fists to her ears. Just like she's blocked out this whole thing about Papa's plan to send us away. Eva did the diplomatic thing, escorted Sister Agatha out of the room.' She sat on the bed, put her hand to my brow. 'What's this about, Guy? Is it about the girl?'

'Leah Meisel? No! How could you think that!'

'Well then?'

'Katya, those ocean-liner tickets? The money's tainted. Papa is trying to cheat Old Meisel.' She didn't say anything. I began to wonder had I gone too far with my accusation, and in such a public way. 'How is the old man? On the warpath?'

'Anything but. You know what he said? Lessons are to resume tomorrow with Miss Ivors.'

'No way! On St Stephen's Day?'

'Two hours in the morning and two in the afternoon, every day until we go, starting tomorrow. We've to make up for lost time, apparently.'

'And that's it? Not a word about what I said?'

'You know what he's like when he's made up his mind.'

'I know exactly what he's like.'

And that was how it happened. On the morning of the twenty-sixth, lessons resumed. On the twenty-seventh, Christmas leave came to an end and Klaus and Eva departed. Father Kaufmann, too, was keen to return to his quarters. But Maman quite simply wouldn't let him. She had such an obvious horror of being left alone in Nerudova Street with a family she no longer understood that the Jesuit demurred. He'd stay on until Friday morning. But then he'd really have to return to his cell.

The gallery wasn't due to re-open before January 2nd. I had the impression that, had it re-opened before then, I would have been surplus to requirements. Generally Papa was out, though we never knew what precisely he was about. On the occasions I did run into him, he looked at me with amused irony. I avoided him.

On Tuesday the 27th, a day of gunmetal sky and powdery snow, once the afternoon lesson was over I wandered over to the Staré Město side. I needed to think. For a while I watched the Vltava, an iron river sliding between snow-upholstered banks. I could no longer think of it as the Moldau. Then I took a diversion to Josefov. I needed to reassure myself that Meisel had not yet set off for the East.

It was curious, traipsing up a deserted Bilkova Street, the pavement dirty with wet snow. I passed the cafeteria where myself and Ivan the Serb had sat so many months before, spying on the shop window. Today both were closed and lifeless. But to my relief, Meisel's van was still parked on the side street, and it was still his name up over the door. Moisés Solomons may have purchased the deeds for the premises, but there was every indication the fine arts merchant resided there still.

On Friday morning, I helped Father Kaufmann pack his things. Sister Agatha had returned to her convent several days before. We'd had such long talks, the priest and I. Today words failed us. We were awkward. Perhaps we both had a sense that this would be the last time we saw one another. From the landing, I watched him say goodbye to Maman. She was dignified, but could scarcely conceal the gamut of emotions running through her.

Then he was alone with Papa.

'Emil. Will you do one thing for me?'

'And what's that?'

There was gravity underlying the raillery in the priest's mien. 'The Jew. Meisel. Give him a fair price.'

Papa took a moment to answer. 'With the greatest respect, Father, that's not your affair.'

'Your soul *is* my affair.'

'My soul?' Papa smiled. He had no wish to part from our old friend on bad terms. 'Ok. I willingly take upon my soul whatever sin you think I may be guilty of.' He made a sign of the cross with his fingers. *'Ego te absolvo.'*

'I wish it were that simple.'

'With respect, you don't know what you're talking about. What would you say is a fair price?'

'For that, you must look to your conscience.'

'Hansi. For twenty years you've been a friend to this family. Please. Leave as a friend.'

'That's precisely how I would wish to leave, Emil.'

'Very good, Hans. In chess, you always had the edge. The last word.' He put an arm about the old priest's shoulder, and steered him toward the door. 'We'll leave it at that.'

The uneasy truce continued until New Year's Eve. At around seven o'clock, Papa asked me to step into his study. His hand motioned to a chair in front of the desk upon which sat a wallet, a map of central Europe, together with sundry papers. 'Sit,' he said, not unpleasantly. I'd been so apprehensive stepping into that room that I'd felt nauseous. This is how it must be, I thought, to be summoned before the principal in a boarding school. His tone wrong-footed me.

He sat opposite me, his hands joined in an arch to support his chin. For several seconds we sat in silence, in silence but for the ludicrous complaint of springs in my chair. Then he pivoted the rail-map about to face me. There was a route traced out in red ink: Prague to Budapest; Budapest to Venice; Venice to Genoa. 'In normal times, one would travel via Vienna,' he commented. 'These are not normal times.'

I remained silent. There was something akin to dread still lurking in my gut.

'Take a look in the wallet. Please.'

I did so. In the left hand compartment were dollars, in the right, Italian lira. His hand made an open gesture, inviting me to count out the contents. I did so. There were twelve ten dollar bills, twelve five dollar bills, twenty ten lira notes, twenty five lira notes. I had no real grasp of what any of this was worth. It seemed a lot.

Papa was scrutinising me, evidently waiting for me to speak. I felt a complete fool. 'Why the lira?' I asked at length, hitting upon nothing else.

'They're for the voyage,' he said. Neatly, he set out several train tickets, turned so that I could read them. 'You arrive in Genoa on the evening of the fifth, the evening before embarkation. You'll have to find suitable accommodation. Then there's the voyage. Genoa to Naples. Naples to Villafranca. Villafranca to Gibraltar. Gibraltar to New York City. That's a little over twelve days in all. The cabin is paid for, but for everything else you'll require cash. Italian lira is the currency on board *SS Stella di Oriente*.' He was still examining me with the supercilious gaze of a school teacher.

'But why tell me? Why not tell Katya?'

'Listen to me, Guido. Your sister is not well. In the first place, she's pregnant. In the second place, she's epileptic. How could one entrust such a sum of money to a person who might... fall down foaming at any minute?'

It was my turn to examine him. Was he mocking me? Was this not precisely what had happened to me the previous week?

'You have no questions for me? Nothing?'

The gears of my mind turned uselessly. 'Why are you so keen to do this for Katya?' I tried. 'When she's not your daughter.'

'I raised that girl as my daughter. In my book, that makes her my daughter.'

Whir, whir went the gears. I felt mortally tired. 'This Gans guy. I mean, he probably doesn't even know I exist.'

'He does know. He knows all about you. Once I booked the

berths, I had a long conversation with Mr Gans by telephone. He's an honourable man. He knows when to expect you, and will arrange for someone to meet the ship when it docks. The husband of his sister, Golda, works for US Immigration, and will help expedite the paperwork. Which is just as well, with so many trying to gain entry.'

'Papa,' I said. I tried to swallow the hard concrete that had set in my throat. 'Papa I can't go.'

'Can't?' he echoed, his equanimity more lethal than anger. 'Can't, or won't?'

'I don't want to argue…' I stopped. My throat was dry as sandpaper. I had no wish for a repeat scene of Christmas Eve.

'I haven't invited you in here to argue, Guy.'

'I can't accept this money.'

'Oh?'

'Papa, I found the letter from Venice. On your desk in the gallery. The letter addressed to Jaroslav Čermák confirming the painting's provenance.'

My father raised his eyebrows in ironic interrogation. 'And so?' they seemed to ask. His fingers had again come together, as though in prayer to some unknown god.

'This money. It's tainted.'

'Tainted.'

Anger began to rise. 'What about *"Always remember our business is people"*. You remember that, Papa? So what about Ezra Meisel. Isn't he "people"? Didn't you once say you admired him, giving up his only son? And now you want to…' I tried but could not pronounce the word 'cheat'. That ugly word. 'I bet Čermák never even collected a sample of red paint to send off to Leipzig.'

A hand slapped the table, not hard, but firmly. 'I want you to listen to me. I won't put up with any more of this nonsense, Guy. Is that understood? I'm not Maman, nor your precious Father Kaufmann, to indulge your schoolboy scruples. Even if what you said is true, that letter has nothing to do with the money I laid out for the Atlantic crossing. For the train tickets. For the currency, to see that you two lack for nothing. Now, I made Meisel an offer. It's a fair offer, considering. If he has not decided to take me up on that offer, that's his prerogative. We're both businessmen. But you tell me. How could a possible transaction which may or may not take place at some point in the future have any bearing on the money set out before you?'

Angrily, I shook my head. He was outplaying me, and we both knew it. 'Father Kaufmann has a word for that kind of reasoning, Papa. It's called sophistry.'

'And I've got a word for that damned Jesuit! Let the priests have a family to look after, as rabbis must. Then I'll respect them.' He'd stood, and now he sauntered around to my side of the desk and began tracing the route on the map. 'The train from Prague leaves at four thirty on Thursday the fourth. It's not ideal, but…'

'Look, Papa. Stop this! I've thought about it. I've thought about nothing else. I've talked about it with Katya. I've discussed it with Father Kau… with Father Hans. You say our country is in danger. Then my place is here.'

'Hunh! You're no fighter, Guido. With respect, once before I asked you to look after Katya. And look where that got us.'

'But I wasn't there that day.'

'No. Too busy chasing after that old Jew's granddaughter.'

I was livid. Choking. 'That's not fair,' I spat out.

'Isn't it? If there's fighting to be done, leave it to Klaus. Klaus is the fighter of the family.'

'Just like Rudi and Franz were the fighters in your family.'

Beside me, I sensed his body go rigid. 'What's that supposed to mean?'

'Nothing.'

'What do you mean by that? Explain it to me!'

I would give the world to be able to take back what I said next. 'I think you want me to run away so I'd be just like you, counting munition trains. Then I could be a coward, too.'

With an agility that astonishes me to this day, he threw himself at me. I was taller than Papa, but he was the stockier man. Sturdier. In a trice he had his right hand about my throat and had thrust me backwards over the desk, while his left hand hurled the chair sideways out of the way. His face, blown up like a bullfrogs, came within inches of mine. 'Don't you say that to me,' he hissed. 'You ungrateful, degenerate brat! Don't you *ever* say that to me.'

My hands were clawing at his, trying to free my windpipe. My eyes swam in pools.

'And what do you think you'd do, when they come, eh? Take up arms against the Wehrmacht?'

'Papa,' I croaked. 'You're choking me…'

'After this, it's finished for you here, boy. Finished! You think I'd let you set foot inside the gallery, after what you've just said to me?'

He pulled me up, shook me like a rag-doll, forced me to my knees. At last my throat was unclamped, and I began to take in great lungfuls of air.

'You'll leave on that steamer, boy. You'll escort your sister to safety. Because it's finished for you here.' Three rough fingers pivoted my chin upward. 'Do we understand each other?'

I nodded. Calmly, slowly, he sauntered out of the study, leaving the door ajar. I was left on my knees, my fingers massaging my throat, gazing at the carpet through hot tears.

XXXII

New Year's Eve

Two hours later, I stood with Katya beneath the great astronomical clock. I wore a scarf, to cover the marks of his nails.

It was just short of ten o'clock, the crowds just beginning to gather. As it might well be our last New Year's Eve together, we'd promised Maman to be back in time to ring in the new year, but by the same token she couldn't begrudge us one last trip to Our Lady of Týn in the Old Town Square.

'Papa was on to me again this morning,' said Katya. 'Guy, do you still think it'd be such a bad idea to go?'

'I told you. He's cheating Old Meisel. I don't mean the usual, the run-of-the-mill creaming off a few hundred koruna. I mean he's fleecing the guy! Destroying him, Katya. And his family! Just because he... look, even Father Kaufmann says he's cheating Old Meisel.'

'I know that. But...'

'Then why the change of heart? I thought you hated the idea.'

'I'm not keen. This is all the home I've ever known.'

'Well then.'

'I got a fright, Guy. A couple of days before Christmas. The contractions started. There was a bloody discharge. I was worried sick I was going to lose the baby. Maman took me to her doctor who gave me something to calm them down. Told me to take it easy. That I was overdoing it. Maman didn't tell you?'

'No. Nothing.'

'I so want to have this baby, Guy. More than anything. Is that wrong?'

'Wrong?'

'It got me thinking. Maybe Papa is right after all.'

'So you want to leave?'

'If it was just me, Guy... but there are two of us, now.' She gripped either side of my face, made me look her in the eye. 'Am I being a coward?'

'That's not for me to say, Katya.'

'But what do you think?'

I removed her hands from my cheeks. 'No, you're not being a coward,' I said. 'Jesus, anything but.'

'Something else has changed. The whole atmosphere in the house has changed. You and Papa, like dogs at one another's throats.'

'Yeah! Who's fault is that?'

'But it's not just that, Guy. The way Maman looks at me. Like at the doctor's, she had this look of distaste. I got the idea she'd have preferred if I'd miscarried outright. It makes me feel like an interloper. A cuckoo in the nest.'

I looked hard at her. 'There's something I never told you. That evening, you remember? It was snowing. I came into your room. You'd left the lights off. You were by the mirror. You had me kneel down and asked me could I hear the baby. Well. Maman saw that.'

A hand covered her mouth.

'When I looked in the mirror, I saw her. Framed in the doorway. By the time I was on my feet, she was gone. God alone knows what she thought was going on.'

Huge cow eyes gazed up into mine. 'What do you mean?'

'I mean, she probably... she might have thought... I don't know, Katya... that the baby was mine, or something.'

'Oh Jesus!' Something halfway between a sob and a guffaw burst from her. 'But that's ridiculous! How could she think...? No, Guy. I don't believe that.'

'I saw her face, Katya.'

Her features became determined. 'Then that's one more reason we should go. Think about it, Guy. What sort of a life is it going to be in Nerudova Street with things the way they are? It's intolerable!'

'Katya. I can't go while he's cheating Old Meisel. It's everything he's got.' I took her by the shoulders and shut my eyes, a catch in my throat. 'You go.'

'No. No way, Guy. Not unless you're coming, too.'

'I can't. It'd be stolen money, Katya.'

'Then we won't go.'

'Solemn vow?'

She blew on her knuckles, pressed them against my cold cheek. 'You still love her, then.' She bit her lip. 'So what *will* we do, Guy?'

'Ok,' I said, once the surge of emotion had passed. 'Here's what we'll do. You'll have to talk to Papa, because I can't. He won't listen to me. He practically threw me out of the house, earlier. So it's up to you. He loves you. Seriously, Katya. He'd do anything for you. So you have to tell him. If he offers Meisel a fair price for that painting, then we'll go. Happily. We'll both go.'

'What's a fair price?'

'Jesus, you tell me! You're the artist. All I know is, fifteen thousand is not a fair price. This thing turns out to be an original, or even a collaboration, it'll clear twenty times that sum. More if it's original.'

'So what will I say then? Papa doesn't have that kind of money.'

'Tell him to look to his conscience. That's what Father Kaufmann asked him to do. He's not a bad man, Katya. It's just this obsession with this painting. Anything I say, it makes him twice as stubborn. But from you...'

'You really think he'll listen?'

'Not really, if I'm honest. But I know for a fact he won't listen to me. It has to be worth a try. Will you do it?'

'Sure,' she shrugged. Then she added in English, "My name is Katerina. I'm very pleased to meet you."

If I'd been in any doubt as to the tension I'd been under over the last fortnight, it was apparent in the relief I felt upon hearing her say this. Suddenly there was a way out. Suddenly, a whole new door was opening. Because Papa was not a bad man. All my life, I'd admired him. Not admired, worshipped. It's scarcely too strong a word. On those mornings when he took me into his confidence and we walked the bridge, I'd felt more light and happy than at any time over the previous ten years.

'Come on,' said Katya, 'we'd better head back.'

It was then, as I ran my eyes over the crowds gathering in the Old Town Square for one last time that I spotted her.

Six months before, in that innocent time when I'd wander the streets of Josefov in the hope of catching a sight of her, it had sometimes seemed to me that our eyes had locked onto each other's across a street, as though attracted by a force field. This is how it appeared to me now. She was standing a good two hundred yards away from me, through jostling shoulders and heads. Beneath her wild black hair, enough hair for two heads, her eyes locked onto mine. I could see behind her Ada, the redhead, laughing with a guy wearing glasses who I didn't recognise.

'Look over there,' I said. 'You see her? There, by the door to the Town Hall.'

'Where? Oh, ok. Who is she, Guy?'

'Can't you guess?'

'Rosalind!'

The name, from that innocent period half a year ago, short-circuited me. 'The very same.'

'Guy? Is she pregnant?'

'It certainly looks that way.'

'It's not... you're not...'

'Not guilty. Unfortunately. I think I'm condemned to be an eternal virgin.'

'Every boy thinks that way. Don't worry, Guido. You're a good-looking guy.' That was the first time, I think, that anyone had ever said the like to me. I felt a warm burn, not unlike the glow that schnapps gives. When I looked again, the bespectacled male companion had left the two girls. 'That makes it ten times times as bad, if you're right about Papa.'

'Come on,' I said. 'I'll introduce you.'

'No, Guy. No. Please don't.'

There was no persuading her. She was ever shy with those she didn't know.

'Ok you go on. I'll catch you up.'

She pushed through the crowd, then turned briefly and held up a hand. 'Solemn promise,' she called. She never looked so beautiful as then.

If I thought that the sloe-dark eyes that had locked onto mine were offering an invitation to approach, I was soon disabused of the idea. 'Fuck you,' Leah said, turning from me. Ada's face had assumed a look of haughty disdain.

'What?' I gasped.

'Fuck. You.' She turned to face me, pointed to Ada. 'She's a thief?' She beat her own chest. 'I'm a thief? Your father is the biggest thief in this city!' As if to punctuate the statement, she spat a cobra-spit at the ground before me.

They made to go. Desperately I clawed at her arm. She spun about, magnificent, head poised, a snake ready to strike. 'But Zeyde is strong. Zeyde is clever. He'll win back that money, every penny of it.'

Zeyde, I thought. A new man. Maybe the companion that I'd seen with them moments before. Another Zak. My heart plummeted.

'How much did he pay them, eh? Your father, the big man. Solomons I know. The thief. His share was the shop. The sole bidder. He stole it from Zeyde for half its value. Half the price. But what about the others? How much did your father pay them not to bid? To pretend the painting isn't real. How much did he pay Kovak, and Sumilov, and Černý? His friend the art expert from the castle. How much?'

Then Zeyde was Meisel! The word must be granddad, in Yiddish. Now, it was the hatred in her eyes that had my heart dismayed. 'Wait,' I pleaded. 'Hold on, would you?' Because they were pushing away from me through the thickening crowd as though I were a repulsive thing.

She shook my hand from her. 'What? What do you want?'

'But he'll come round. You'll see! We'll make him come round. Katya and I.'

'What are you talking about?' Then to Ada. 'What's he talking about?'

'That offer. That fifteen thousand. That's only a ploy. A trick. Tell your grandfather to wait. To hang on. He'll raise the bid. You'll see. He'll come round.'

She turned to Ada. 'What is he? Is he crazy?'

'I think so. Let's go.'

'No. Wait.' I held my hands out before me in supplication. 'I'll make him double that bid. Treble it.'

She stared at me as if, for the first time, she were trying to understand me. 'Don't you know it's too late?' Her brow frowned interrogatively. 'Don't you know he's bought that picture?'

'Your grandfather sold it!'

'Zeyde had to. Tomorrow we must leave.'

'But when?'

'When? What does it matter when? He sold it.' She was still examining me, but her features had softened somewhat. 'On Wednesday they went to the bank. They needed the money to be transferred to Odessa.'

I swallowed sand. He'd betrayed me. He'd betrayed my trust. All the time he was showing me the route on the map, he'd never let on that Meisel had been cheated. My heart was hammering recklessly. 'How much?' I croaked.

'How much. Eighteen thousand five hundred.' Once again, she spat at the ground. This time the disdain was not aimed at me.

'Does that include the portraits?'

'Tsst! The portraits are *drek*. Zeyde is leaving the portraits with Solomons.'

'But why? Why did he agree?'

'Tomorrow, we leave.'

'Tomorrow? But…'

'Solomons has insisted we leave the shop. His shop. Your father knows this.'

I stood, winded. It was as though I'd received a blow to the solar plexus. Christ, what now? Where could I go, now? Twenty minutes before, my heart had soared at the thought that Katya might convince the man. Then we'd sail on together to a new life. A new world. But the man had betrayed me. He'd betrayed the old merchant, and he'd betrayed my trust. There was no going home, now.

The two heads, black and red, pushed away through the crowd in the direction of Týn. I swam with my arms through the masses to catch up. 'Leah!' I called. 'Ada! Leah!'

Just short of Týn I caught up with them. 'Take me with you!' I panted. Her gaze was almost amused. 'Please! Take me with you.'

'He is crazy,' said Ada. 'Go home, boy.'

'I'll help you. I'll do whatever Zak did, just teach me…'

Arm in arm, just as they used to walk, they began to move away.

'I'll bring money!' I cried. They stopped. Leah turned her head. 'I have money. You can have my money. Just take me away from here.'

'You have money?' she doubted.

'I have. I have four thousand eight hundred koruna. I saved it.' Frantically, I ran through the contents of the biscuit tin. That was the princely sum. 'You can have it. You can have all of it.' Wildly, my imagination searched the house. The study. 'There's more! I can get more…'

'And you can get this tonight? We leave tomorrow, at dawn. First light, we're gone.'

'I can get it tonight,' I said, 'just so long as you take me away from here. I have a passport. I can bring my passport.'

'Ok,' she laughed. She put her open hand against my cheek. 'Ok, crazy boy! You bring the money. Bring your passport. At the other side of the Štefánikuv Bridge, we'll pick you up.'

'Yes!' I cried, already turning. 'I will. I'll do that!'

'First light, crazy boy. After that, we are gone.'

XXXIII

Flight

It was after two when I arrived home. I'd wandered the streets for hours, to be sure that everyone would be asleep when I got there. Snow had begun to fall, and my shoulders were matted with it. The entire house was silent, eerie, illuminated by that curious lunar glow that comes off fresh snow, even at two in the morning.

It hadn't been my intention to steal anything. What I'd said to Leah Meisel, those wild and whirling words, had been just that. But as I tramped the streets that slowly emptied of living beings, the words descended on me and gathered as the snow had on my coat.

Now my father kept a strong-box in the basement. That was out of bounds. Even had I known the combination, which I didn't, or where he kept the great key, which I could probably have guessed, the contents of that strong-box belonged to the family. That was theirs, and who was I to take it from them like a thief in the night? But in Papa's study, behind the Kandinsky lithograph, Papa kept a night-safe. Often, when he was entertaining clients or art dealers at the dining table, he'd dispatch me in there to fetch some paper or other, so that I knew the combination by heart. I also knew that there was every chance he'd placed the wallet in there earlier that evening, with its dollars and Italian lira. That money was intended for a journey. Very well then, let it serve to pay for this journey!

I mounted the stairs painfully, dreading every creak, then moved like a phantom to my room. There I changed out of my wet clothes, pulled down a knapsack, and placed in it a second set of dry clothes. Before it popped open, the biscuit tin made a sucking noise that had me on tenterhooks. I counted out the notes, laying them in tens, twenties, fifties. Four thousand eight hundred koruna. I divided the sum in four, put three of the twelve-hundreds inside a sock, and spread them throughout the various pouches and pockets of the knapsack, the other I stuffed in my wallet in my pants pocket. My passport I slipped into my coat pocket, through a hole that led into the lining. Should I take the stamp album? The photo of the family on my bedside table in which I'd have been about six? With an adult ruthlessness that pleased me, I decided against.

I stood by my doorway for a moment and listened. In the still of night, a house gives out curious noises. The gurgle of a pipe, the click of furniture. Lightly, I could hear my father snoring. I crept like a cat to the door of the study, eased it open, the spring in the door-handle groaning horribly. I set down the knapsack, eased the door shut behind me. The room was the monochrome dream of a room, familiar and unfamiliar. I paused at the desk, where the silver-blue rail-map of Eastern Europe sill lay open. There, I tried to map out the journey to Odessa, through the Slovak provinces, Hungary, Romania, Bessarabia, the USSR. Once there, the Black Sea would be the first I'd ever seen. How many days' journey was that? A week? More?

I tiptoed across to the Kandinsky lithograph, prised it open. My fingers were so damp when I touched them off each other that I had to wipe them in my pants. I was so nervous, so damp with perspiration, that it took me three goes to hit upon the right combination. The door clicked, I pulled down the handle, eased it open. There lay the wallet. Hands trembling, I flicked it open. There were the monochrome dollars, there the lira, washed to grey-blue. I slid the wallet into my coat pocket, shut the safe, returned the Kandinsky to the wall. Just before I turned, I was seized with the certainty that there were a pair of eyes upon me.

For a moment, I thought it was the old priest, the eyes rimmed red. But it was nothing. It was a stack of laundry that the maid must have inadvertently left on the stool behind the door. Just above it, a vase twinkled. I must have caught a reflection of it in the window, my fevered mind conjuring a face and body out of it.

Breathlessly, too nervous to breathe, I crept down the stairs and out of the door. I think I knew, then, that it was the last time I'd ever see the house on Nerudova Street.

The snow had stopped, but it was deathly cold. For about another hour I tramped about the streets, stamping my boots to stop the slush gathering on them. It was still only twenty past three. Then it came to me where I could go. I hurried along the deserted footpaths of Josefov, made for the warehouse by the Štefánikuv Bridge. Body clenched against the cold, I prised open the door and slipped inside. The great trunk of old clothes and costumes was still there, so I buried myself in their midst and watched the sky slowly lighten in the broken panes above the entrance.

I suspect that whoever it was who said that the darkest hour is just before the dawn never spent a sleepless night. From about four thirty, there is a gradual lightening of the sky, so faint at first that it might be a hallucination, a trick of the night. By five o clock I was too restless to stay put, too apprehensive that the mother of pearl then beginning to overwhelm the stars to the east might mean Meisel's van was already setting out on its journey. I gathered my rucksack and tramped across the bridge, the whole city silent and asleep. Virgin snow lay everywhere, an unmarked page upon which the New Year had not yet begun to write its history of jackboots and tank tracks.

It would be a mistake to imagine that I had no thought for Katya. Quite the opposite. They flitted about me like bats, driven by the awful knowledge that I was abandoning her. Betraying her trust, even as my father had betrayed mine.

But was that accurate? She'd said she had no intention of using the tainted money Papa had now stolen. We'd made a solemn vow, that very night under the astrological clock. I wasn't stealing it. This was an act of restitution, and scarcely the tenth part of what Papa was cheating the Meisels out of. And there was this. Suppose the worst came to the worst. Suppose the Germans annexed Bohemia. Might she not come to me in Odessa just as well as to a stranger in New York?

Was I rationalising? Was this not the very sophistry I'd accused Papa of using? The Devil's babble? A mere balm to my conscience? Even now, after so much has happened, I can't say. Besides, I had other concerns. Suppose there was no room in the van for me. Suppose Hookworm was with them, and was to accompany us into exile in distant Odessa. Suppose they didn't show.

Gradually the sky brightened. A wind that would skin you swept mercilessly along the surface of the Vltava. I stamped my feet, slapped arms about my chest. My cheeks were stinging, my chest muscles clenched. Only two or three stars now persisted in the white sky. And still they did not come.

What if, when they pulled up, they asked me to pass in the knapsack? After all, if the van contained Old Meisel, Leah and Hookworm as driver, where was I to sit? I pulled open one of the pockets, removed a roll of koruna wrapped inside a sock and thrust it into my coat pocket. Then I felt that the gesture might somehow put a jinx on the whole thing, and I replaced the roll in the knapsack. Where were they? It was now a quarter to eight.

I would have liked to have said goodbye to Maman. It was the least she deserved. I would have liked to have said goodbye to Marta and Jula, those companions of my childhood. It had not been possible. Then there was Katya. And Father Kaufmann. I would write a letter from Odessa. I would write to each of them, separately. Even Papa. What numbed my sense of shame at slipping away without leaving so much as a note was the gut-punch of betrayal my father had dealt out. My throat still smarted from the rough grip of his fingernails. Did he really think so little of me?

The hands of my watch moved on. The first, infrequent traffic of the New Year began to dirty the innocent snow. And still there was no sign.

Meisel's van was a Škoda dating from the early 20s, the

front radiator slatted like a venetian blind. It was a dull, olive green, with the letters *Meisel: Antiques & Fine Art,* spelt out in cursive gold on either flank. For about a minute I watched a green Škoda van putter along the far bank, but then it turned in toward the city.

A new feeling began to overwhelm that of Papa's betrayal. It was made up of two emotions: anxiety, which heightened with every minute that passed; and self-loathing, that I'd been taken in by Leah Meisel's laugh. By her hand touching my cheek. It had been a joke, one last, gratuitous, cruel joke. And I'd fallen for it. I'd crept through the family house like a thief and had stolen money at her bidding. What disdain she must feel for this adolescent fool.

Papa had called me a degenerate brat. That was how I felt that morning, huddled against the east wind sweeping up the Vltava.

A horn tooted, twice.

I looked across the road to see the van, pulled up at a junction I'd not anticipated. I could see three figures spread across the seats, and as I heaved up the knapsack and trotted over toward them, the driver resolved himself into Meisel's nephew – not Hookworm. The other one.

Once we were outside Prague and into the countryside, progress became tortuous. I doubt we averaged twenty kilometres an hour. I was hunkered in the rear of the van, back pressed to the side, rattling with every vibration that came up through the floor, gagging on the sweet stink of diesel, propping up boxes with my elbows, my left flank hard against the seats, my knapsack clutched between chest and thighs as though it might give a modicum of stability at every jostle and gear-change and slide. And I was happy as a child. I imagined the van as a bird might see it, a drab green bug crawling over the white expanse of Bohemia.

My travel companions didn't talk much, and when they did, it was largely in Yiddish. I made out the odd term and phrase, no more. The word Bratislava cropped up quite a number of times. It seemed that Meisel had some business to transact there, and I understood that we might be stopping over for the night. I'd never been. In my childish way, I associated the Slovak capital with the diminutive art dealer, overwhelmed by a beaver collar, who'd asked us about the Jewish question. Slovakia was agitating for a break-up of the country. It was enough to turn me against the city before ever I laid eyes on it.

The engine gunned hysterically, the tyres whined, and we careened sideways into a bank of snow. I extracted myself from a confusion of boxes and antiques, clambered out after them over the seats.

It took a quarter of an hour in the raw air for myself and Meisel's nephew to dig the van out and set it back on its slow journey through winter. Aaron, they called him. He always said Meydl when talking to her. 'What do you call yourself?' he asked as he tossed me a snow-shovel so roughly that I fumbled the catch. I thought for a moment before replying, tried to catch Leah Meisel's eye. 'Daniel,' I replied. It was the name she'd given me on that distant summer's day outside the café by the Čertovka millwheel.

She snorted, tossing her mane as a pony might. 'The boy's a Yutz. That'd be perfect, telling the customs officers your name is Daniel when on your passport is written Guido Hayek.'

'Guido,' leered the driver. 'What sort of a name is Guido?'

'Italian,' I blushed. 'My mother's Italian.'

'So, Guido, do you drive?'

I shook my head, no.

'What I mean, could you learn to drive?'

'The van?'

'The van. The van.'

'Sure,' I shrugged. 'Why not?' Then, 'You mean today?'

'Pfffft! Today he wants to learn to drive! You're right, Meydl, the boy is meshugga.'

I knew I was being joshed. All the same, it was glorious to be out in the fresh air, away from the claustrophobic city with its guilt and deceptions, shovelling snow and watched by a solitary raven in a leafless tree. I felt as Jim Hawkins must have felt, climbing out of the apple-barrel on board the *Hispaniola*. I was one of them now.

It was dark by the time we pulled up at an inn in Bratislava. Never before had I been in such close proximity to the Third Reich. Only the mighty Danube separated us. I levered myself out of the torture chamber, dizzy on diesel fumes, and rubbed blood back into lifeless limbs. The air was warmer now. Sleet, falling obliquely through the brown night, was galvanised by each streetlamp into a cascade of sparks.

Leah Meisel was left behind at the inn, to sort out arrangements for the evening. For the next several hours, Meisel's van puttered about the streets of the unknown city. I had taken her place in the front, seated between Aaron Grossmann and the old merchant, helping to unload such merchandise as he could offload for cash. The old man scarcely seemed to count the payments. When I'd approached the van that morning, Leah had not asked how much money I'd brought. In fact the whole rationale for her allowing me to join them on their journey appeared to have been forgotten. This had come as a relief. But the old man's indifference? Had my father's subterfuge dispirited him so much? It did strike me that the following day, there'd be a good deal more space in the rear compartment. How long, I wondered, would it take me to pick up the rudiments of handling the van? The rudiments of Yiddish?

By the time we got back to the inn I was ravenous. All I'd had all day was a withered apple and half a bread-roll that had been passed back to me. The inn was a dingy, smoky place, low-ceilinged and ill-lit but stifling thanks to a huge-bellied, wheezing stove. I avoided any eye-contact with the shadowy occupants scattered about the corners.

We were served a bony fish soup, which after long hours in the van tasted of petrol, and slabs of black bread tough as plywood. Nevertheless I wolfed it down. Then came a tray with a bottle and four glasses, brought by a slatternly barmaid who looked down at me with ironic disdain. I knew, before I tasted the eye-watering spirit, that it was vodka. Hours passed, but no more food arrived, with the exception of one diminutive dish of pickled cucumber with each refill of the bottle.

Time and again, Aaron poured our glasses. It was a mirthless affair. Perhaps the knowledge they were leaving their home for good had struck home to my travel-companions. At some point during the second bottle, we were joined by a bearded giant with pockmarked skin who looked at me as though he were considering purchasing me. The conversation switched to Yiddish. I longed for the evening to end. I was aware we were all four to share one bedroom, wondered vaguely what the sleeping arrangements would be. My mind was hazy, my eyes swimming. I didn't at all like the glances of this peasant who had joined us. I pushed myself up from the table, to go once more to the toilet. Before I took two steps I doubled over and disgorged a mess of fish soup and vodka over the stone flags.

I was aware of teetering stairs. I was aware of several hands, laying me on the bed. Of voices, one of them Leah's. A taste of sweet saliva fought with the bile I'd vomited. The ceiling reeled drunkenly. I clamped my eyes shut and gripped the woozy bedframe.

I woke with a taste of ashes in my mouth and a clattering in my brain. It was my first hangover, the pain so overwhelming when I moved my head that for a while I didn't dare. I listened, but heard nothing but a pulse, somewhere in my temple. I pulled my arm from my eyes. The room was dusky, a single shard of morning light, dust-filled, stabbing in through the broken slat of a shutter.

Even before I propped myself onto my elbow, I knew. I fought the axe-pain in my forehead, levered myself onto my feet, pressed my fists to my temples. A tongue of sandpaper tasted the stale air. One question only hung in the stale interior. How long had they gone?

Of course, the knapsack had been rifled. The coat. The trouser pockets. They had taken everything. Even my watch was gone. The only thing that had been overlooked was the passport, which had slipped down into the lining of my coat.

Outside, there were all the signs of a thaw, runnels of

melt water dripping from every roof. From the courtyard, dirty tracks led out through the slush in several directions. The van had long since gone.

XXXIV

Degenerate

Eight days it took me to walk back from that accursed city. Eight days in which I almost starved. Eight nights in which I all but froze.

I might have greatly shortened the journey if I'd attempted to thumb a lift. I didn't. It was a punishment. A penance. Looking back, there was a masochistic determination driving this act of contrition. I foraged hen's eggs, pig-feed, prised swedes and mangels from the frozen earth with blackened nails. At dusk I burrowed into haylofts, where the damp ferment gave a sickly warmth. In the course of each day, a thaw came on. In the course of each night, a freeze.

By the time I reached the outskirts of Prague I was in rag order. It was some hours after midnight. I stumbled like a sleepwalker through the unreal city as far as and then across Štefánikuv Bridge. There I prised open the warehouse door sufficiently to squeeze in, pulled boots from ruined, water-logged feet, fell into the chest of old clothes and burrowed under them.

Dawn woke me. I was famished. I had longed to be overtaken by oblivion. Oblivion was short-lived.

Of one thing I was certain, during that long tramp through winter. I was no prodigal, to beg my father's forgiveness. When I'd shut the door on the house of Nerudova Street, I'd shut it on my childhood. I would make it as a man, or I wouldn't make it at all. There was no going back. It was not lost on me that *SS Stella di Oriente* had embarked for America several days since. Another door had closed, this one on the future.

What I'd decided to do, for want of any other prospects, was to seek out Ada. Through her, I might work again with Goran. Play the passer-by who unfailingly finds the Queen of Spades, the pea under the shell. Maybe even learn the art of picking pockets. I had been robbed. I'd been left destitute in a distant city. It had blunted my scruples. Would Ada come here? Did they still use these old costumes, dream up scenarios? There was no sign that the place had been entered since I'd first broken in here, nine long nights ago.

The more immediate problem was how to stanch the hunger gnawing at my insides. I'd had plenty of time to consider this as I approached Prague. There were two soup-kitchens that I was aware of, probably many more during the topsy-turvy period in the wake of the Sudeten annexation. The Jesuits ran a charity kitchen to the rear of St Niklaus Church in Mala Strana, and I'd come across another in the great, echoing foyer of the Hlavní Railway Station. The latter would be more anonymous. There was less chance I'd run into anyone who knew the Hayek family. But nothing would be open before the early evening. In the meantime, as I'd done several times on the weary trek through frozen Bohemia, I sucked on splinters of wood to take the edge off the hunger-pangs.

This became my pattern for the next several days. After

a cold morning wandering Josefov in the hope of a chance encounter with Ada – if that was her real name – I mooched about in the cold interior of the warehouse, waiting for the hour when the soup-kitchens would open. It struck me that I might find a channel to contact her if I called back to Nana Levy's, where they'd brought me for that abortive assignation. But the thought of the place, and the harridan who'd answered the door, made me shudder.

The shanty-town of refugees that had grown up between the Masarykovo and Hlavní stations was somewhat reduced from its October dimensions, but substantial nonetheless. There was a mobile kitchen set up in each, where a mess-tin of stew and a bread-roll could be had for a half-hours' queueing, no questions asked. I alternated between the two, rebuilding my strength on two hot meals each evening an hour apart. St Niklaus Church on Mala Strana was too close to home to chance it. Home, with the guilt it exuded, was something I'd managed to block from my consciousness. I'd learned that you shun people not so much for the hurt they've caused you as for the hurt you've caused them.

On the third day, just as I was being handed a watery goulash inside Masarykovo, a hand gripped my shoulder. I turned rapidly, wielding the spoon as though it might be a weapon. I was disarmed by a stubbly grin beneath a Russian shapka, its flaps protruding like donkey ears. It took me a moment to place the grin. The Good Soldier Švejk.

We sat on the floor with our backs to the wall, hands still cradling the last ambient warmth from the empty mess-tins. By this time, after almost two weeks alone inside my head, I craved human company almost as keenly as I craved warmth and nourishment.

I was astonished to learn that he knew the basics of my situation. That I'd had a heated falling out with my father. That I'd failed to return home in the early hours of New Year's Day, had likely absconded with Meisel and his granddaughter. 'How do you know all this?' I asked.

'Your sister.'

'Katya?'

He replied that every evening since I'd gone missing, she called round to the artists' squat in Vyšehrad. If I were still in the city, it was the only place she could think of where I might go. 'Where *do* you go?' he asked.

I'd no wish to tell him. Not as yet. 'Will she be there tonight, do you think?'

'If I had any money, I'd lay every cent on it.'

'Will you do something for me? Will you tell her I'm ok? I'm doing ok.' I shut my eyes, pressed my head back against the wall. My Adam's apple throbbed. 'Tell her I'm sorry.'

'Sorry?'

'Just that. That I'm sorry. I let her down.' I opened my eyes. They were dry and hot. 'How does she look?' I asked.

'You mean the...?' He mimed a bump with his hands. 'Fine, I guess. She looks pregnant, you know?'

'Tell her, listen,' I was speaking even as the thought was forming. 'Tell her not to stop. To keep dropping by the Vyšehrad tenement. One evening I'll meet her there. Tell her, I swear it. On my...' The word honour stuck in my throat.

'One evening?'

'Not today.' I levered myself up from the floor. 'I can't, today.'

'Tomorrow?'

'I don't know. Maybe tomorrow.'

It was only as I hurried away from him and out into the twilight that I realised I'd forgotten to ask him his name.

Another three days passed before I could bring myself to face her. This sounds absurd. She was my sister, the last person in the world who would hold this against me. She understood what Papa had been trying on. The violence of the row we'd had. The robbery he'd pulled off, that put mine in perspective.

She hadn't even wanted to go to America.

I think what I was most afraid of was her disappointment in me. I still had sent no word directly to anyone. Not to Maman. Not to Papa. Not to Klaus. Not even to Father Kaufmann. And only indirectly to her. I had tried to write notes, on numerous occasions. They were still-births, hurting and frustrating with each failure.

The knowledge that I was to meet her gave me renewed determination. I had to do something about my useless situation. So the evening after meeting Švejk, I bit the bullet and called around to Nana Levy's. The same woman of fifty with the look of a drag queen squinted out at me suspiciously. The black-lined eyes and powdered face called to mind a macaw. 'Ada Meier?' she asked.

'I don't know. Yeah. Maybe Meier.' A figure, it may have been the girl I'd been with, was watching from the interior. 'The redhead,' I added.

'She's not here.'

She made to shut the door but my boot blocked it. For a second I saw something like fear flit across her features at which I experienced a tiny thrill. 'Look. Lady. I need you to give her this.' I pulled a note from my coat, and with the stub of a pencil, scribbled the name. 'Ada Meier. I need you to give her this.' I pulled her bony hand up and slapped the note into it. 'Yes?'

She didn't reply. She squinted at me with enmity. But she took the note.

The following evening Ada was waiting in the warehouse when I got back after my second stew. A guy in a pinstripe suit too large for him – I recognised it as one that Zak used to wear – was behind her, the same I'd seen talking with them on New Year's Eve. I'm not sure what got into me. He was a weedy specimen, with an owlish look behind his glasses. I guffawed, eyed him with open disdain.

'So,' she said, 'you want to learn how to make money?'

I nodded. 'A lot of money.' I jerked a thumb at the skinny guy in the suit. 'What does Kašpárek do?'

She chose not to answer. Instead, she sauntered up to me, pinched my bicep. Her spoor of musk was Leah's. I ached to smell it. She must have inherited her perfume. 'And what is it you're prepared to do to make a lot of money, Guido Hayek?'

'Whatever it takes.'

Two evenings later I waited for Katya at the old artists' commune. It was, if anything, more dilapidated than before, broken glass scattered over the floors and a stink of stale urine in every corner. It had become the hang-out of tramps and down-and-outs, characters with glazed eyes and beards dangling from weather-cudgelled faces. There was little evidence now of artistic activity, though one or two of Ivan's plaster death-masks still haunted a couple of walls.

We found a room on the first floor that was empty save for an overturned bathtub upon which we sat. 'You look different,' she said. Her hair was long enough now to cover her birthmark, but she wore it pulled back in a ponytail.

'Skinnier?'

'Not just. You look…' She placed a hot palm against my cheek. 'Older.'

'I've been learning how the world works,' I snorted. 'How are things at home?'

'Terrible. Really terrible, Guy. It's Papa. It's as if he's gone crazy. Ever since you left. No. Even before you left. But afterwards, it's got so much worse. It started when he bought that painting. It's up under his bed, that's where he keeps it now.'

'So what's the problem? Didn't he clean off that botched hand?'

'That's the first thing he did. Then he brought it home.'

'Well then? What's the problem?'

'It's like he's totally obsessed by it, Guy. Ever since you've gone. He talks of nothing else. You know he's fallen out with Jaroslav Čermák?'

'No. How would I know that?'

'He's convinced that Čermák is trying to cheat him. He won't say the attribution is definitive, or something. Papa says he's trying to cheat him. But I don't think he is. He told Papa the castle is prepared to go the full amount that Meisel paid. But Papa insists he wants twice that. He's holding out for a quarter of a million, which is crazy. But it seems he's been talking to this guy in Germany. This curator for the Alte

Pinakothek in Munich. This guy says he's prepared to go the full quarter of a million, or whatever that is in Reichmarks.'

'I don't believe you! How could he even talk to them? What does Klaus say?'

'Klaus doesn't know. But, Guy. That's not the worst. He's told Jula and Marta that we can no longer afford to keep them on. He's given them a month's notice.'

'No! But who's to...'

'Cook and clean?' She turned her troubled eyes on me. 'I am. I'm to stay home and learn to cook. Marta is to teach me. After all, I'm going to be a mother. A single mother. I'm not going to get a job anywhere.'

'I don't believe you, Katya. He wouldn't do that. And what about Marta and Jula? As a kid I used to play hide and seek with them.'

'He took it very bad that I refused to take the ocean liner. I think it's a punishment.'

I dropped my voice. 'And Maman?'

There was a silence. Katya turned away from me. 'Maman's in hospital, Guy.' I had no need to ask. Her inflection told me. Maman was back in the psychiatric ward.

'Jesus,' I said. 'It must be hell, for you.' I'd had plenty of time to think about what I was to say next. All the same it came out clumsy. 'Katya, you can't stay there.'

She shuddered. 'I can't come here!'

'No. That's not what I'm saying. Listen. What savings do you have?'

'Savings?'

'From your time in the typing pool.'

'I don't know. Two thousand? A little over.'

'Ok. Listen to me. We'll go away. I'll make two thousand. I'll match what you have. Then we'll go away from here.'

'Go away? Go away where, Guy?'

'To your father. To America.'

'If we asked Papa, perhaps he…'

I stood up, my fists clenched. 'I'd rather starve.' I walked to the broken window. A bitter wind struck my cheek. 'So what do you say? Will you come with me? Because Papa was right about one thing. There's going to be a war. A war to end all wars. You can't bring your baby into a world with that hanging over it.'

And that night, that's where we left it. She'd consider it. Much depended on Maman. How she progressed. 'But Guy. Where will you get two thousand koruna?'

'That's my affair. When I have it, I'll let you know.'

The apprenticeship Ada Meier had in mind for me was short and brutal. Rolling drunks. The other guy, Samuel was his name, was to graduate from that to the packed tram routine with Goran. But I was too clumsy for that. With my hammer sized hands I was far more suited to rolling drunks. On Thursday, Friday and Saturday, Ada Meier would select and accost a target leaving a bar, tickle his lust, waylay him down a side street away from the light. Then, once his trousers were down or, at the least, his flies open, I was to appear. The jealous boyfriend. 'Don't leave it too long,' she warned me. 'I'm not a whore.'

Some would cave in at once. If not, they'd be no match, in their inebriated state, with their pants around their ankles. A shove, a slap to the head, a dig under the ribs. A quick boot once they were down. In two minutes flat they'd be fleeced. We'd leave them lying in their puke, for there was no poetry in these scenarios. The best part, few if any would ever report the theft. Who wanted it known that they'd been led down a side street by a redheaded whore and her pimp?

This was a new low point of my life. And a part of me revelled in it. Every black eye or bloody nose that met me in the mirror I wore as a badge of honour. I was becoming hardened. That February fourteenth I turned sixteen. Valentine's Day. I'm sure there's an irony there. I was by this time just one hundred koruna shy of the two thousand.

Ada Meier got wind of the fact it was my birthday. It was a Tuesday, but with so many lovers about, it was too good an opportunity to miss. 'What age are you, anyway?' she asked.

'Seventeen,' I lied.

The last of the drunks we rolled that night fought back. Pulled out a knife. I took a stab to my forearm before he backed away from us, back into the light. It was only a flesh-wound. All the same it had Ada's full attention.

That night, for the first and only time, I brought her back to the artist's squat. Or she brought me. It was my first time to be with a woman. On a filthy mattress, it was all over within minutes. But an hour later, as I lay watching her, the long locks tumbled over her naked back and legs still in stockings, I again became aroused. I kissed the white moons of her backside. I turned her, tasted her all over. I gripped her hands, wrestled her into the mattress. She fought back, scratched, bit. At one point a series of sobs racked me. She licked away the hot tears.

Two days later, Katya and I left Prague on the night-train to Budapest.

XXXV

Cigno Nero

We spent the best part of a week in the port of Trieste, holed up in a dingy fleapit over a bar while we bartered and negotiated with the touts and traffickers some sort of passage to America. Even for that straw-packed mattress on a floor and a single blanket, they charged as though for a boutique hotel. All Europe, it seemed, was converging on the seaports, fearful of the great conflagration about to engulf the continent.

I'd been cheated once before. I wasn't about to let that happen again. I was wary of everyone. Inside my coat I carried a crowbar, in case anyone should take it into their head to mug me. At night it lay beside the mattress while we slept. Or tried to sleep. I was too wary to sleep. The wallet containing our money I kept inside my shirt while I pressed up against Katya's back, the one source of heat in that draughty room. All that week, there was a cruel wind coming in off the Adriatic.

The first full day after our arrival, having divided the money between us into equal parts, I left Katya to wander the Parco della Rimembranza, while I set off for the waterfront alone to watch the goings on. Merely to observe. I was determined not to trust or talk before I had a feel for the place; for the scam artists that invariably converge on any port.

My apprenticeship with Leah Meisel and her cronies would stand me in good stead. I could spot a scam at fifty yards. I watched shysters who'd arrived together that morning let on to be strangers. Stage rows and expose lesser scams in order to win a greater confidence. I watched uniformed officials arrive opportunely, could only assume how much they creamed from the frightened refugees. At one point a character in a soutane ushered a family of seven or eight to one corpulent shyster with a lazy eye I'd watched operating earlier – a sort of Mediterranean version of Goran. I'd lay odds neither of them had seen the inside of a chapel in years. Any time I sensed that I was being observed, I moved to a different wharf, where I'd cast an eye over the freighters and tramp steamers pulled variously alongside.

That night I filled in Katya on all I'd seen as we lay on the mattress, her back pressed to my belly. She'd been chilled to the bone, she said, wandering around that God-damned park. Had spent most of the afternoon inside churches to get out of the wind. 'So you didn't actually talk to any of them?' She pivoted about, so I could see her frown.

'That's tomorrow's work. Just getting the lie of the land for the moment.'

'I got talking to this Jewish couple, Guido. From Brno. They're sailing out tomorrow evening.'

'Yeah? How much they pay for that?'

'They didn't say. What they did say was, look out for a guy called Stavros. He arranges passages. They said it was the Rabbi something-or-other back in Brno told them to look out for this Stavros character.'

'Good Samaritan, is he?'

'He was a refugee himself at one time. From Smyrna, I think they said. That's all they knew about him.'

'So now he goes about doing good turns? You see, Katya, that's just what I'm telling you! That smells of a scam.'

'How do you know! You didn't even see them…'

'"Some guy called Stavros"? Come on! They see this pregnant girl on her own. Of course they're going to take advantage!'

I felt her body tense. 'I'm going down with you to the docks tomorrow.'

'I'd rather you didn't.'

'If I see the inside of one more church, I swear to you…'

The next morning a fine drizzle was blowing in off the sea. But there was no dissuading her. A few discrete inquiries told us where Stavros could usually be found. We approached a fat man standing at the corner of an arcade with hat pulled low and collar turned up against the drizzle. It was none other than my friend with the lazy eye. 'That's just perfect! Katya, I watched this fellow yesterday. He's some operator.'

'We *are* talking to him, Guy.'

'Whatever you say.'

I approached him. 'You Stavros?' He turned on me a stone-wall 'who-wants-to-know' face. Though her Italian was far more hesitant than mine, Katya took charge. She'd lost all her former shyness. 'We understand you organise passages? To America?' He looked away, the lazy eye trailing the other as though it might pick up anything the good eye had missed. 'Or have we got the wrong man?'

He slowly examined us, took in Katya's bump. 'You want to go to America?'

'There's a ship sailing tonight. Is that right?'

At this point, another character slinked around from the other side of the arcade. The two began to argue, to berate one another in a Triestine dialect that was all but impossible to follow. 'Come on,' I steered Katya by the forearm, 'we'll leave them to it.'

We stood in a nearby Piazza, at a loss where to go. At least the drizzle was lighter, here. 'I've seen it a thousand times, Katya. Those guys know each other. That argument is all for show.'

'So what do you suggest we do? We can't stay here indefinitely.' She had a point. 'And what if you're wrong, Guido? What if the second guy was the real trafficker, and he was pissed off at Stavros for stealing his pitch and being too honest.'

'Too honest. Right! We don't even know for sure his name is Stavros.'

'We have to trust someone. For Christ's sake, Guido, I'm not having my baby in fucking Trieste.'

'Ok, ok. I'll go back. We'll get a bowl of soup somewhere, and afterwards I'll go back, I promise. I'll ask him how much. Ok?' She didn't seem impressed.

After lunch I set off again for the waterfront. There was no sign of him where I'd left him. I walked up and down, agitated. Increasingly soaked. Annoyed. Annoyed as much at myself as at Katya or this Stavros individual. I was on the point of giving up when I was arrested by a whistle. He was seated at a café, his hat pushed back, a glass of grappa and an open *Corriere della Sera* on the table before him. 'You the kid wants to take his wife to America?' Afraid my voice would betray the agitation in my breast, I nodded. 'How much you got?'

Now, there was no way on God's earth I was going to answer that one. Instinctively, my left hand gripped the crowbar inside my coat. 'You tell me. How much does it cost?' He made no move to reply, lifting instead the newspaper. 'Come on! Two to America. How much?'

'My friend,' he said, laying down the paper and caressing it, 'it's a question of when. And how. And on what ship. Everything has its price.' His voice was heavily accented, as though Italian were an acquired language.

'Suppose we want to go this evening.'

'Impossible.'

'There's a ship this evening.'

'It's full.'

'Ok. What about tomorrow?'

'My friend, this is Trieste. There is not a ship to America every day of the week. And even if there were, there is not a passage to be found so easily.' He smiled, sipped at the grappa. A drop glistened from his fat lower lip. 'All the world wants to get to America.'

'So when's the next ship *with* a passage?'

He shrugged. His playacting was really getting on my nerves. The more I saw of him, the more he reminded me of Goran. 'Stavros. What is that, Greek?'

'If you like.' He sat back. 'There is a ship that sails on Friday.'

'Friday! But that's not for four days!' He nodded, then

readdressed the newspaper. I watched his game with deep loathing. 'Ok. How much?'

He sighed. 'I tell you already, my friend. Everything has its price. You'll want a bunk for your wife. She is with child, no?'

A bunk! What sort of passage were we discussing here? I copied his shrug, trying to look hardened. He pushed the hat still further back on his head, assessed me with his good eye, then named a sum that was so uncannily close to the combined wealth of myself and Katya that its accuracy wrong-footed me entirely.

I grunted, turned on my heel and walked away.

That evening we returned to the seafront. The drizzle had eased off. There was no particular purpose to our visit other than to get out of the den where we slept. We were passing a liner drawn up by the wharf when a voice called down from an upper deck. Katya peered up, then waved. 'That's them!' she cried. 'That's the couple from Brno I met in the church.'

As if fate wanted to laugh at me, at that moment I saw a priest usher a family of seven toward the gangway, the very family I'd seen the day before talking to the lazy-eyed guy with the passing resemblance to Goran. It was the priest whose soutane I'd doubted. I never told Katya about that. For her part, she never berated me that we might have had a berth on that ocean liner.

Next morning, we sought out Stavros to secure a passage on whatever ship was leaving port that Friday.

Sometimes, I look back on those cold, miserable days spent in Trieste, a ball of anxiety in my gut that we'd been swindled out of everything. What was it I felt, when the trafficker had assumed Katya was my wife? That her child was our child? What was it I felt, pressing into the body-heat of her back, a hand protectively on the soft bump of her abdomen? Pride, certainly. It was a different manhood I was growing to, a thousand miles from scowling and rolling drunks. It was love, if I'd dared to give it a name.

On board, too, it was assumed that I was Katya's partner and a father-to-be. We gave over pretty much everything we had for steerage on a rusted carcass of a troop-ship that had struggled through the last war on the side of the Austro-Hungarians. *SS Cigno Nero*. As we left port, one hundred and eighty-eight of us crowded below-decks into its foul-smelling hold.

'Cigno Nero?' Katya snorted. 'A regular swan covered in an oil-slick, more like.' For an extra five hundred lira I'd managed to secure a bunk and blanket for the passage. There were sixty bunks all told, so that like most of the refugees, we'd take turns resting there in a system they called hot-bunking. We had precious little cargo. Katya had a single suitcase, while everything I possessed fitted into a kitbag.

We stopped at Puglia, where unbelievably, another forty-four refugees were squeezed into the hold. Though it was scarcely fair, those of us already aboard treated these intruders with resentment. They had to make do with whatever space they could find on the floor of the deck. Misery might make for strange bedfellows; when one had so little, one clung to it with the jealousy of a sultan.

Once we left the Mediterranean and set out into the open Atlantic, the *SS Cigno Nero* rolled and shuddered with every wave. Great, ringing vibrations juddered through the bulkheads any time there was a swell. The air was stifling, but it was dangerous to go up on deck. After one protracted swell, rust-stained water sluiced about our feet and possessions.

About a week into the voyage, cholera swept through the hold. Drinking water was tightly rationed, a half-cup each day per person, and such water as they gave us tasted of mould and rust. Saltwater drawn up from the sea in buckets was used for all cooking and washing, so that even before the cholera, most of us were weak with dehydration.

Cholera is a dreadful death. The body expunges all fluids relentlessly through both ends as though it were poison. Within forty-eight hours, the healthiest body might be dead. And we were far from healthy. Every day, corpses were taken out of the hold and slipped overboard with the most cursory of services.

For the first time in months, I prayed. Katya refused absolutely to take any of my ration of water. The most I could get her to agree to was to take the bunk for the majority of the time. Every hour, we'd examine one another for symptoms; and I prayed God, if one of us is to be taken, let it be me.

We were already in sight of land, of the great continent, when Katya went into labour. Hour after hour, I clutched her hot hand, mopped the perspiration from her brow. A woman from Yugoslavia who had been a midwife stayed by us, though we shared not a word in any language. A day passed. From above decks came the word, New York was in sight! You could all but touch the lights of the city!

But the ship wasn't allowed to dock. Although there hadn't been a single fatality in two days, it would be quarantined. The news was mitigated somewhat by the arrival of a launch with fresh fruit and vegetables and, miracle of miracles, gallon cans of sweet water.

Katya's labour pangs continued. I believe it's not unusual with a first time mother. After thirty hours, the baby, a bawling, bloody thing, was delivered. The Yugoslav midwife wiped it clean, then wrapped it in her own headscarf before passing it to Katya.

She was terribly weak. I knew from her forehead she was fevered, and prayed to God that the cholera had spared her. 'What is it?' she panted.

'A boy. It's a little boy.'

She shut her eyes. 'Tell Gans I want him named Emil. Be sure, Guido. *Emil*. Promise me you'll do that, Guy.'

I squeezed her clammy hand, swallowed a hard lump. 'What are you talking about? For heaven's sake Katya, you'll tell Gans yourself.'

But she knew. She sensed it. Three days later she was dead. An Italian woman who had lost her own baby to the cholera suckled the infant until quarantine was lifted.

XXXVI

New World

For several weeks more we lingered on that death ship under the dismal yellow flag. Not the full forty days the word quarantine implies, but a lifetime all the same. Of the two hundred and thirty-two who'd embarked, scarcely one hundred and sixty of us queued at the tables of Ellis Island to be processed. There, we were met with hostile eyes. Among Katya's possessions was a letter embossed with the United States Immigration and Naturalisation Service logo. It was written in English, but contained both our names. Letter or no letter, I was made to feel a gate-crasher. The New World had no great appetite for refugees, and such sickly specimens.

On the second day of April, I finally boarded the ferry from Ellis Island to Battery Park, New York, the precious bundle clutched to my chest. While we were still quarantined on that accursed ship, news had overtaken us that the Germans had annexed the remainder of Bohemia and Moravia. But by that time I was so punch-drunk with the blows of fate that it scarcely registered.

For more than three years now, I've been living in Brooklyn, in the residence of Mordecai Gans. It would be untrue to say we ever really warmed to one another. But what Papa said of him is true. He is an honourable man. He tolerates me because I'm the teenager who brought his grandson to him. What we have in common, what makes my stay tolerable for me, too, is a shared love for baby Emil. Above the cot, pasted to the wall, is that photo of myself and Klaus and Katya with Maman and Papa, the one I'd had in my bedroom in Nerudova Street. It was one of the few possessions I salvaged from the voyage.

Around the same time as our flight from Prague, Father Kaufmann was transferred to the Curia in Rome. It's from his letters that I'm kept abreast of the news from home. The Father Provincial in Prague writes to Rome, and Father Kaufmann sends on the news to New York. It seems the Catholic Church is bigger than the war.

That's how I know that Papa died. In July, after Reinhard Heydrich was assassinated, the Germans came down pretty hard. An entire village, men, women and children, was sent to their deaths. Elsewhere, vast numbers of suspected partisans and sympathisers were swept up. Many were tortured. Someone must have given them the name of Mikuláš Hayek. Eva's name too, for she's also active in the resistance. Frustrated that they hadn't captured either of them, they took it out on the families. One morning Papa was dragged out of bed, along with Špotákov the wine-merchant and about a half-dozen others. They were summarily executed, hanged from a temporary scaffold erected in the square outside the castle gates, their bodies left for several days to serve as a warning.

Had Papa gone to his death still blaming me for Katya's?

Of Maman, Father Kaufmann hasn't been able to get any news. Last he heard, she was in a private sanatorium near Kutná Hora. He hopes that no news is good news.

On a map on a wall in the dining-room, we move flags eastward as the newspapers report the German advances. Last October, Odessa fell. If the Meisels remained, have things gone any easier under the Romanian divisions? The Romanians were once our allies. Or were they among the thousands evacuated by the Soviet Black Sea Fleet to the Crimean port of Sebastopol? If they were, what does it matter? In July, on the very day that they hanged Papa, Sebastopol fell to the Germans.

And **Sandu and Mihaela, in their colourful clothes, have they been swept up too by the relentless tide? And Ivan the Serb, the Muslim who'd loved Katya?**

Often I think of those days, in Prague. Of that summer, when we dressed up and played at thieves. Of the days I'd look for her, wandering the crowded streets of Josefov. How many of those faces have they rounded up? Sent off to detention camps, or forced labour?

After the attack on Pearl Harbour, I tried to enlist. I was almost nineteen, I'd been living in America for more than two years. But Papa was right. My heart is wired wrong. Papa, whom I'd called a coward. Whom I'd do anything not to have called a coward. Maybe I knew I'd fail the physical, just as I'd always known that any talk of joining the partisans was posturing. The Devil's babble. Maybe I'm the only coward here, brave enough to deal out a few furtive blows on a drunk in a darkened alley.

Had I listened to him, had I not been so caught up with

the Meisel girl, so intoxicated, so finely principled, would Katya be alive now? She died of puerperal fever, the same hazard Leah Meisel's mother died of. All the same, a passage in a cabin on a proper ocean liner, arriving in New York two months before the baby was due? It would have given her a fighting chance.

And what have my scruples led to? The German stain spreads ever eastward. It's hard to see how it will be stopped. The Americans held off from joining the fight for two years, and now have an enemy of their own to fight. So unless Leah Meisel and her baby keep fleeing forever, I don't see how they'll survive.

So what was it all for?

I speak to baby Emil in Czech. Gans doesn't like it. He's only three, he says. Besides, English is the future. What need of Czech? Gans' English is excellent, though it carries an accent. When he grows up, I told him, he may wish to visit the city of his mother. But I think that's precisely why he doesn't want his grandson to learn the language. When he grows up, says Gans, who knows what the world will be?

When we're alone, I persist. Even if he never leaves here, Czech is part of who he is. Katya would have wanted it.

There are weeks when I can barely face the world. Weeks of lethargy. Weeks of anxiety. Of enormous, debilitating guilt. I look at baby Emil, then, and I whisper, 'One day, I'll tell you all about your Uncle Guido, and how he brought you here to live. One day.'

Recommended Reading

If you have enjoyed Dara Kavanagh's *Prague 1938* you might like to try other books we have published which are also set in Prague:

The Golem by Gustav Meyrink
Walpurgisnacht by Gustav Meyrink
The Angel of the West Window by Gustav Meyrink
Prague Noir (The Weeping Woman on the Streets of Prague) by Sylvie Germain
Infinite Possibilities by Sylvie Germain
Invitation to a Journey by Sylvie Germain

You might also like to try Robert Irwin's novel *My Life is like a Fairy Tale* which is set in the same period but in Berlin.

If you like novels written by Irish authors you should read:

Le Fanu's Angel by Brian Keogh
The Failing Heart by Eoghan Smith

For further information about all Dedalus' titles please visit our website: www.dedalusbooks.com or email us at info@ dedalusbooks.com or contact us for a catalogue at Dedalus Limited, 24-26 St Judith's Lane, Sawtry, Cambs, PE28 5XE

The Golem – Gustav Meyrink

'A superbly atmospheric story set in the old Prague ghetto featuring the Golem, a kind of rabbinical Frankenstein's monster, which manifests every 33 years in a room without a door. Stranger still, it seems to have the same face as the narrator. Made into a film in 1920, this extraordinary book combines the uncanny psychology of doppelganger stories with expressionism and more than a little melodrama... Meyrink's old Prague – like Dickens' London – is one of the great creation of city writing, an eerie, claustrophobic and fantastical underworld where anything can happen.'

Phil Baker in *The Sunday Times*

'Gustav Meyrink uses this legend in a dream-like setting on the Other Side of the Mirror and he has invested it with a horror so palpable that it has remained in my memory all these years.'   Jorge Luis Borges

'A remarkable work of horror, half-way between *Dr Jekyll and Mr Hyde* and *Frankenstein.*'   *The Observer*

£8.99   ISBN 978 1 910213 67 4   280p   B. Format

Walpurgisnacht – Gustav Meyrink

Comic and fantastic, gruesome and grotesque, *Walpurgisnacht* uses Prague as the setting for a clash between German officialdom immured in the ancient castle above the Moldau, and a Czech revolution seething in the city below. History, myth and political reality merge in an apocalyptic climax as the rebels, urged on by a drum covered in human skin, storm the castle to crown a poor violinist 'Emperor of the World' in St Vitus' Cathedral.

'It is 1917. Europe is torn apart by war, Russia in the grip of revolution, the Austro-Hungarian Empire on the brink of collapse. It is *Walpurgisnacht*, springtime pagan festival of unbridled desire. In this volcanic atmosphere, in a Prague of splendour and decay, the rabble prepare to storm the hilltop castle, and Dr Thaddaeus Halberd, once the court physician, mourns his lost youth. Phantasmagorical prose, energetically translated, marvellously evokes past and present, personal and political, a devastated world.'   *The Times*

£8.99   ISBN   978 1 907650 17 8   165p   B. Format

Prague Noir (The Weeping Woman on the Streets of Prague) – Sylvie Germain

'An intricate, finely crafted and polished tale, *The Weeping Woman* brings magic-realism to the dimly lit streets of Prague. Through the squares and alleys a woman walks, the embodiment of human pity, sorrow, death. Everyone she passes is touched by her, and Germain skilfully creates an intense mood and feel in her attempt to produce a spiritual map of Prague.'   *The Observer*

'Firmly rooted in magic realism, Germain adds her own strain of dark romanticism and macabre imagination to create a tale poised between vision and elegy.'

Emily Dean in *The Sunday Times*

'Hallucinatory, lyrical in the extreme, it's a post-modernist playground for literary game-playing. It seems, at first, a radical departure for this gifted tale-teller but no, this is a teasing meditation on her familiar themes: history, place, creativity, death and desire.'   James Friel in *Time Out*

'The figure of this bereft woman develops into a memorable symbol: her sudden appearances – on a bridge, in a square, in a room – haunt the book like history, moved to tears.'

Robert Winder in *The Independent*

£8.99   ISBN 978 1 903517 73 4   112p   B. Format

Le Fanu's Angel – Brian Keogh

The life of Kieran Sheridan Le Fanu, a young Dublin advertising agency director, is abruptly upended when he is the sole survivor of a gruesome car crash. In the aftermath, he develops a form of Cotard's Syndrome, the belief that he is dead and possibly experiencing the drawn-out delirium of a mind hovering between consciousness and extinction.

He meets and loves the enchanting and enigmatic Aoife and struggles to differentiate between memory, fantasy, and reality, with bizarre and inexplicable encounters where he is attacked by strangers, pursued by a vicious stalker and transported to a haunting afterlife dimension. In a final showdown, he faces real and paranormal foes and is given an astounding revelation.

Le Fanu's Angel is a novel full of excitement, mystery and the unexpected. It is a literary delight set in historic and contemporary Dublin, with its vibrant business and social life, and hidden underworld of vice and crime.

£11.99   ISBN 978 1 912868 45 2   368p   B. Format

The Failing Heart – Eoghan Smith

'Brilliant! Dark and atmospheric. It's a compulsive account of how it feels to be tortured and mired in anxiety.'

Sue Leonard in The Irish Examiner

'Reading *The Failing Heart* is like taking a trip; part escape into another consciousness, part suffocating delusion. The story – or rather the scaffolding upon which Smith displays elegant philosophical architecture – follows a young scholar whose mother has just died. Estranged from his father after stealing his money, hounded by the ominous figure of his landlord, and oppressed with images of his ex-lover's impending labour, he wanders into an existential purgatory. "All these open mouths, living or dead, they never shut up." Death is everywhere, through the needs and revulsions of the body, its smells, secretions, drives. The narrative circles in on itself in an ever-decreasing gyre, examining ancient and modern ideas about existence, subjecting philosophical scholarship itself to a sardonic inquiry using its own tools of scrutiny. The writing is self-aware and wry, with rare flashes of humour amid a claustrophobic search for meaning and desire to confess. Time expands and contracts; it is unclear what is real, what is internalised: at the end of this brief novel there is the sensation of having witnessed the dark dream of a stranger.'

The Irish Times

£9.99   ISBN 978 1 910213 91 9   152p   B. Format